Sweet Thing

The tip of the creamsicle drew slippery pictures along the inner lips of Jessica's pussy, kissing her with ice. She shuddered, but Kelly didn't stop. He pushed the tip inside her, and the ice cream confection started to melt from the heat of her body.

'The sofa –' Jessica said softly, her last rational thought of the afternoon. They would stain the fabric with the sticky-sweet juices, but Kelly didn't seem to care. He simply pushed the popsicle further inside her. Then he got down on his knees behind Jessica and started to lap the dripping juice and ice cream from her thighs, placing his mouth just under her and catching each dulcet droplet of the melting sugar and cream . . .

Other titles by the author

Learning to Love It
Strictly Confidential

Sweet Thing
Alison Tyler

BLACK LACE

Black Lace books contain sexual fantasies.
In real life, always practise safe sex.

First published in 2002 by
Black Lace
Thames Wharf Studios
Rainville Road
London W6 9HA

Design by Smith & Gilmour, London
Printed and bound by Mackays of Chatham PLC

ISBN 0 352 33682 X

For Sam

Contents

Boys, boys, it's a sweet thing.
— Bowie

Prologue

On one of the hottest days of the year, Kelly and Jessica connected at the grocery store. They often found out-of-the-way places to meet, like the back alley behind Read My Lips, where Kelly bartended, or a lush mirrored dressing room in the men's section of a Beverly Hills department store. But this particular location had been Kelly's idea, and Jessica didn't know exactly what to expect. All he'd said to prepare her was, 'Meet me at The Cheshire Market. And bring your appetite.'

Now, as Jessica wandered the aisles looking for him, she tried to guess his plans for today. Would he fondle her personal peaches in the produce department? Or could he possibly intend to fuck her in a deserted corner, bent over a steel metal shopping cart, the rubbery black wheels squeaking each time he thrust forward?

After walking through the store, Jessica finally found her man in the frozen-food section, where he stood admiring the colourful array of popsicle choices as if he were just another mid-afternoon shopper. In silence, she observed him from behind. Kelly had on a pair of well-worn Levis that fitted his athletic body to perfection. Jessica thought about sneaking up and copping a quick feel, cradling his tight rear cheeks in her hands and squeezing, but he sensed her presence and said her name.

'Hey, Jess.'

She approached and stood next to him.

'Which is your favourite flavour?' he asked, not looking over to meet her eyes, but gazing instead at her semi-transparent reflection in the glass window of the frozen-food compartment. She tucked a wayward strand of her shoulder-length dark hair back into her ponytail, aware of the chill in the air, the fact that she was braless, that her pert round nipples were already standing up firm and erect from the cold.

'Orange.'

'Juice, or creamsicle?'

'Creamsicle,' she answered, naming the type of decadent popsicle filled with vanilla ice cream. Why was she getting hot from discussing frozen treats?

He picked up a box. 'Ready?' he asked.

Jessica looked into his basket. There was nothing else. 'That's it?'

'That's all we need.' His slow-spreading smile made him seem momentarily innocent, when they both knew what a kinky mind he possessed. This was one of Kelly's best features – he looked wholesome on the surface while the soul of a pagan lover burned like brush fire within him. It was the same way with Jessica. She had a naive air about her, but those who knew what to look for could tell that she played dirty.

'Trust me?' he asked, and she nodded, then lifted up on her tiptoes to kiss him. Although it was obvious that he wanted to control the situation, he gave in to her, wrapping one strong arm around her lithe body and meeting her tongue with his. Kelly knew how to tease, working slowly to build the arousal within her. Jessica felt his mouth move slowly southward, as he licked to the hollow of her throat, then pressed his lips there for a moment to feel her pulse racing rapidly beneath her skin.

When he released her, he smiled again and led her to the checkout stand to pay for their purchase. The round female cashier made small talk about the sudden rise in temperature, and the Indian summer in October driving people out to the beach and to the store for ice cream and popsicles. Jessica did her best to respond politely, but her mind was focused on the box of creamsicles as the teenage bagger placed them in a special paper wrapper to keep them from melting on the ride home.

What did Kelly have in mind?

He wouldn't tell her. Not in the store, or outside in the parking lot where heat waves melted the ribbons of black tar that criss-crossed the paved concrete surface. All Kelly said was, 'My place,' before climbing on to his shiny Harley, the colour of Jessica's favourite crimson lipstick. He blew her a kiss, then drove down San Vincente Boulevard towards his apartment in Santa Monica.

Jessica followed Kelly in her roommate's tiny denim-blue Triumph, cruising past the various numbered streets that bisected the tree-lined boulevard. As she approached his building, she grew wetter at each inter-section. By the time she pulled her car into his double parking space, her panties were soaked, and she still had no idea what her man had in mind. Would they feed each other popsicles while standing naked in the centre of his kitchen? Or trace the treats along each other's bare skin, a creative way of keeping cool on such a scorcher. Although sexy, these ideas didn't seem up to Kelly's level of erotic surprise.

When Jessica got out of her convertible, her man was waiting for her, looking like James Dean with one hand tucked into his pocket, the other holding the bag from the store. Jessica was a fan of old movies, and it was easy for her to cast him as the classic rebel. He possessed a sense of self-assuredness that she found intensely attractive: a 'don't fuck with me' attitude that made him stand out from the rest of the LA actors. Others were obviously acting. Kelly's persona seemed real.

Now he motioned for her to follow him to his apartment. Neither one said a word as they walked up the wooden stairs. When they got inside, Jessica thought that Kelly might tell her his plans, describing every sexy detail in advance. One of his favourite tricks was to use dirty talk as foreplay, not touching her, but standing across the room and staring at her as he spoke. He didn't do that today. Instead, he simply told her to undress.

'Strip for me, baby,' Kelly said, his voice low. 'You know how I like to watch.'

Yes, she knew. Kelly had a thing for playing the voyeur. With his eyes focused on her, Jessica pulled her flimsy blue-and-white floral slip dress over her head. Her fingers trembling, she slid her silky, pale-pink panties down her toned thighs and stepped out of them. Then she stood there, waiting. Kelly was wearing his faded jeans and a lightweight blue workshirt. The fact that he was still clothed excited her more than if he'd been nude.

'You're wet,' he said, stroking her pussy lightly with the tips of his fingers and finding the liquid cream centre between her thighs, like the secret vanilla ice cream hidden within the popsicles he'd just bought. 'What do you think I'm going to do?' he asked. She shook her head, unwilling to guess, and her hair came loose from the ponytail, covering her shoulders in a mink-coloured curtain. The softness of her straight mane tickled over her naked skin. Every move, every gesture, seemed tinged with sex.

With finesse, Kelly bent Jessica over his coffee-coloured sofa, his hands lingering at the indent of her slim waist, then sliding down to cradle her lovely ass. Her breath came faster as Kelly continued to trick his fingers along the slippery split of her body. For a moment, it seemed that he would stay here and play – might bend on his knees and fuck her with his warm, knowledge-able mouth. Sometimes, he would eat her until she reached climax over and over, making her whole body shake with the spirals and circles he traced with his tongue. But, today, after a moment of his playful caresses, he got himself under control.

'Stay still for me, Jess,' he said. 'Don't move.'

She turned her head to watch as he ripped open the pack of popsicles and pulled one out. Was it because she wanted to be a writer that she was so in tune with every small detail? She didn't know, but she always grew more excited when she could process all parts of a story. Like now, as she watched Kelly put the popsicle in his mouth as he carried the rest of the package to the freezer. She could see him through the open hatch from the living room.

Returning, he took the treat out of his mouth. The popsicle had a well-crafted point on the end, like a miniature rocket ship. 'This is going to be cold,' he said in a warning tone. 'It's going to be cold and hard and wet inside you.' She held herself steady as he used one hand, fingers icy from the popsicle, to part her already slick lips.

And then she felt it.

The tip of the creamsicle drew slippery pictures between her legs, kissing her with ice. She shuddered, but Kelly didn't stop. He pushed the tip into her, and the ice-cream confection started to melt from the heat of her body.

'The sofa –' she said softly, her last rational thought of the afternoon. They would stain the fabric with the sticky-sweet juices, but Kelly didn't seem to care. He simply pushed the popsicle further inside of her. Then he got down on his knees behind her and started to lap the dripping juice and ice cream from her thighs, placing his warm, ready mouth just under her pussy and catching each dulcet droplet of the melting sugar and cream.

'Oh, yes, lick me,' she moaned, as she felt the heat of his breath on her. If only he would touch his tongue to her clit. Kelly didn't. Not yet. He always took things at his own pace, refusing to rush to the finish line. Now he removed the popsicle, and Jessica's pussy felt suddenly empty. She wanted the dessert back inside her, or something else –

Before she could beg for the treatment that she needed, he leaned forward, replacing the popsicle with his mouth. His tongue was cold from the ice cream, but much warmer than the frozen treat. The two different temperature sensations, one right after the other, made Jessica feel weak inside. Tremors of pleasure ran through her as Kelly continued with his skilful ministrations.

With his lips parted, he met her desperate clit and flicked the point of his tongue against it – just once, as a little wake-up call. Instantly her pussy began to heat up. Next he thrust his tongue deep inside her body, licking in long strokes on the inside walls. Tasting her. Teasing her. Making her squirm and moan against him. She wanted too many things at once, and all she was able to do was squeeze her eyes shut and hope that Kelly could read the language of her body.

He did. Again, his tongue pressed to the front to find her clit, tapped on it, then picked up a delicious in-and-out rhythm within her pussy until Jessica found herself gripping on to the velvety brown sofa cushions, pushing back, pressing her cunt to his face. The only thing that she wanted now was release.

'Sweet thing,' Kelly murmured, speaking into her body. 'Jessie, baby, you taste so fucking good.'

That extreme sense of pleasure was almost too powerful to bear. For a moment, Jessica didn't think she could take it. Except she *was* taking it, obviously could take it, and immediately started visualising what was going to happen next. With Kelly, she never knew. All she could be sure of was that he had a plan, and that it would undoubtedly make her come.

And that was all she really needed to know.

Book One:
Falling Hard

Sweet thing, with your champagne eyes
And your saint-like smile.

– Van Morrison

1

Every good news story has a who, what, when, where, why, and how. That's what Jessica reminded herself as she walked along Westwood Boulevard towards the newspaper office. Pyramid format means an editor can cut from the bottom. That was another tidbit she'd learned in her journalism class. Put the important facts first to capture the reader's attention. What else? Newspaper stories always begin with lead statements that tell the main concept of the article.

Busy mentally prepping herself for the appointment, she found herself filled with the type of bubbly anticipation she tended to get before riding a rollercoaster, or climaxing on the tip of Kelly's tongue. Even so, there was no reason for her to feel insecure. Her achievements, even at the tender age of nineteen, were worth bragging about. She'd been a top writer on her award-winning private-school newspaper before spending two years in Paris working on an underground 'zine devoted to the nightlife of the city of lights. This was a job she'd spent years dreaming about.

But as she stood in the doorway of the *Zebra* office looking in, all she saw was disarray. Alexander Harris, the managing editor, had told her over the phone that Friday afternoon would be a quiet time to interview. The staff put the weekly paper to bed by 4 a.m. every Friday, and only a few people hung around the rest of the day. People like Alex and Josh Charles, the lead ad man, who had to be there, and people like Pete and Todd, lonely staff members who had nowhere better to go, according to Alexander Harris. Jessica watched through the open door, listening intently to the dialogue these guys were throwing at each other as two of the men in the room squared off.

'Come on, Alex,' Josh whined. 'What are you? Scared?'

'You're on some weird testosterone kick,' Alex told him, sounding tired.

'Get it over with and shut up, the both of you,' Todd muttered, sleeking his greasy, fifties-style haircut back in place with one well-practised gesture. 'I'm sick to death of this. Some stupid macho contest every single Friday –'

To quieten Todd, Alex stood back to back with Josh and put his palm flat on top of Josh's sunstreaked blond hair. 'You're at least two inches shorter,' Alex informed him.

'You've got lifts in your loafers,' Josh shot back.

'Pete?' Alex asked, summoning assistance from the mountainous figure seated nearby. Without looking up from his laptop, Pete said, 'When you're horizontal with your lady, it won't matter. So why the fuck should you care?'

'He's taller,' Jessica said.

'Told you,' Josh sneered, not concerned with who was speaking, only with the fact that he was right.

'Not you. *Him.*'

Alex looked over as she pointed his way. There she stood in the doorway, staring at the two men, then glancing past both to take in the sprawling, L-shaped office. Alex and Josh were instantly mesmerised. Jessica had on a cornflower-blue micro-skirt, her favourite white-fringed cowboy boots and a pink angora sweater the colour and softness of freshly spun cotton candy. Her long hair, up in a ponytail, revealed a slender neck encircled by a deep blue velvet choker.

Without moving away from Josh, Alex turned to take in the office from Jessica's perspective. Pete sat on one of the chewed-up black leather sofas, surfing for porn on his laptop. Todd lay comfortably on the other sofa, talking vigorously into his miniature cellphone. On Alex's desk was a large, empty pizza box. Crumpled balls of paper and dirty napkins littered the floor. Copies of *Zebra* magazine were everywhere. A dartboard hung on one wall, a photograph of Josh's face tacked to the centre. Alex swivelled his head back towards the young girl in the doorway. As she walked in, she said, 'Now, tell me which one of you has got the bigger cock.'

Josh stepped away from Alex. 'I have to get back to work upstairs,' he told nobody in particular. On his way out of the room, he ripped his photo off the dartboard. There was another stapled directly beneath it, but he didn't bother tearing that down. He simply stalked out the doorway, muttering about lack of respect. In the courtyard, he turned around and checked Jessica out with interest from behind.

'Can I help you?' Alex finally asked.

'My name's Jessica Taylor,' she said. 'I called.' Her voice was soft, semi-husky and shy all at the same time. 'I talked to Alex,' she added, staring pointedly at the tall, striking man with the sleepy-looking hazel eyes.

'I'm Alex.' He seemed to slowly realise that he'd arranged for someone to come in. Jessica could tell from his expression that he hadn't expected someone like her. 'You're right on time,' he said. Rapidly, as if afraid she might flee, he launched into his spiel. '*Zebra* is a small, entertainment weekly paper. This is a hands-on job. Working here would be a great opportunity for a person who wants to learn everything there is to know about journalism.'

'Oh, I do,' she said, and her blue eyes glowed.

'There's plenty of potential for promotion, and the hours are flexible. We can definitely work around your college classes,' he assured her. 'What year are you?'

'Freshman,' she said, and Pete choked from the depths of the sofa. 'I took two years off after high school to work in Europe,' she explained. 'I'm a late bloomer.'

'Come by at seven-thirty on Monday night,' he told her. 'We're having our weekly staff meeting. You can get acquainted with the whole cast of characters. Then, if we haven't frightened you off, next Friday is the big staff Halloween party. More than just the staff, actually. All of our advertisers, neighbours, friends –'

'Ex-lovers,' Todd added, winning an instant scowl from Alex.

'I wouldn't miss it,' she said honestly, then waited for the questions. Certainly, he'd want to read through her clips, which she had carefully arranged in a new violet portfolio. But Alex didn't seem to care about any of that. With finality, he shook her hand and told her he looked forward to her coming along.

'I'm sure you'll fit in perfectly,' he added.

As he held her hand, she felt a flush creep along her jaw. What was going on? This man with the circles under his eyes and the rumpled, mismatched outfit had obviously gotten no sleep in the past 24 hours. Yet he had an oddly disarming air about him. Writers, she thought, always turned her on. Especially ones who had actual ink on their hands from holding freshly printed papers. In the extended silence, she was suddenly aware that there were two other men in the room. She also realised that Alex might think it odd that she'd been holding on to his hand for several long beats. 'It's a costume party, right?' she asked, as if that's where her mind had been.

He nodded, and she extracted her hand and said she'd

see him on Monday. She left, quickly, before she could embarrass herself further.

Thoughtfully, Alex watched her walk out the door, through the courtyard, and on to Westwood Boulevard. Once she was out of sight and hearing range, Pete said, 'You'll ruin her.'

'If Dashiell doesn't get her first.'

The intercom buzzed, and Alex went over to his desk. 'Yeah?'

'She still there, Harris?' Josh asked, his voice all innocence.

'You know she's not,' Alex said patiently. 'You've got a clear view of the courtyard from your window.'

'So who was she? Some stripper hired for your birthday?'

'She was here about a job.'

'I know those kinds of jobs,' Josh said. 'Off comes the sweater, down comes the hair, the skirt's on the sofa and she's squirming in your lap and calling you "Daddy".' He sounded nostalgic.

'She's our new intern, Josh, a journalism major.'

'I bet she was sent by Exotic Escorts. They just placed a monster ad with us. Back page. Four-colour. No money problems this week, man. We are set.'

'She came from UCLA. She's a freshman.'

'Oh, Christ,' Josh sighed, his voice hoarse. 'I remember freshmen.'

Alex released the intercom button and moved away from the desk. If Josh was going to take a perverted trip down memory lane, Alex knew better than to ride in the tour car with him.

Dashiell Cooper was taking his own perverted trip in a luxurious private cabin on a transatlantic flight. Reclining on his stomach, he was being attended to in one of his all-time favourite ways: a full-body massage with plenty of sweet-scented almond oil. And nobody knew how to please him like Gizelle. Her graceful fingertips, dripping with the oil, stroked gently along the back of his neck, slid along the powerful muscles of his back, then trailed down on either side of his spine. For nearly forty, Dashiell was in fine shape. Best shape of his life, he thought. His well-muscled body was hard and lean, and he worked out daily to keep it that way. Although right now, he wasn't thinking much of his own build. He was concentrating on Gizelle's.

She straddled him easily, poised on the seat created by his ass, her willowy form adding just the right amount of weight. He thought of how it would feel when he rolled over, her body in the same position as he slid into her beneath the crisp sheets.

Nothing beat fucking on an airplane. And he should know. He'd had a chance to try just about every different sexual fantasy. Money could get you where you wanted to go. He'd received a blow job in the elevator on the way to the top of the Eiffel Tower. Easier than one would think. You only had to arrive early in the morning, before the regular tourists showed up, and pay off three people for the chance of taking a frisky private ride. Years before in his misguided youth he'd done it on a gondola, nearly tipping the boat into the filthy waters of the Venice canals with his exuberance. What else? Screwed one of the Crazy Horse girls up on the stage after hours. But sex in the air, in his opinion, was the best. It was the closest thing there was to fucking in space.

They could look out the window at the sky in a near permanent sunset as the plane headed west, the golden glow creating a halo in Gizelle's metallic-brown hair. Her face still carried a gingery warmth from spending the past week on the yacht. Sunbathing nude, her glorious small breasts, just enough for a mouthful, had been on constant display. The girl possessed one fuck of an amazing body, and she didn't mind showing it. There were no hang-ups about nudity, about being exposed, though that might have been because she was a catwalk model. At 24, she'd already had years of experience being on display. Nothing could be more natural than the way she moved around, naked except for an emerald and diamond necklace he'd given her and the platinum hoop piercing her perfect navel.

Suddenly, wanting to see her azure blue eyes, to kiss her full lips, he rolled over. She helped him by lifting up on her streamlined thighs just long enough to get situated before slipping back down on him. Now his cock was beneath her, shielded by the crisp white sheet and nothing else. She rubbed herself languidly against him, and he thought about how he wanted to fuck her.

This might be their last time for a while. As soon as they landed, she'd have to board a plane to Italy for a photo shoot. The girl was hot and in demand. Not only by the top designers, but by all of those other model-worshippers who flocked to the shows. Dashiell wanted her to remember him in the best possible way, so that the next time he called, she'd slip away again; cancel her appointments and be at his beck and call for the length of his visit, as she had done for the six years that they'd known each other.

It didn't take him long to decide how he was going to stay in the forefront of her memory. He'd fuck her clit. That was his favourite method of leaving a woman – a way to leave her wanting more.

'Put it in me, Dash,' she whispered, sliding the sheet back and exposing the rock-hard erection towering up towards her. 'Fuck me, baby.' Her British accent was delicious to him, the way her tongue seemed to caress every word, especially the dirty ones, bestowing them with a little added sexy charge. Still, he wouldn't give her what she asked for. To her obvious dismay, he shook his head.

'Spread your lips,' he commanded, and she reached down automatically at his instruction and parted herself for him. He placed his cock between them so that she could feel the length of it pressing against her clit. Using only her personal wetness for lubrication, he began to fuck against her body, sliding his hard cock back and forth between her juicy soft lips but not entering her, despite the fact that she was primed and ready. Gizelle sighed and leaned her head back, her long, straight hair nearly brushing the mattress behind her.

'I'm going to fuck you until you come,' he promised, giving her the exact pressure that she craved, his cock rubbing along the seam of her body. 'And then I'm going to fuck you until *I* come.'

'Please –' she said. Just that one word. He understood that it didn't have any meaning at this point. She didn't want him to do anything other than what he was doing, but she had to say something. Had to arch her back and moan, looking like a magazine advertisement come to life. Each time she shifted her body, she reminded him of a different photograph he'd seen: Gizelle selling perfume, Gizelle selling suntan lotion, Gizelle selling anything.

The pleasure on her face was sublime, and it made Dashiell's cock even harder as he watched the beautiful woman grow closer to climax. The heady, uncontrolled picture of ecstasy that radiated from her was priceless. But Dashiell owned this look; this moment. It was all his, for his own pleasure. And, for Dashiell Cooper, life was all about pleasure. Giving it. Taking it. Flooding the senses with it. Some people didn't understand that, but Gizelle most definitely did. As she came, breathing fiercely through her open mouth and sliding her body against his in a rapid rhythm, he finally entered her, letting her contractions swallow him up.

The warm rays from the never-ending sunset bathed their bodies in a golden sheen, and Dashiell closed his eyes and let the light wash over him.

When Jessica got home, her thoughts remained focused on *Zebra*'s managing editor, on his greenish-brown eyes and sharply defined cheekbones. As always, she played her private game of mentally casting a new acquaintance as a movie star. But this time she failed. He was unique; didn't remind her of anyone she'd ever seen. Categorising his features, she remembered his hair was as dark as hers, worn nearly down to his shoulders as if he couldn't be bothered to get a cut. Jessica had always liked the rock-star style of long hair on men, and she wondered what his hair would feel like beneath her fingertips ...

A full moment passed before she realised that Kelly was sitting on the concrete front steps of her apartment, waiting for her. When she saw him, her cheeks grew pink with guilt at the fact that she'd been so consumed by thoughts of another man. But that was silly. She and Kelly were little more than a summertime fling that had amazingly survived through autumn. They'd made no promises to each other.

'You walked to the paper?' he asked.

She nodded. She lived only several blocks from *Zebra*'s offices, in a pale-blue building on a jacaranda-lined street. Although October, the trees were in full flower, their heady petals falling down from the sky like purple confetti. Kelly held several of the blossoms in a make-shift bouquet.

'For me?' Jessica asked coyly, still trying to recover from her visions of Alex. Thinking back, she could hardly believe that she'd asked the 'who's got the bigger cock' question. But a room filled with testosterone, like the *Zebra* office, tended to bring out the rebel in her. She wouldn't tell Kelly about *that* part of the interview.

Kelly had his tortoiseshell Wayfarer sunglasses on, and he tilted them down to look at her as she walked towards him. Her hips swivelled seductively, making the short skirt look as if it had been painted on to her body.

'So did you land it?' he asked as she reached the step.

She nodded.

'Want to celebrate?'

Now Jessica grinned at him, waiting. No man had ever managed to surprise her as much as Kelly. Not her boyfriend in high school, not her lover in Paris. Even though he was young, Kelly had a wealth of experience to borrow from.

'Champagne,' he said innocently, pulling a bottle from behind his back.

'Sounds good.'

'Oh, it's not for you, little girl,' he told her, standing and waiting for her to open the front door to her building, then following her up the stairs. 'It's for me,' he continued when they reached the top landing and she unlocked the door to her apartment.

'Aren't I the one who's supposed to be celebrating?'

'You get to be my glass,' he said. 'That's celebration enough.' Jessica giggled as he lifted her into his arms and carried her through the apartment and into her bedroom. This was going to get wet, messy and potentially loud, she could tell, but she didn't care. Her roommate, Sasha, was at the beach working on a movie shoot, and wouldn't be back for hours.

On the centre of her floor, Kelly spread out a fluffy white bath towel. Then he waited for her to undress. She moved slowly, tossing him her mini-skirt, her petal-pink sweater, the lilac garters and matching G-string she had on underneath.

'Put those white-trash boots back on,' he said. 'I like the way they look.'

She slipped on the fringed cowboy boots, cocked her hip like a cowgirl, and waited for her next instruction. Kelly didn't give her one. For a moment, he was silent, admiring. Jessica had a dreamy body. Unlike most women in southern California, she didn't believe in tanning. The contrasting quality of her pale skin with the rest of her features made her hair seem even darker, her eyes shine a more brilliant blue. Kelly looked her up and down, taking in the way she kept her chestnut-brown curls well manicured in a thin little drag strip of fur over her pussy. She didn't mind him staring, and stayed in her confident position until he moved from the bed.

Instead of speaking, he silently spread her out on the towel. Then he popped open the champagne and let the first bubbly sip pour into the basin of her concave belly. Jessica shivered at the sensation. The bubbles burst against her naked skin, and she could both hear them and feel them pinging against her.

Kelly bent to drink from her, using his tongue to lap at the liquid as if he were a cat drinking from the saucer of her body. Jessica squirmed, loving the way it felt. They might not have too much in common – he was a bartender with fantasies of becoming a famous actor, while she hoped to be an investigative journalist – but they definitely lit up the bedroom together. Lit it up like the vibrant neon lights along Sunset Boulevard.

'You're delicious,' he said.

'It's the bubbly.'

'No,' he disagreed. 'The way your skin tastes. Like some tropical fruit.'

He reached for the bottle again, refilling the indent of her body with the smallest amount of liquid. She wondered what it would feel like if Kelly poured the champagne between her legs. Luckily, she didn't have to wait long to find out.

'Where do you want this?'

He asked the question in a teasing manner, and she guessed that if she named what she most craved he would make her wait. That was one thing she'd learned in her summer with him. Opening her eyes wide, she waited silently to see what he would do.

'Let me guess –' he said, and slowly he let a light waterfall of the champagne rain over her small, firm breasts. Carefully, he licked away every drop. Her nipples instantly responded by growing as hard as tiny, sea-worn pebbles. Kelly playfully licked one, then the other, and then he brought the champagne bottle up again, pouring a sparkling river between Jessica's breasts. He drank heartily, and she squirmed and shuddered at his touch. The feeling was magical.

'You like that,' he said. It wasn't a question, and Jessica didn't respond. She simply watched as he made sure to drink every drop of the champagne from her naked skin. Even though it felt transcendent, her mind was already lost in the future, imagining what it would feel like when he finally gave her what she wanted.

Now, Kelly rewarded her for her good behaviour, letting the bubbly liquid pour in a waterfall over her pussy. It was like nothing else she'd ever felt. Yes, they'd played in the shower at his apartment before, with the hand-held nozzle that sent vibrating streams of pressurised water pounding against her clit. And they'd made love early one summer morning on the lawn while the sprinklers had covered them with a spray shot through with rainbows. But this was different. As the champagne poured between her legs, it sparked against her skin. The tiny bubbles burst as they met her pussy, and Jessica thought she might come from that feeling alone.

Again, Kelly bent to lick her clean, lapping to taste the mix of the liquor and her own fragrant juices. His tongue, flat against her, added to the pleasure of the popping bubbles. 'Intoxicating,' he announced, as if he were speaking at a wine-tasting party. She laughed, liking the vision of Kelly getting drunk off her. 'A subtle bouquet, with a fruity afternote,' he said, sitting back on his heels before adding, 'I think I'd like another swallow.'

This time, he let the bottle tip and a larger wave of liquid splashed over her. Jessica shivered at the cool sensation, then closed her eyes as Kelly resumed his activities between her thighs. His tongue was well versed in this behaviour. He knew how to make all the different designs that she liked best: figure eights that traced over her clit and had her straining; loopy circles that worked gradually inward; and then a different rhythm – a tap-tapping like a drum beat in an oval all around the pulsing gem between her thighs. He played tricks with her, slipping his tongue deep inside her body, then using it to draw invisible pictures on the inner walls of her pussy.

But just when she thought she'd reached her limits, she needed something else. Kelly was a step ahead of her, adding a new trick to the festivities. He moved her on to her hands and knees, and he gently spread her bottom cheeks slightly apart. Then he tilted the bottle again, pouring the remaining champagne in a sparkling flood between the cheeks of her heart-shaped ass. While Jessica held her breath at the rush of pleasure, Kelly brought his mouth back again, this time tickling her hole with his tongue. This move made her arch her back, pressing against him, but he stopped what he was doing and told her to behave herself.

'Trust me.' This was Kelly's favourite phrase. 'Let me set the pace.'

He was going to take her there. But he was going to take his time doing it.

Jessica focused on keeping herself still. When she obeyed him, he would always reward her, as he did now, getting her into a proper position so that he could enter her from behind. The feeling of his warm, hard cock between her lips made Jessica moan out loud. She wondered how Kelly would react. Sometimes he liked her to let go. Other times he preferred her to stay contained.

'Be loud,' he said now, as if reading the thoughts as they entered her mind. 'Let me hear how excited you are.'

She sighed with relief, and then, as he started to fuck her harder, she found it inside herself to make noise. Her moans grew in volume, becoming more intense.

'That's my baby,' Kelly said, urging her on. 'You let it all out.'

Jessica's head was down, her eyes still closed, her arms locked into place. She shuddered as he fucked her, and then she said his name. That was the way to please him. 'Kelly,' she murmured, 'I love your hard cock inside me.'

She was taking back a bit of the power, because this was his secret weakness. Kelly adored it when a girl called out his name as she came. It transformed him inside, and now he worked Jessica even harder, slamming into her with each thrust.

They were going to come together. Jessica sensed it.

'Fuck me, Kelly,' she groaned. 'Oh, fuck me good.'

He did exactly what she wanted, and then he took her one step higher, slapping her pretty ass in rhythm to the motion of his cock. He left handprints on her silky skin, prints that quickly turned a purplish hue rivalling the jacaranda blossoms outdoors. With his other hand he reached beneath her waist to stroke her throbbing pussy.

His fingers slipped between her lips as he played them lightly over her clit. Just a back and forth motion, a pattern that seemed to match the pounding of her heart beat in her ears. Then his fingertips made sloppy circles, sometimes touching her clit, sometimes intentionally missing it, making her want to feel his fingers there even more. Finally he pinched her slippery clit between his thumb and forefinger, touching her more firmly as he sensed she was about to reach climax.

'Oh, God, yes,' she sighed, and she opened her eyes, staring at the pink-painted wall of her bedroom as she reached the final goal. Seeing, but not seeing: the open window, the lacy white curtains shifting slightly in the late-afternoon breeze. Pleasure emanated throughout her body, but just as the orgasm surged through her, she felt a nagging ball of unease rocking in the base of her stomach.

Why had she pictured Alex's handsome face in her mind when she'd come?

2

'Nice shirt,' Avalon said, perching on the edge of Alex's desk. 'Is it new?'

Alex looked down at the striped grey shirt as if he'd never seen it before. 'I've had it for a while,' he lied. Avalon, the paper's gossip columnist, was a pro at sniffing out the truth in any situation. It was obvious from her expression that she didn't believe him, but Alex ignored the look in her eyes. So what if it was a new shirt? No way in hell that he was going to describe the experience he'd had buying the thing. Standing helplessly in one of those hipster stores on Melrose, surrounded by overly cool eighteen-year-olds, he'd searched for something that might make him look as if he knew how to dress. Rather than share this with Avalon, he spoke to the crew around him, trying to gain control.

'People, please,' he said, attempting to get their attention by raising his voice. The ploy didn't work. As usual at story meetings his staff continued to ignore him. Alex banged one fist on his desk, but that only served to knock a stack of *Zebra*s on to the floor. Avalon laughed and quickly helped him pick up the pile of papers.

Monday nights were the only times the whole editorial staff got together. It was a fairly crazed event, but for once Alex found himself looking forward to the occasion. And all because of the new intern. Sure, she was pretty, but that's not what was keeping her in the forefront of Alex's thoughts. There was an energy to her that he found enticing, and this had caused him to dress nicely in preparation for seeing her again. That was truly crazy. He had a steady girlfriend. Well, an on-again off-again girlfriend. A girlfriend who he broke up with repeatedly, but who always seemed to wind up back in his bed again, despite their best intentions of going separate ways.

Still, his heart raced when Jessica showed up right at 7:30. She wasn't going to flake out. You never knew with these young interns. The paper had already gone through several kids in the past year. Some lasted for a few weeks. Some never came back to the office after their initial interview. But Jessica looked as if she were serious about learning the trade.

She stood for a moment in the doorway, looking in at the turmoil, and Alex smiled at her in what he hoped was an encouraging and not lecherous manner and motioned for her to enter. 'Take a seat anywhere,' he said, indicating the sofas, the floor, and the desk tops littered with the newspaper paraphernalia that went with the job: crumpled notes, expired movie passes, laminated press packages.

While she looked around, Alex watched her. Jessica was wearing a crisp white shirt, navy-blue skirt and a checked blazer. Her hair was up again but, instead of a choker, she had on a skinny red tie. On her, the 'Annie Hall' style worked beautifully. After a moment, Alex realised that he wasn't the only one appraising her looks. Josh's eyes roamed up and down her exquisite body, and Todd had his gaze firmly attached to her breasts. Alex wanted to smack the hungry look off both men's faces, but he stifled the urge. Finally he cleared his throat and said, 'Everyone, this is our new intern. Jessica...' He hesitated, unsure how to continue. 'This is everyone.'

A few other people looked up, but most continued discussing what they'd done the weekend before and what they were going to do on the upcoming one. Nobody seemed to notice when Josh stood and moved to

Alex's side. 'Let me give you the real introductions,' he said, and Alex grimaced.

With a wink to Alex, Josh pointed to Pete, who was seated in his normal spot on the far edge of the sofa, surfing for porn. 'That's Pete,' Josh told Jessica. 'Our page designer. His claim to fame is that he can't fit in an airline seat.' Pete didn't comment. 'Next to Pete is Hank who writes video and music reviews. In a previous life he had the name Rock Solid.' Hank flexed his biceps at Jessica, and Josh continued. 'He was named for flexing an entirely different muscle.' Hank gave Josh the finger.

Todd had his cellphone glued to his head. 'On the sofa is Todd, our resident musician. Wherever Todd goes, his cellphone goes too. Then there's Avalon. Sweet Avalon. She was sleeping her way through the staff, but she's currently on hiatus.' From Avalon's expression of accepting bemusement, it appeared as if she and the ad man had a relationship where statements like this were the norm.

'Next we have Barton,' Josh continued. 'He's our sports editor, someone who pretends to be a real man's man. But Barton's deeply guarded secret is that he's a lesbian trapped in a man's body.'

'Think of me as one of the girls,' Barton said, sitting up straighter to show off his T-shirt. Beneath a thin horizontal line, a sentence read, 'You must be this tall to ride this ride.' He smirked as if he could physically feel Jessica's eyes reading the words emblazoned on his strong chest.

Next, Josh looked over at two men playing quarters in a corner. 'Tom Collins and Jack Daniels are two of our ad executives. Don't ask them about their pasts, because they'll only lie.'

'I'd tell you about myself,' Tom explained, looking up at Jessica with bloodshot eyes, 'but then I'd have to kill you.'

'A few people are missing,' Josh continued. 'Our editor-in-chief, for one. Dash's in Europe, but he'll meet you soon. But that's the crew for the most part. You did get all that, right?' Without waiting for her to answer, Josh added pompously, 'If you're going to be our intern, you really need to have a good memory.' It seemed as if he were trying to get Jessica back for her 'cock' comment the previous Friday.

'Done?' Alex asked Josh, glaring. The ad man obviously thought he was being funny, but Alex wasn't amused. 'Now,' the managing editor said, addressing the staff, 'I call this meeting to order.'

'Excuse me, Alex,' Jessica said, interrupting him. 'I think I got it, Josh. That's Pete. He's a big guy with a big . . .' She hesitated before adding '. . . heart', which won her a grin from the large man and a burst of laughter from the rest of the staff. 'Next to him is Hank, the person I'll go see if I ever need help picking an X-rated video. On the phone is Todd, the lead singer for the rockabilly band Third Leg. I've caught his show at Sammy's Mango Hut. I'm a fan.'

Todd moved his phone away long enough to give Jessica a humble bow and less humble wink.

'That's Avalon,' she continued, pointing to the panther-like blonde now stretched out on one of the leather sofas. Avalon had been staring at the heavy gold watch around her wrist, as if contemplating how much more time out of her life this meeting was going to take. At the sound of her name, she shot Jessica an interested look. 'She's a woman and you guys are threatened by her. Next is Josh, shorter than Alex by two inches, but we don't know about his height . . .' As she continued through the staff, the room fell silent. At the end of her speech, she pointed modestly to herself and said, 'Freshman,' and then added, 'But you can call me Jessica.'

'How'd you do that?' Josh asked in awe.

Instead of answering, she glanced over at the managing editor and said, 'The thing is, Alex, you're the only one I don't know anything about.'

Feeling the heat in her radiant eyes, Alex was momentarily speechless. He opened his mouth, meaning to tell her about his nearly optioned movie, about his stint writing for a literary New York magazine, about anything except what the other voices hollered out.

'He's a wannabe writer.'

'Since he can't write, he reviews.'

'He exclusively dates ice queens who treat him badly.'

'Modern dance makes him want to kill someone.'

'He's only nice to you because he wants to get in your panties.'

The voices overlapped for a few moments and then suddenly, in synchronicity, as if they'd planned it, the group yelled, 'But what he really wants to do is direct!'

Read My Lips was part karaoke bar, part college hangout, and all hipster dating scene. Dimly lit enough to create a sexually charged mood, but bright enough to make a love connection, the bar was always packed with the young and lovely creatures who light up the Los Angeles nightlife.

With his matinée-idol good looks, Kelly fitted right in, as did Jessica. After finishing her first editorial meeting at *Zebra*, she walked the few blocks to the bar, intending to describe the events of the evening to her boyfriend. Sharing what had happened would make it all seem more real. But there was something else she wanted to tell him as well. Although she'd aced the first meeting, it hadn't been by chance.

For over a week Jessica had studied the masthead of the paper, memorising the names of the writers. In her mind, she could picture the entire masthead.

Zebra: Staff Members
Dashiell Cooper – Editor-in-Chief
Alexander Harris – Managing Editor
Avalon Granger – Senior Columnist
Josh Charles – Advertising Executive

And on down to the minor players, the writers and advertising sales people who made up the bulk of the staff. After learning the names of the people she hoped would soon be her co-workers, she'd read several issues from cover to cover, paying attention to the individuality of each staff member's writing style. Finally, she'd done research on the Internet, gleaning more background information about Avalon Granger, about Todd X, the musician, even about the past life of Barton. She couldn't wait to tell Kelly that her plan had worked.

Kelly, serving up drinks, grinned as Jessica approached him. She wasn't of legal drinking age yet, would only turn twenty this Halloween, but he'd worked out a deal with the bouncer. If Byrd would look the other way when Jessica showed up at the door, then Kelly would occasionally slip him a joint. It was Kelly's opinion that good Columbian marijuana could get you almost anything you wanted in life. So far, he'd been right.

Sliding up to the bar, Jessica took the offered tall drink that Kelly handed her.

'It's a Screaming Orgasm.'

'How do you make it?' she asked after taking her first sip.

'I can tell you,' Kelly drawled, 'or I can show you.'

Jessica waited for the punchline.

'Back room,' he said. 'We've got all the ingredients.'

Jessica nodded, and Kelly told his co-worker, Sienna, that he was going on a quick break. Sienna winked, as if she understood exactly what that meant, watching as Jessica slipped off the leather barstool and followed Kelly to the private room just to the side of the bar. As Jessica waited while he locked the door behind them, she looked around. The space was sparsely decorated: fake wood walls, an old battered desk and a leather chair on wheels. There were no liquor bottles here, but Jessica hadn't thought there would be.

Once inside the room, Kelly looked her over, then silently undid the red tie around her throat. Without a word, he pulled off her jacket, then spun her around so that she was facing the wall, her palms flat against it.

'A "Screaming Orgasm",' she reminded him softly.

'That's what you'll need the gag for,' he said, slipping the red tie between her parted lips. 'Keep that in place, baby, and I'll treat you right.'

Jessica nodded, then waited while he raised her skirt past her thighs and stroked her supple ass through her dove-grey panties. Would he really make her scream at work? The flimsy red necktie might muffle her moans, but if she truly let loose others would definitely be able to hear, even over the raucous music blaring in the other room. Suddenly Kelly slipped her panties down, leaving them just below her bottom cheeks, and then he gave her a firm spank that made her breath catch. As he did, Jessica stopped thinking about the customers at the bar and started paying attention to Kelly.

'How long has it been since you had your last spanking?' he asked. 'Last *real* spanking,' he added, apparently not counting the little game of pat-a-cake he'd played on her ass after her interview. She understood the difference. When Kelly gave her a true spanking, he took the job seriously, generally putting her over his knee and tanning her ass so that she could really feel it afterwards, knowing that the flush of pain always intensified the feelings of pleasure for her.

'How long, Jess?' he asked again, and his voice held a

tone that let her know he meant for her to answer. Immediately.

It had been less than a week, out at the beach. Jessica had been horsing around, teasing him, and he'd picked her up, sat down on a bench facing the sparkling blue Pacific Ocean, and spanked her bikini-clad bottom until she'd promised to behave.

At first, when Kelly had done things like that in public, Jessica had been mortified. Someone would see, and she would melt from the embarrassment. But, after a few instances of playing in plain view, she realised that people rarely cared what went on around them. That afternoon at the beach they had been in a fairly secluded area, obscured by several dwarf palm trees. Yet other beachgoers could have watched if they'd wanted to, and that was the thought that always made her the wettest. Kelly had coaxed out an exhibitionist side that she didn't know existed.

'How long, baby?' Kelly asked, bringing her around to his line of questioning.

She couldn't really answer. Not with the tie in place. But she made some attempt at a murmured response to appease him, and Kelly instantly said, 'I think it's been too long, Jess. Way too long.' Then he began the spanking in earnest, really letting her have it.

With her hands still flat on the wall in front of her, Jessica tried to behave the way that Kelly most appreciated. He liked her to steel herself and absorb whatever pain he had to give her. Because the pleasure always worked in direct proportion to the pain. An ass-tingling spanking was rewarded with a climax that rumbled powerfully through Jessica's body like the aftershocks following one of southern California's trademark quakes. Kelly knew her main secret – the more he spanked her, the wetter she got.

But, as Kelly punished her, Jessica couldn't stop her thoughts from returning to Alex. She thought about his eyes, and the stark features of his interesting face, and then compared the way he looked to Kelly. She couldn't help herself. With Kelly's surfer-boy looks and blond sun-god innocence, his kinky side seemed that much darker. In contrast, Alex had a troubled, sorrowful look to him, which Jessica thought might simply be from lack of sleep. Working on a paper kept editors up all night. She knew this from experience. But what if that soulful yearning came from something else, something deeper?

She wondered whether he would like to play the way she did. If she pouted and played the brat, would he know that it was time to give her a bare-ass spanking? It was obvious to her that he was enamoured with her; she could tell by the way he watched her move, cautiously, carefully, as if he didn't want her to know that she'd captured his attention. Jessica was a pro at understanding when a man wanted to fuck her. She could play naive, pretend that she couldn't read the signs, but men were so transparent. At least when it came to deciphering the language of their cocks.

Now she envisioned Alex sitting in the chair at Kelly's boss's desk, observing as Kelly spanked her. Not actively participating aside from offering advice. Simply watching. Would that turn Alex on? She didn't know. But it definitely turned *her* on. In her head she could hear Alex talking to Kelly: 'Spank her harder. She can take it –'

At the fantasy of being punished for the pleasure of her managing editor, she had to bring one hand between her thighs and stroke the outer lips of her pussy. Starting slowly, she tickled gently between her legs, not going immediately for her clit, but taking her time. Kelly would have none of her solo pleasures. Quickly he reached for her hands, capturing her wrists behind her back. Pinned like this, she was at his will. He kept her balanced and continued to spank her ass, the blows stinging each time his open palm connected with her blushing bare skin. How long would he keep it up? Would he fuck her afterwards, or would he send her home yearning, forcing her to wait until he got off his shift? God, she hoped not. She didn't think she would be able to wait for three more hours before coming.

Apparently Kelly didn't think he could wait either, because soon he was moving her, positioning her on her back on his boss's desk and spreading her thighs wide open. His hard, ready cock slipped easily into her. The spanking had lubed her up, made her pussy warm and pliable and, as he slid inside, she squeezed him tightly, embracing him with her cunt.

Kelly reached for the tie, still between her lips. He pulled it free and used it to bind her wrists so they were captured over her head. She stared up at him, eyes wide as he pinched her nipples tightly, twisting them slightly to make her moan.

'A screaming orgasm,' he reminded her suddenly. 'That's the goal.'

He was going to make her come from the heady combination of pleasure and pain. Out of all the games they enjoyed together, this was how Kelly most liked to play: sparking their interactions with a hint of danger, with a slight darkness that made the final breakthrough into bliss that much more powerful. Now Kelly let his fingers move down her body, firmly spreading her slippery pussy lips wide apart and running his thumbs along the edge of her clit, capturing it.

Jessica sighed from deep within her, realising that he was going to let her come. He knew how much she could take, because he stopped teasing and neatly pinched her swollen clit between one thumb and forefinger, using his other hand to keep her lips spread wide. This brought the climax rushing forward, the feeling of being opened combined with Kelly's cock pulsing inside her, his hands on her.

'That's it,' Kelly said, encouraging her. 'Come on, baby.'

As she came, Jessica realised she'd told Kelly nothing about her meeting, about the different staff members and what they'd discussed. But maybe that was OK. She and Kelly had always been casual in their relationship so far. No promises. Perhaps there were simply some things that they didn't need to share. Like the front-page news that she was going to the paper's annual costume party the following weekend. And the fact that she was going without him.

3

Friday night couldn't come quickly enough for Avalon. Gossip in Los Angeles was generally plentiful and easy to find, but sometimes Avalon felt that she had to work too hard. What she hated the most was running into dead ends, coming across sources who wouldn't confirm things that she knew to be true. That didn't make sense to Avalon. If you were famous, then you should roll with all that fame brought with it. Welcome the rewards. Make life easier for people like Avalon whose entire living was based on sniffing out secrets.

After a week spent chasing several gossipy leads to no fruition, she was ready to relax. And relaxation for Avalon generally began with a strong drink and often ended in a bedroom. Hers. Her roommate Ian's. Occasionally even Josh's Malibu condo. Didn't really matter, as long as the person knew how to fuck. Mornings after, her conscience occasionally got to her, requiring her to answer the question she hated the most: what was she doing with her life? But morning was such a long way off. She didn't have to worry about that now.

With a steady hand, Avalon used her favourite turquoise kohl pencil to outline her deep-set eyes. Next she added several coats of coal-black mascara, pausing between each application to let the liquid dry. This trick made her curled lashes almost impossibly long and thick. For a moment she took in her reflection beneath the several rose-coloured bulbs that lined her large, oval bathroom mirror. No question about it – she looked like a movie star.

Her impressive body was more revealed than concealed in a silver-spangled outfit that appeared to defy gravity. Exactly how was the tiny strapless number attached to her breasts? Only Avalon knew for sure. A blue-black, bob-style wig hid her shining blonde hair, completing the Halloween costume. At least, almost completing it. Her roommate Ian was the one to add her final accoutrement.

'Hey, baby,' he said, opening the bathroom door without knocking. Ian didn't believe in false modesty – what secrets did he and Avalon have from each other at this point? Besides, honesty was much sexier to Ian than hiding behind a false front. He saw enough fakery in his day-to-day life as a soap-opera stud.

Stepping into the room, he glanced from her fancy reflection to his own. He had dark eyes and darker hair, and he possessed a slightly mussed look, as if he were constantly on the move, never taking the time to care for himself. In reality, he spent hours in front of the mirror, preening. Being at the top of his game meant that even at 31 he still occasionally made the cover of some teen magazine. And in his world, that was important.

Now focusing on Avalon instead of his own mirror image, he nodded his approval. His date for the evening looked amazing and, even if she already knew this, it didn't hurt to add his own accolades. 'Awesome, baby,' he told her. 'Couldn't have chosen a better Cleopatra for my Marc Antony.' Avalon smiled, pleased with the compliment, but she wasn't expecting what came next. 'You know that I'd never travel all the way from Rome to Egypt without bearing gifts.' As he said the words, she looked down at his palm, where a miniature vibrator rested innocently, waiting for her. The toy looked tiny in his large, open hand.

'You're kidding.'

But he wasn't. Leaning against the wall, he said, 'I want to be in charge of your pleasure tonight. I want to turn you on as no other man will be able to. Literally. And from past parties, I know that many will try.' He said this with a wink, and Avalon remembered the previous year's Halloween party, when Ian had suddenly walked into the men's room, catching Avalon fucking Josh against the door of one of the cream-coloured stalls. Her roommate had gone into the next stall without making eye contact with her, as if he didn't even know her. Josh hadn't thought there was a connection between the two, not recognising Ian in his Spiderman mask.

The thought that Ian was listening to her fuck another man had turned Avalon on so much that she had come twice in several minutes, grinding against Josh and then biting back on the hoarse moans of pleasure that had threatened to turn into screams. Much later that night she and Ian had done it back at home, rutting savagely, both imagining her with another man while Ian listened to her come. It had been a particularly memorable Halloween.

So, on this evening, at his sweet insistence and under his intense observation, Avalon carefully slid her dress past the dangerous curves of her hips and positioned the petite device within her already wet pussy. Ian watched, his brown eyes narrowed in concentration, as Avalon's fingers disappeared up inside her velvety slit. She did a little sexy hip-hop move just to make sure that she wouldn't be embarrassed with an unexpected revelation while gyrating on the dance floor. The tiny toy stayed put, nestled deep inside her.

'How do I turn it on?' she asked, her breathy voice letting him know exactly how excited she was at the thought of her secret plaything.

'Don't worry about that, beautiful. Leave the mechanics up to me.'

Then he tilted his leafy headpiece in a gentlemanly fashion that made Avalon laugh. 'Your chariot is ready, madam,' he said. With one hand around her waist, he led her down the hall and out the front door, where his shiny gold Range Rover sat in the driveway. 'We wouldn't want to make your subjects wait.'

Jessica wore her tightest red dress to *Zebra*'s Halloween fiesta – her magic dress. It rested off-the-shoulder with a black band across the top and faux silver buttons running down the front. Even with her short red-hooded cape over it, the dress cast its spell. As Jessica walked down Wilshire Boulevard, several drivers honked in approval. A man in an ice-blue Jaguar even took his hands off the wheel long enough to applaud. This made Jessica smile as she entered the office building on the corner of Westwood and Wilshire and rode to Mathilda's Steak House, on the top floor, in an elevator decorated with paper streamers and spider webs.

She hadn't told anyone on the staff that today was her birthday. That was something she wanted to keep to herself. Yet this was the perfect way to spend the evening, she thought, at a party that was bigger than any she could have thrown in her honour. Kelly hadn't been upset they couldn't spend the evening together because he'd landed a well-paid freelance bartender gig, filling in for a friend. He'd promised they would celebrate together, later.

As she stepped out of the elevator to a crowded lobby, Jessica attempted to get swept through the restaurant doors with a large group of partiers. No such luck. A thick hand grabbed her wrist and pulled her back. 'ID,' the bouncer demanded. Although his expression made it obvious that he liked the dress, his eyes told her that he wasn't going to lose his job over it. There were plenty of adorable girls over 21 already inside.

'I'm an employee of *Zebra*,' she replied, as forcefully as possible. The man shook his head, denying her passage until her boss wandered out of the party, as if on cue.

'She's with us,' Alex assured the bouncer. 'There's no problem.' Even in his bright red velvet suit and extra padding, Alex commanded instant, if begrudged, respect.

'The problem's yours, Santa, if she drinks.'

'On my honour,' Alex replied, 'and the honour of all of my reindeer.' He quickly dragged Jessica by the arm into the restaurant, calling over his shoulder, 'On Dasher, on Prancer, on Dopey, and Sneezy –'

Once inside the large room, a busty coat-check girl dressed as Betty Boop took Jessica's cape and batted her eyes at Alex, who ignored her. Jessica smiled. Alex was different from the cookie-cutter boys who were already lined up at the bar. Jessica made out the standard costumes: football player, pro wrestler, and a dapper man in a tuxedo who must have been going for James Bond.

'Now behave yourself,' Alex told Jessica, pushing her in front of him until they reached the dance floor. 'I'll find out if you're naughty.' He paused and gave her a sexy smile that made Jessica's heart race. 'It's my job.'

'And if I am, will I get a lump of coal for Christmas?' Jessica asked shyly, working to rise to his playing level. 'Or do naughty girls get something else?'

Alex's eyes lit up at the obvious challenge in her voice. He could hear the words in his head before he said them. 'Naughty girls go over my knee,' was what he wanted to tell her. 'They get their little red dresses pulled up and their tiny little panties pulled down. And then they get to feel my sturdy hand connecting firmly with their –' But he felt his date watching him from across the room. Didn't matter that this was a date of convenience rather than love, he wasn't the type of person to act so impulsively. Instead of flirting with Jessica, he offered her over to an Elvis in his later years, assuring her with the words, 'Remember, I'll be checking my list later.' Then he walked back to the other end of the bar to appease Mrs Claus.

Marina had insisted on accompanying Alex to the Halloween party, using the argument that they'd already rented the matching outfits. Besides, she'd continued in her self-righteous vein, everyone would expect to see her there. In reality, nobody from the paper expected to see them as a couple, because Alex had been adamant about the fact that they had finally managed to break up permanently. He'd dreaded the look that he knew would greet him in the eyes of his co-workers. Especially Avalon. Was he so weak that he couldn't say no to her?

Yes, apparently, because when it came down to party time, there she'd been at his side, dolled up in a short red velvet skirt, scarlet fishnet stockings, and white-trimmed jacket as a fiery Mrs Claus. And from the look on her face, it seemed as if she was plenty ready to use those claws if any girls got too close to him.

By 11.30, Avalon had forgotten about the vibrator inside her pussy. She was enjoying the party, especially a new drink called an Octopini – a martini with a tiny pickled octopus floating in place of an olive. She wasn't actually enjoying the drink herself, but she had a great time watching other people try to swallow the briny cocktail without flinching. It was something she'd definitely mention in her next column. As she saw a well-known starlet take a swallow and then make an unhappy face, Avalon mentally wrote the opening to the piece, 'Mathilda's is the last place on earth where you'd expect to come face to face with an eight-legged antagonist...' when suddenly, and surprisingly, the little sex toy inside her pussy hummed to life.

Unprepared for the instant blast of pleasure, Avalon let out a gasp – one that Alex's annoying girlfriend noticed. Why was Marina even here? Alex had sworn to the staff that things were finally over between him and his incubus-like girlfriend. God, but she managed to drain the life out of a room. Everything about her, from her watery green eyes to her cadaverous dancer's figure to her emaciated personality irritated Avalon. Now Avalon had to deal with her because Marina turned towards her in alarm.

'You OK, Ava?' Marina cooed.

Avalon winced. More than almost any other pet peeve, she hated it when people who weren't close to her used that nickname. She kept it in reserve only for the special few who really knew her. Ian. Josh. Friends and lovers.

'Cleopatra,' she corrected Marina, with what she hoped was more smile than sneer. 'And I'm just fine, thank you,' she said next, turning around slowly to see where Ian stood in the crowd. He had to be close by, she knew, but she couldn't immediately locate him. After a moment, she spotted him leaning against one wall, his hand casually tucked in the side vent of his toga, no doubt on the remote control device. The man always kept her guessing, didn't he? Well, she could keep him guessing as well.

Sliding off the polished leather barstool and making her way across the room, she saw Ian shoot her a smile. It was obvious that he thought she was coming his way, perhaps to snag him and drag him off to the nearest deserted corner of the restaurant where she could sit in his lap and let him ride out the rhythm of her pleasure. Or maybe she would lead him out to the open-air balcony, where they could watch the city lights twinkle while they rubbed their bodies against each other.

Not in her plans. She kept walking right on by him,

heading towards Josh, who was in a heated discussion with two young and lovely bunny girls. This evening, Josh was wearing a burgundy silk robe over paisley-print silk pyjamas. He had on a pair of leather bedroom slippers and carried an unlit pipe. His double-dates were both blonde, both blue-eyed, both tipsy. Yes, they were pretty, but there was no contest in Avalon's opinion. She'd always be the winner in Josh's eyes.

'Mr Hefner.' Avalon grinned at her co-worker, bending down so that he could see her ripe, full breasts peeking out of the silvery sheath. 'Would you like to dance?'

Josh responded exactly as she'd hoped, kissing off the bunnies in a brusque, but friendly fashion, and joining Avalon on the dance floor – a dizzying pattern of colour- ful squares lit from below in homage to the seventies disco craze. He held her close, even though it was a fast song, and Avalon wondered whether he'd sense the internal motor vibrating within her. She wasn't worried about her secret being discovered, only excited at the prospect, and charged up by the way that Ian was watching her fixedly from his spot across the room.

Men. You could never let them think they were in control. That was Avalon's number one rule.

Elvis was into skin: the bare skin of Jessica's shoulders above the band at the top of her dress; the pale skin of her arms and back. 'No tan lines,' he yelled above the music. 'I like that. It's rare in LA.' He began a ragged dance step, his white polyester suit glowing blue and then green beneath the flashing lights. Jessica nodded to him and kept moving to the beat, her eyes scanning the room for familiar faces. Most of the partiers were in costume, and many had masks on. She looked for Avalon, but couldn't find her. The gossip columnist had promised to introduce her around at the party.

'You should do an ad for body lotion,' Elvis insisted.

'I'm not a model.'

'Just your skin.' He reached out to touch her but she danced backwards, away from him. This move seemed to make him more interested because he strode forward, pursuing her until she reached the edge of the bar.

'One touch,' he begged. With his gold wraparound shades on, Jessica couldn't see his eyes; couldn't tell if he was serious or playing. She shook her head and took a seat on a red leather barstool, next to a man dressed in a heavy brocade jacket, a buoyant white wig, and a simple black mask that covered three quarters of his face.

'Go away, Presley,' the bewigged man said. 'The girl's obviously not interested in what you have to offer.'

Elvis put on a sad puppy face before catching sight of a slender girl in a Geisha costume, the back of her kimono dipping low to reveal the cosmetically whitened nape of her neck. Off he went through the throng, sniffing for skin.

'You saved me,' Jessica said, putting out her hand.

'Mozart,' the man told her, squeezing her fingertips. She felt spangles of warmth flood through her, starting at the base of her stomach and working lower. Before she could speak, Alex reappeared, glass in hand. 'Early Christmas present,' he said. 'Pretend it's grapefruit juice.' He gave Mozart a look that Jessica couldn't decipher.

She sniffed the drink. 'Isn't it?' she asked Alex.

'And vodka.' He waggled his eyebrows in a Groucho Marx impersonation, made sillier since his brows were painted white to go with his cotton beard. Then he slid past her towards the dance floor. Jessica drank half the Greyhound quickly, before anyone could stop her.

'Who are you supposed to be?' Mozart finally asked.

'Little Red Riding Hood,' Jessica said, 'all grown up.'

'Where's your wolf?'

'I gave him the night off.'

'And your goodies?' the man mused as a tall redhead

approached and attached herself to his arm. Curved, crimson nails dug into the skin of his inner wrist. The man seemed accustomed to it.

'Little Red Riding Hood,' Mozart said, by way of introduction.

'Mozart's wife,' the woman replied, offering her free hand to Jessica.

'Mozart's "date",' he corrected her. The 'date' was dressed in a matching brocade gown and jacket, her hair piled high in elaborate, shiny curls. When she looked at Jessica, her green eyes were cold. 'Are you from the university?'

Jessica nodded, adding, 'But I also work for the paper.'

'New?'

'This is the end of my first week.'

As the bartender, dressed in a rubbery Frankenstein's monster mask, made his way to their corner, Jessica finished the rest of her drink in several large swallows. Mozart held up his fingers to indicate three, paid for the round, and then hustled both women to a nearby booth. He sat between them, apparently enjoying the tension that vibrated in the air. When Jessica looked at him, he winked, and she instantly started to relax. The vodka was already working, and the man's calm demeanour fascinated her.

Mozart said, 'I've heard about you.'

His companion seemed interested in this tidbit of information, and she leaned forward, asking sweetly, 'Exactly what did you hear, darling?'

'I heard that she's got quick fingers,' Mozart said, reaching for one of Jessica's hands. He squeezed her fingertips again, and his touch made Jessica shiver.

'A typist,' the woman announced. She sounded pleased. More than that, Jessica decided, she sounded as if she had killed the competition. Jessica didn't bother to explain that she wasn't a typist but an intern, and that she hoped one day to work her way up to staff writer. Would any of that matter to this woman? Probably not. Besides, this was Halloween, a night of fun and frolic. No need to let someone else's attitude get in her way of having a good time on her birthday. Now the woman slid her way out of the booth, icily excusing herself for the 'ladies'. Jessica watched her leave, and, as she did, she felt Mozart's hand on her thigh under the table.

Avalon's number two rule was to roll with things when they got interesting. And it didn't take too many more twirls around the dance floor with her co-worker before things had reached a decidedly interesting level between Ian, Josh and herself. Was she standing too close to a potential inferno? Maybe, but she didn't care. There were no wedding rings on any of these fingers. Avalon was free to fan the flames as she wished.

Moving in tightly she danced hip to hip with Josh, caressing the skin of his face lightly with her fingertips to let him feel the heat that pulsed throughout her body. She couldn't wait to see what would happen next.

Ian watched as Avalon and Josh danced in front of him. The DJ was playing one funky song after another, and Ian stared, transfixed, as Avalon used her most erotic dance steps, causing a stir not only in the crowd, but beneath Ian's crisp toga.

Thank God for skirts, he thought for the first time in his life, gratefully aware that his erection was well concealed beneath the folds of ecru fabric. Was that why Scottish men wore kilts? There was no time to consider that query for long because now, to Stevie Ray Vaughan's trademark croon, Avalon started to slide her hips against Josh's. 'She's my sweet little thing, she's my pride and joy,' came the words from the speakers. When Avalon was practically fucking her partner on the dance floor, Ian could take watching no longer.

For a moment, he considered his options. The biggest sin in Avalon's world was to be boring. It was why she never lasted long in a relationship. As soon as she reached that comfortable plateau stage with a man, she was off in search of the next best thing. So instead of acting the jealous type, Ian used his head. Suavely, he invited the two lonely bunnies from Josh's table to join him on the floor, making sure that both Avalon and her slick advertising buddy could see him. The girls, instantly recognising Ian from his soap-opera status, were more than happy to keep him busy, taking turns rubbing their cute little cotton-tailed asses against him, book-ending his lean form between theirs and giving him decadent fantasies of becoming a sexual sandwich. He steered them to the centre of the floor, directly in front of the DJ station. From this point they could feel the beat blasting out of the speakers; could soak in that raucous tempo with their skin.

Something was going to happen tonight. The pulse of sexual energy in the room told him that much. Didn't really matter to Ian what happened. As long as it was memorable.

Mozart sighed as he watched his date stalk angrily across the room. 'Andrea has a flair for the dramatic,' he said almost sadly when they were alone. 'You have to understand, she's an actress.'

Jessica nodded, as if that explained everything, as if the word 'actress' was some sort of catch-all term for 'queen bitch'. Rather than dwell on it, she said, 'You know, I've never met a classical composer before.'

'Any questions?' he asked. 'I can tell you a lot about Prague.'

'Didn't Mozart live in Vienna?'

The man didn't seem to hear her, instead saying, 'You've made an impression on the staff. Alex says you're good.'

'He likes everyone,' Jessica said, 'as far as I can tell.'

'That's probably true,' Mozart said, 'but he says you're *good*. The last few interns could barely spell their own names.'

'I do know my ABCs,' Jessica said as Andrea suddenly reappeared at the table.

'They teach ABCs in pre-school, don't they?' the actress asked, slipping into the booth and sliding so close to Mozart that it looked as if they'd been connected at birth.

'Have a quick drink at the bar?' Mozart wondered innocently.

Andrea's eyes narrowed. 'Not so quick. You two seemed busy here. I took care of myself. Have you forgotten how good I am at making sure I'm cared for?'

Jessica interrupted, trying to save the situation. It would help nobody to have a fight in the centre of what was supposed to be a happy occasion. 'Have you been in anything I might have seen? He said you're an actress.'

'Actor,' the woman said, stressing the second syllable. Jessica tried to look impressed, but couldn't. All she felt was sorry for the lady. Again she turned her attention to the dance floor. Where was Avalon? Through the crowd, she spotted her co-worker in a Cleopatra costume. Avalon was busy dancing with two men and two women, and as the fivesome disappeared in the throng of dancers, Elvis stopped in front of their booth and hit a button on his belt buckle. 'Love Me Tender' started to play.

Mozart said, 'It must be time for your next love affair, right, Presley?' He nodded towards a nearly naked girl dressed as the devil. Elvis headed instantly in her red-tailed direction while Andrea refocused her attention on Jessica. 'Do your parents know you're out so late, honey?' She sounded concerned about Jessica's well-being.

Jessica nodded and sipped her drink.

'Isn't it past your bedtime?'

Now Jessica shook her head. She tried to pay attention to what the woman was saying, but Mozart had his hand on her thigh under the table again, exploring, and the secret quality of his touch tantalised her. Subtle, whisper-soft tickles were followed by tender strokes on the inside of her thigh. Then his fingertips slipped up and down the front of her lacy panties. The difficult part was staying still, acting as if nothing indecent was going on, when, in reality, all she wanted to do was close her eyes and bask in the feeling of being so intimately and expertly fingered.

Turning, Jessica stared at Andrea, who was discussing her latest stage production in great detail. As the woman blathered on about the theatre, Jessica felt that her expression would give away her pleasure. Any moment, Andrea would realise that her date was up to no good. But somehow, Jessica maintained her poker face as Mozart's fingers found the wetness between her thighs and probed more firmly now up between her panty-clad pussy lips. Jessica wished they were alone, that he would pick her up, spread her out on the table and continue with his tongue what he'd started with his fingers.

When she looked away from Andrea and met his gaze, she couldn't tell what he was thinking, with his face mostly hidden from view by the mask. He seemed simply to be having a good time, interjecting a few comments into Andrea's long-winded story and occasionally greeting people he knew as they stopped by the booth. He appeared, Jessica decided, to be holding court. Was he someone important, someone she should know?

Halloween was the perfect time to hide behind an assumed identity, but she wondered who Mozart was when out of costume. He couldn't be serious about his date, or he wouldn't be playing with her like this, would he? Suddenly, she had to stop thinking as his fingers finally broached the hidden area under her panties, sliding in the private wetness that awaited him, ever so lightly brushing against her clit and sending an intense jolt of pleasure through her. A moan filled her throat, desperate to escape, but she stifled it by taking another sip of her drink.

His fingers continued on their dangerous trip, now making soft circles over and around her clit. The best feeling was when he put his middle finger directly on top of it and then captured the sides with his ring finger and pointer. Up and down went his middle finger, stroking, rubbing, while his other fingers added delicious pressure. Suddenly, Jessica forgot how to breathe, how to blink, how to speak. She nibbled on her bottom lip as he pressed harder, understanding precisely when to change the rhythm, to give her something new to process.

As Mozart brought her closer to climax, the music in the room seemed to grow louder, the dancers twirling faster as they passed the table. Everything seemed infinitely clear as she came to the crest of orgasm. At this exact moment, Andrea reached under the table, gripping on to Mozart's hand just as he prepared to thrust his fingers deep into Jessica's slit. The woman's own fingertips actually brushed against Jessica's lips, and Jessica sucked in her breath at the intrusion.

Andrea's emerald eyes burned darker than they had all evening, and she looked as if she wanted to say something cutting and memorable, but as an actress without a script, didn't have the words to capture her feelings. Instead, she stood up and stormed away from the booth.

Mozart didn't appeared fazed in the slightest by this turn of events. Taking his time, he leaned forward and kissed Jessica once on the lips, lingering and slow. Jessica flushed and stared at him. The DJ had put on 'Sympathy

For The Devil', and the famous words made it into Jessica's head above the pounding rush of her heartbeat: *Pleased to meet you. Won't you guess my name?*

'You're a sweet Little Red Riding Hood,' the man said. 'Stay that way. It won't be easy for you in LA.' Then he was gone, following slowly after the train of the Actor Andrea. Jessica took the time to finish her drink before standing and shakily making her way through the crowd to retrieve her cape from Betty Boop. She brushed off Elvis as he made another play for her, saying that she was tired and had to get home.

Alex, who had been watching the evening's interactions with great interest from a distance, caught up with Jessica just as she wrapped her crimson velvet cape around her shoulders. They stood at the front door by the bouncer, their backs to the party. 'Mozart wasn't bothering you, was he?' her boss asked.

'He was just having a little fun, Alex,' Jessica said, hoping that she sounded unconcerned. 'See you Monday.'

As she headed towards the elevator, Alex stood next to the bouncer, and both men watched Jessica until the last possible moment when the doors closed in front of her. 'Mozart is a wolf in sheep's clothing,' Alex said, thinking aloud.

'Maybe so,' the bouncer replied, as if he completely understood Alex's dilemma. 'But I'll tell you this, man. You don't need to worry about that one.'

'Why not?'

'Little Red Riding Hood outsmarted the wolf, remember?'

4

Frankenstein's monster had a problem. A big problem. The thick rubbery mask that hid Kelly's identity from those around him allowed him to mutter to himself without anyone hearing. In a low tone, he said, 'What the fuck is going on?'

After getting paid for the evening, he made his way to his Harley, only remembering the mask when he tried to put the helmet on over it. His mind was a jumble of confusion that made simple actions difficult to focus on. Jessica had told him early in the week that she had plans for Halloween. When he'd accepted a bartending job at Mathilda's, taking the place for a friend, he hadn't lost any time thinking about what Jessica's plans might be. It wasn't as if they had to spend every moment together. He'd promised they'd have their own special kind of birthday celebration later: twenty spanks against her beautiful bottom.

But as he'd watched her work her way through the party, he'd felt a painful jolt of insecurity shake his normal confidence level. To get into the mood, Kelly had worn an old costume. With his mask in place, and his manner of grunting to all those placing orders, he hadn't caught Jessica's eye once during the whole evening. But she'd definitely caught his. Flirting with the wigged man, with Santa Claus, and even with a paunchy, unattractive Elvis.

As he rode home, he tried to work out the situation in his mind. Yes, he knew that they'd never made a commitment to each other. To Kelly, no pressure equalled no problems. That didn't explain the jealousy that throbbed through him as he'd watched Mozart lean in to kiss her at the end of the evening. To his surprise, he'd had to force himself to stay put, not to vault over the bar top and bust in on her. Wouldn't that have been a sight? It would not only have meant the end of his job, but undoubtedly the end of their relationship.

Now he couldn't even confront her with the facts, because if he'd been at the party in total innocence, why hadn't he simply gone over and said hello at the first sight of Jessica in her Little Red Riding Hood outfit? That was an easy one to answer. He'd wanted to see exactly how she'd behave when she didn't know he was there. Secrets. Once you let them begin it was difficult to get them under control.

Home again, he sat alone in his apartment with a beer in one hand and the end of a joint in the other and looked out the window at the Santa Monica night. He stared, without seeing, at the stars in the sky, the bands of white light cutting across every so often, heralding some after-hours Halloween event at a nearby club. With past girlfriends, he would have gone after instant pay-back, searched for a little fling of his own this evening. But Jessica was different. There was something unique about her combination of intelligence, sweetness, and that unbelievable naughty side . . .

He had to learn from this experience. It was up to him to let her know his feelings were growing. Maybe their summer fling would turn into something real. With these thoughts in his mind, Kelly began to mentally prepare a special evening for the next date he spent with Jessica. Not on the weekend, since he worked both nights at Read My Lips. He'd have to wait until Monday to give her an experience that she would remember the next time a man looked at her in that way. Yearning. Hungry. She'd have something to think about before she decided whether she'd act on those feelings. He wasn't worried. Not yet. He was only aware, and that was exactly how he needed to be.

Avalon was reminded of that old joke about clowns and VW bugs, except this evening's comic relief had a slightly different query: how many people could fit comfortably in Avalon's bed? More when they were naked. That was for sure. Costumes had been thrown off in a hurry, and two forlorn bunny tails lay discarded like used powder puffs on the floor next to Ian's toga, Avalon's glittery dress and black wig, and Josh's silk bathrobe and pyjamas.

As she grew accustomed to the situation, Avalon momentarily lost count of the new members who had found themselves on top of her sheets. Josh. Ian. Bunny One. Bunny Two. Including herself, the total made five. An uneven amount for ballroom dancing, but a perfect number for an orgy. As Avalon watched, one bunny girl sat astride her co-worker while the other moved into a 69 with her roommate. Ian's playmate opened her pink-lipped mouth around his cock and took his tool down her throat. Then she flicked her little tongue out to meet his balls, and Ian thrust forward, hard, moaning.

The sight was so arousing that Avalon had to bring one hand down her own body, touching herself in a sensual line along the way to reach her pussy. Her fingers meant business. They didn't stop until she had hold of her clit, squeezing gently, then making circles around it with her fingertips. Fast and then slow, alternating the pressure to make the ride last. She could have come simply from watching, stroking her pussy as she viewed the erotic exhibitions unfolding in her bed like an audience member at a live sex show, but suddenly a voice said, 'Let me do that.'

It was Josh. He wanted to eat her out while fucking

the pretty co-ed, and Avalon had no problem with that idea at all.

'I need you on my tongue, Ava,' Josh murmured, and Avalon nodded to let him know that it was what she wanted. Effortlessly, Josh moved himself up on the mattress and adjusted her body. Avalon helped, parting her thighs and perching herself delicately over Josh's lips so that her waiting pussy was perfectly situated over his mouth. Now that they were in the prime position, her handsome co-worker began to trace his tongue up and over her clit, making several rotations to get her good and ready before sliding it deep within her. From this new vantage point, she found herself face to face with the bunny girl astride Josh's mammoth prick. The two women shared a momentary smile of almost sweet embarrassment at fucking the same man without even knowing each other's name.

Here was a situation Avalon had never read about in any advice column. She pictured the question in her mind. 'What is the proper way to introduce yourself to a woman who is fucking the same man you are, at the same time, in your bed?' She grinned as she envisioned the start of the answer: 'Dear Slut...'

But in Avalon's bedroom, there were no such worries. With the type of finesse that only came from having lived through such sexy situations in the past, she easily smoothed over the minor awkwardness. 'You're beautiful,' she whispered when she was breathing so close to the other woman she could smell the girl's musky perfume, could see the lightest dusting of golden freckles crossing the bridge of her nose. 'So pretty.' Leaning forward slightly, she gave the girl a full, wet kiss on her parted lips, then let the kiss extend as her new bedmate opened her lips wider and met Avalon's tongue with her own.

That was all it took – the physical key to unlock the rest of the evening's events. The bunny reached cautiously forward and tentatively touched Avalon's breasts, ran her fingertips lightly from one nipple to the other, stroking gently. When Avalon closed her eyes and moaned, the bunny grew more adventurous. From Avalon's breasts, the girl moved her hand down the flat of Avalon's firm belly, searching between her pussy lips to find her throbbing clit while Josh lost his tongue within her cunt. The vibrator had already been removed and discarded, but Avalon suddenly felt as if she had her own personal motor inside of her.

Oh, yeah, she thought. Can't get better than that –

Except that it could. Because Ian wasn't able to let the evening continue without joining his duo to the trio, connecting the parts in the most interesting ways. It simply didn't seem fair to him to remain an island alone, when the five together could create so much more intense friction. Directing his new lover, he had the girl kiss her bunny mate and then kiss Avalon.

'Make nice,' he whispered. 'Get to know each other.'

Mouths pressed together, slipping against one another, and the women joined lips in a sexy three-way kiss that made both Ian and Josh suck in their breath in awe.

Men were so easy to please, Avalon thought. But women – women were far more complicated. They needed more touching. More talking. More everything in order to reach their pinnacles. Maybe that wasn't fair, but it was true. Still, on this evening, each of the partiers seemed to know a range of tantalising tricks to help the others along. They worked together as if part of a well-choreographed X-rated production and, within minutes, the five playmates were joined in extreme positions. Hands overlapped, tongues met, limbs entwined in the most delicious and decadent ways.

Avalon found herself touching one of the bunny girls in a soft, lilting manner, while using her free hand to tug on Josh's cock in a much more powerful rhythm. She couldn't believe how effortless everything felt, even when she no longer could tell who was connected to who, or how. As she stared at the mess of limbs around her, she understood that untangling the playmates would have been next to impossible, while tying each other up in silky, sticky knots was simple.

In the glow from the streetlight and from several twisted candles, the lovers moved and glided as they danced together to a private and unrepeatable song.

The sun was starting to rise by the time Mozart and his date had finished fighting and finally started fucking outside, on the open balcony of his Hollywood apartment. Light-sensitive streetlights winked off on the avenue below as dawn painted the sky in pastel streaks. The beauty of the morning wasn't lost on him. It simply enhanced his desire to add to the buoyant feeling by climaxing within his cold yet stunning date.

The black iron railing that ringed the outdoor patio was just high enough to lean comfortably against. Perfect height, actually, for fucking one of his frolicking female friends. Now, he lifted his date's heavy brocade dress to discover no panties beneath it. This was Andrea's way of showing him how adventurous she was. *See?* she seemed to be saying with her actions. I'm wild. I'm frisky. I'm free!

But that was a lie. Just another role that she was trying out for, hoping to get cast in a lifelong gig. If he guessed right, she had taken off her knickers in the ladies' room at the party, realising that she was losing his attention to Little Red Riding Hood and wanting to jumpstart his interest in her. He knew all of these things as facts, the same way he knew that he and this woman would never be together for long. She was another in his long list of lovers to call when he was lonely. That didn't take away his pleasure at being with her. Andrea knew the rules to the game. They were both users. She was using him as a leading man in her mental fantasies. He was using her as a way not to admit that he needed a life-time partner.

'You're so big,' she murmured now as he took her from behind. 'So big and hard, baby,' she cooed, and that made him smile. Who didn't find it erotic to hear some beautiful, classy woman use words you generally heard only in porno films? But he could stay mentally clear enough to realise that she was an actress. How was he supposed to know when she wasn't playing a character? Like now, starring in the role of the willing slut, allowing herself to be fucked doggy-style in the clear morning light on his balcony.

With one hand, he reached under her dress in the front and began to carelessly tickle between her pussy lips. He was one of those very good lovers who made everything seem easy. It took him no time to find her clit; to play with the sensitive pearl as if it were a ball of modelling clay from which he was moulding a master-piece. Andrea sighed when he found the right rhythm, moving two fingers over the rise of her clit as if rubbing a polished stone.

Even as he played her, his mind was somewhere else. But as usual, he was not at all disturbed or guilty about the thoughts that ran through his consciousness the entire time he pumped hard into his date. What was the use of feeling guilty? He took life as he saw it. And what he most wanted to see at this very moment were the undergarments beneath his new fantasy's dress. Not Andrea's, but the lithe and flirtatious girl he'd met at the party. More specifically, he wanted to know what Red Riding Hood's panties looked like.

And, even more important than that, he wondered who the lucky man was who got to slide them down her sweet, young thighs this evening. Did he know what a prize he possessed?

5

Slowly, Jessica undid the buttons on her leopard-print dress. Her fingers trailed down the opening, parting the material so that her boss could see the lack of bra and her perfect, round breasts beneath. Just waiting for him to lick, to suck. He had plans for her this evening. Intense plans. Those beautiful nipples would be kissed, pampered, and then captured between two clothes pegs so that Jessica could really feel it. She'd look down, he knew. She'd blush and squirm. But she'd love every fucking second of it.

As he drew her closer to him, she put her hands around his body and murmured –

'Alex?'

Jessica was making it difficult for the managing editor to focus. In his mind, he created chapters from a fictional novel, a dirty story that starred him and this new intern in a wide assortment of sexually intriguing situations. None of which was remotely possible in the current environment.

What he ought to do was excuse himself from the meeting and make a quick sojourn to the men's room. Jack off for the three and a half fucking minutes it would take, and then come back with a tired hand, a pounding heart and a clearer mind. Because at the moment, he was getting nothing done. Literally nothing. Jessica would look at him with those large, inquisitive blue eyes, and he'd want to lean over and kiss her. His lips pressed to hers, then pulling her bottom lip into his mouth to bite hard and make her moan –

Wouldn't that have shocked everyone? The managing editor losing his mind right in the middle of a meeting. They'd run a front-page article on it, a mea culpa to the many readers who had put their faith in him for all of these years. 'Managing Editor Melts Down'.

To hide his feelings, Alex assumed an extra-serious act. Without once cracking a smile or giving into the general silliness that pervaded these meetings, he discussed the deadlines with the page editors gathered at the table. For once, he was thankful for being so well organised. Yes, his desk might look like an explosion had gone off somewhere in the epicentre, strewing papers and files in its wake, but he had a mental list of what needed to be done by whom and when.

Once he'd checked in with each editor for brief status reports, he dismissed everyone to work on their individual assignments, speaking more sternly than usual and winning questioning glances from Barton and Todd. Glances he chose to ignore. After the rest of the writers had dispersed, Jessica stayed where she was. She didn't have an assignment yet.

'What should I do, Alex?' she asked.

Get on your knees under my desk, was his first thought. Or better yet, strip out of those clothes and let me bend you over the sofa. No, not *let me*. That sounded too ineffective for what he wanted. Which was to take off her clothes himself. Quickly, tearing them in his haste, hearing the fabric rip in his hands. Today, she was wearing a long-sleeved leopard-print dress made of some stretchy material, black opaque stockings, and leather pumps with high, square heels. She'd won approving glances from all of the male staff when she'd entered the office, but what Alex wanted was to get her out of her clothes immediately, and then spread her out on the floor and just fuck her. Hard. Fast. Get it over with the first time so that he could then work slower the second round, letting the electricity between them flicker.

OK, so none of these suggestions was particularly workable, but that didn't mean he didn't wish every vision in his mental movie would come true. Finally, he regained his sense of decorum and said, 'I need to see your writing style before I know how we can use you. When I feel that you're ready, I can send you out on assignments. First, I think you should start with something simple.'

Simple, like opening your pretty lips and sucking, sucking, sucking –

Man, he was losing it. He felt eyes on him and looked up to see Avalon strutting minx-like through the office. She lowered her rhinestone-studded sunglasses and gave him a wink behind Jessica's head, as if she could read the ticker tape of Alex's X-rated thoughts. Just what he needed. Only someone with a mind as filthy as Avalon's could possibly guess what Alex desired. Hurriedly, he shuffled through the mess of files on his desk until he found the one that Josh had handed him earlier in the morning. Filled with information from this week's advertisers, the file bulged with random papers. Alex opened the folder and showed the information to Jessica.

'We do a feature each issue that reads like a real article, but is actually another form of advertisement,' he explained. 'Little paragraphs in a chatty, friendly style about how good a particular restaurant is, or what great service a dry cleaners gives. Why don't you read through these press releases and see what you can come up with.' He reached for an old issue of *Zebra* and handed that to her as well. 'You can use this for reference,' he said, pointing to the previous week's write-up, a half-assed version done by Josh. 'I know there's not much to it, but I think you'll do great.'

Jessica smiled. Alex saw easily through her facade. It

was obvious that she didn't want to spend her time writing advertising copy.

'Don't worry,' he said kindly. 'I know that you're far better than this. I read the clips you left for me, and I can tell that you'll move quickly through the ranks. But it's standard practice. Prove how good you are with this assignment, and I'll give you something else to do. Something you can sink your teeth into.'

Like my shoulder as I fuck you.

Again, Avalon shot Alex a look, as if she sensed that the 'something else' he truly wanted to give Jessica happened to be the nearly eight inches tucked serenely away beneath his neatly pressed khakis. He frowned at her, and then pointed Jessica to a free computer in the corner of the office. 'Show me what you've got –' That won him another smirk, which he ignored; Avalon was known for having sex on the brain. 'Then we'll talk.'

The flowers arrived after lunch, a bouquet of long-stemmed white roses spilling out of an expensive cut-crystal vase. The fragrance filled the entire downstairs office, but nobody mentioned the bouquet until Avalon re-entered the room, slightly tipsy from spending a two-hour Cosmopolitan lunch pumping one of her favourite sources for information. Flushed with a combination of success and alcohol, Avalon's senses were in high pitch. At the sight of the flowers, the gossip columnist instantly moved to Jessica's side.

'From your boyfriend?' Avalon purred, reaching forward to stroke one fingertip along the ridge of a satiny open blossom. It was in her nature to learn the scoop on the lives of her co-workers, even if the rest of the world didn't care. But some of the other people in the room definitely did care. Avalon knew that Alex, for one, was listening carefully to every word. His eyes must have roamed repeatedly to the card when it had arrived, trying to make out the words from a distance. Poor Alex was too easy for Avalon to spend any time deciphering. He wore his desire openly.

'He must love you,' Avalon continued when Jessica hadn't answered. "Or he must have done something very wrong," she added, laughing to soften the words.

Jessica shook her head and handed over the card. 'Nope. Not from Kelly. It just says 'Looking forward to seeing your goodies'. Can you believe it? All I can think is that it's from Mozart – the man dressed as Mozart at the Halloween party.'

At the name, Alex coughed loudly, and his expression darkened. He squinted at his computer screen when Jessica looked his way, but Avalon wasn't fooled. Again she started to laugh, but this time she couldn't stop. Pretty soon, she was sitting on the floor, collapsed in a fit of giggles. Her blush-pink skirt rose up on her thighs, revealing the lace edges of her garters, but she didn't bother to fix the hem. By this point, she didn't care who on the staff saw what. They were too close to be embarrassed about something as silly as showing her panties.

'What's so funny?' Jessica finally asked, looking down at her.

'You're only here a week, and already you're the star of the soap opera,' Avalon said when she caught her breath.

'I don't get it. Do you know him?'

Now Avalon got a sly look to her face, and as she stood, she brushed her hands along the front of her short skirt, smoothing the fine material. 'I know everyone, Jessica. Haven't you heard? My sources are all over the city.' She shot the managing editor a look, but he didn't bother to meet her gaze. 'I would have thought that Alex would have given you a little more behind-the-scenes information than the brief intro from the other night.'

Uh-oh, Jessica thought. Did that mean that Avalon

had slept with Mozart? She wished she could ask more questions, but from the way Avalon was staring at her, she decided to keep quiet. She wanted to know more about the mysterious musician, but she'd put her own journalistic skills to good use to find him.

She didn't need Avalon's help, did she?

For the rest of the day, Jessica focused on the menial task that Alex had given her. She read the press releases, stunned at the fact that in Los Angeles, even dry cleaners hired PR agencies. Then she worked to build a column around the different factoids. Then she dived into the lead:

> *Wouldn't you like to rub up against your favourite movie star? Your jeans sliding against those worn by the celebrity of your daydreams. T-shirt pressed to T-shirt. Undergarments dancing and entwining ... All right, so maybe you won't be going on a date with Brad Pitt or Julia Roberts any time soon. But if you bring your clothes to Out, Out Damned Spot, your laundry may have a fantasy life of its own. Out Out, located at 5 North Beverly Boulevard, is the cleaners to the stars. So why not make the secret dreams of your bras and panties come true.*

When she was finished, Jessica gave Alex the story on disk, then excused herself to get a cup of coffee at the cafe down the street. Although the work day was almost over, there was the large weekly staff meeting that evening. She wanted to be mentally aware for it. Last time, she'd been the newcomer, and her nerves had run freely. Now she hoped to learn more about the obviously complex relationships taking place between the staff members.

If she was going to fit in, she needed to use her wits.

* * *

As Alex looked over Jessica's file, he felt inordinately pleased. Past interns had simply shuffled around what was on the press releases, but Jessica had made the piece her own. With guidance, she would easily become one of his top writers, which meant that he could do a lot for her. Not, perhaps, what he wanted to do for her, or *to* her, holding her up against the wall of his office, sliding what he was certain would turn out to be her filmy panties aside, probing her silky pussy to see whether she was wet enough. And of course, in every single one of his fantasies, she was dripping, his fingers glistening in the light when he removed them. When he licked them clean . . .

Yes, that's what he wanted to do, and it was out of the question. At least, until he got his own love life straightened out. But what he could do right now was help her in her career. Sitting back in his plush leather chair, he reached for an emergency cigar from the back of the bottom file drawer of his desk. Avalon would have given him a double dose of shit if she'd walked in at the moment he brought his silver lighter to the end of the stogie. For over a month, since Avalon's 28th birthday bash, they had been after each other to quit smoking, Avalon with her addiction to mentholated Kools and Alex with his Freudian fixation on cigars. But finding himself momentarily alone in the office, he caved. If he couldn't get what he wanted physically, at least he could enjoy an occasional Cuban.

Closing his eyes, he savoured the first rich taste of the cigar, while trying to figure out how he would help his new writer. A choice assignment. That's what he would give her. Maybe *she'd* be the one to move forward, utilising the paper as the stepping stone that he'd always thought it would be for himself. He'd never have believed it if someone had told him that he'd be sitting at this same desk six years after he'd taken the job. No, his plans had included movie deals and the high-flying lifestyle that went with them.

Wasn't really his speed, anyway, was it? He'd had several fights with Dashiell on the subject, Dash telling him to get used to it, he was a newspaper man through and through. Alex rebelling and saying that Dashiell was simply a party boy, playing at running a newspaper. That Dashiell was the one who should re-evaluate his goals. Look at him, with his fucking tally of the women he'd done, and the places he'd done them, collecting sexual experiences the way some people collected stamps.

But Jessica was different. He could see her –

Naked, that's right. Every goddamn time he closed his eyes, that's how she appeared. No matter what cute outfit she'd put together to wear to work – and she'd shown off quite the flirty wardrobe during her first week on the job – he mentally removed the items one by one, viewing her from the front, the back, the side. That Little Red Riding hood outfit she'd had on at the office party was his particular favourite. Although tight-fitting, it had been sweet none the less, perfectly suited for her personality and her appearance. In his mind, he peeled it off her, revealing her nude form and then taking his time to appreciate her beauty.

Jessica was so different from the normal LA girls. She didn't look like the type who would destroy herself to get ahead. How refreshing was that?

At quitting time, to top the events of the day, Mozart called.

'Is this Little Red?' he asked.

'Speaking.' She couldn't believe how calm she sounded. Since Friday night, her feelings about the events at the party had fluctuated dramatically. Even after discussing the situation in depth with her roommate, Sasha, Jessica couldn't decide whether the man's actions at the party had thrilled or repulsed her. Still, whenever she closed her eyes and imagined the way he'd touched her under the table, a small shiver ran up her spine.

'I'd like to apologise for the behaviour of the Actress Andrea the other night. Jealousy has no place in a friendship.'

'I've already forgotten about it,' Jessica lied. 'No need to apologise.'

'But I have to warn you. When you play with the big kids, you might get burned.'

She wondered if he thought he sounded tough. Could someone who dressed in costume as Mozart actually play a heavy? The two concepts didn't seem compatible.

'Is that what you guys are?' she asked. 'Big kids?'

'I don't think you're ready for us yet,' Mozart told her. 'You're too nice.'

'Much too nice,' Jessica agreed. 'Compared to your girlfriend.'

'Ex. –'

She waited for him to tell her more, but when he said nothing, she tried to take charge of the conversation. 'Was that what you called about? To apologise?'

'No,' he said, and she could hear the smile in his voice. The tone again made her remember the way it felt to have his fingers wander between her legs, touching her pussy in front of all those other people without any fear of the consequences. That's why she wasn't hanging up on him now. Men who ignored the boundaries always impressed her. She waited to hear what he would have to say.

'I was calling to hear your adorable voice,' he told her, 'and to let you know that I'll be ready for you. Ready and waiting. When you grow up a little. You're a sweet kid, but I'm nobody's teacher.'

Then he was the one to hang up the phone, leaving Jessica listening to the empty sound of nothing but air. It took her a moment to set the phone down in the cradle and try to figure out exactly what she was supposed to be doing.

Alex wandered by her desk at this precise moment, and he stopped in front of her desk as if he wanted to tell her something. Something important. Then he shrugged and gave her a half-smile that was completely unreadable. 'Ready for the meeting, Jess?' he asked softly, and Jessica looked into his eyes, now green, now brown, and wished he'd share with her the secrets hidden behind them.

'You have to understand how things work around here,' Avalon told Jessica. The two were seated at Read My Lips, where Jessica had gone to wait for Kelly to get off work. Avalon had trailed her to the bar from the office, and she'd bought the first round of tequila shots without bothering first to ask what Jessica drank.

'Around where?' Jessica asked, speaking loud enough to be heard over the poor rendition of 'Papa Don't Preach' being wrung to death by some pretty, and drunken, blonde co-ed on the stage.

'*Zebra*. Things look one way on the surface, but you have to watch out. It's sort of like quicksand. You'll get sucked into the twisted little employee dramas before you realise what's going on. And then it will be too late. You'll be fucking stuck.' Pausing in her rant, Avalon reached deep into her purse for a cigarette, then simply held it between two fingers, unlit, like a prop.

Jessica was grateful that Avalon had appeared to have taken an interest in her, but at the same time, she wondered what was going on. The senior writer had followed her out of the office after the staff meeting and invited herself for an after-work drink. Now it seemed that she was simply issuing a warning – and doing so in such a vague style that Jessica didn't know how to process the information. Exactly what was Avalon trying to tell her?

Kelly, making his way towards the women, brought free refills with him. Avalon didn't seem to notice that he and Jessica were acquainted, and Kelly gave Jessica a kind smile, letting her know that he wasn't offended by the assumption that he was nothing more than a barkeep.

'The flowers were one thing,' Avalon said as Kelly moved down the bar again, 'but I know that you got a call tonight as well.' Suddenly, Jessica understood that this was why the woman had asked her out. All the rest of the talk was fluff. Avalon, a gossip columnist extraordinaire, had sniffed out the fact that she'd received a private phone call from a secret admirer. Someone who didn't seem to be secret at all to Avalon. Once again, Jessica found herself desperately wondering who Mozart was, and why he was making a difference in the way that people treated her.

'Watch out for him,' Avalon added, and to Jessica, her voice took on the hushed quality of actors in 1940s mystery films. The ones staring Bogey or Bacall, actors clad in ankle-length trench coats, featuring sinister villains who talked with lisps and walked with limps.

'Who?'

Avalon grinned broadly, as if that was the perfect answer. 'Exactly,' she said, nodding as if she were proud of the intern. 'Treat him as if he were just another one of the many men in your weekend line-up and you'll do fine. In fact, he won't know how to deal with you.' The unlit cigarette danced between her fingers as she tapped the edge on the bar. 'What I'm saying is this: He can't break your heart if you don't offer it up for him first.' She set the cigarette on the counter, as if deciding that she wasn't going to light it after all, then downed the shot of tequila. Before Jessica could reach for her wallet, Avalon motioned to Kelly that she was ready for the check. She paid for the drinks, and slid a five-dollar bill beneath the empty glass.

'Gotta run, Jessie,' Avalon said, squeezing Jessica's shoulder in an older-sister type way. 'You just keep up that attitude and you'll do fine.'

Jessica watched Avalon leave the bar, feeling as if she had not understood anything that the woman had said. But now Kelly was walking towards her again, and from the look on his face, she knew that he was ready to play. She wondered for an instant if he had heard Avalon mention the flowers, but then put the previous conversation out of her head.

'New drink,' he said, sliding the menu forward and letting her look. His finger pointed to the title written in on the very bottom. 'Sex on the Beach.'

'Yeah, I've heard of it,' she told him.

'Wanna find out how we make it?'

The drink itself required vodka, peach-flavoured brandy, several fruit juices and a glass filled with ice. The ingredients for creating this type of sex, however, were totally different. Kelly had come prepared. After punching out, he waited while Jessica slipped into a spare pair of jeans and a long-sleeved black T-shirt that he'd brought for her. Then he rode her on the back of his Harley to a deserted beach near Zuma. The rumbling vibrations of the powerful engine pulsed through her body, concentrating on the space between her legs. She could practically come simply from sitting on the back of his bike.

With hardly any traffic, they made good time, cruising along Pacific Coast Highway by moonlight, manouvering easily around the few other drivers on the road. There was no attempt at conversation during the twenty-minute drive, but Jessica felt that Kelly was telling her everything she needed to know by the way he slid the cycle around the curves, pushing hard, striving forward. He parked the bike in an empty lot and helped Jessica off the back. By day, the sandy dunes were crowded with sunbathers. At night, the couple had the space all to themselves.

'Sex on the beach,' Kelly whispered, taking a wrapped blanket out of his leather sidepack and carrying it with him to the sand that sparkled beneath the yellow moonlight. He spread out the blanket and waited for Jessica to join him at his side.

'You were going to show me how you make it,' Jessica prompted him.

'It's fairly simple,' he assured her, sliding her T-shirt slowly over her head and then helping her peel down her jeans. With only the light of the moon above, Jessica's nearly naked body took on a heady glow. Kelly traced his fingertips along the rise of her collarbones, working his hands down behind her back to undo the clasp of her lavender lace bra and release her breasts. He moved closer, wanting to kiss her nipples, to tease them with his lips and tongue.

When Kelly kissed her breasts like that, her body no longer seemed under her own control. Sighing loudly, she arched her back, pressing herself firmly against him. She wanted him to touch her harder, to switch from those soft kisses to more dangerous lovebites. Kelly understood and instantly used his teeth as she wished, gently marking her pale skin as he now moved lower along her belly to the waistband of her turquoise panties. They were trimmed with black lace and he admired them for a moment before sliding them down her thighs and having her step free.

* * *

He'd made a decision on Friday night. Forget Halloween. Chalk it up to a lesson learned. Focus on the future and what he and Jessica could do together. But that didn't mean he wasn't going to punish her. Now, he said, 'I'm going to make you come, Jessie. I'm going to make your whole body tremble. My mouth against your pussy. My tongue deep in your slit. I'll do everything you say. Anything you ask. But you have to do one thing for me.'

'Yes,' she said quickly.

'You haven't heard it yet.'

'Whatever,' she promised. She didn't care what he wanted from her, as long as he kept true to his word and made her come exactly the way he'd just described. But Kelly wanted her to know what she was agreeing to. Standing, he tilted her chin upward with two fingers, forcing her to look deep into his eyes.

'Listen,' he said, 'then decide.'

'What, Kelly?' Jessica whispered. 'What should I do?'

The first request was simple. He wanted her to remain upright in the sand while he made her come. He knew that she'd be desperate to lie down on the blanket, to lose herself in the wonder of his transforming kisses. But that's not what would give him pleasure. He liked it when she could do as he asked, when she restrained herself enough to obey his requests.

'You stay like that,' he explained. 'Don't move. Just let me play.'

Jessica nodded and closed her eyes. He was going to tease her until her legs buckled, until the pleasure slammed through her and made her weak. And she was going to let him.

'That's not all,' Kelly said. 'I'm going to put my fingers just under your pussy –'

'Yes –' Jessica said, her voice already begging.

'I'm going to flick my fingertips against your clit, tickle

it, and make you so crazy you won't know what to do, what to think. Then I'm going to run my fingertips up and down your ribs and under your arms, tickle your inner thighs, and the backs of your knees –'

She was squirming slightly in the sand as he spoke.

'Stay still,' he admonished her, and Jessica squeezed her eyes even tighter shut.

'I'm going to tickle you lightly, all over your naked skin,' Kelly murmured, 'and I'm not going to stop, my bad little girl, until you wet yourself.'

Her eyes opened quickly, and she stared at Kelly in disbelief. But before she could speak, he continued, 'That's the deal. Do you accept my offer?'

She nodded immediately. She couldn't stop herself. Just nodded, because she wanted everything he'd said. If she took the time to think about it, to analyse her feelings, then she might back out. As soon as she'd agreed, Kelly assumed his position in front of her and did exactly as he'd promised. His tongue found her clit and licked it, and then, as he played hide-and-seek games within her pussy, his fingertips searched restlessly for the ticklish parts of her ribs and the sweet indents at the backs of her knees, anywhere that might be a point of release. At first, Jessica controlled herself commendably. She stayed statue-like as Kelly tricked his tongue along her clit, matching the pressure with his fingers and palms against her ribs and over her thighs.

But then he started to work her harder with his mouth and tickle her more seriously with his fingertips. His fingers roamed at the indents above her ass, then parted her cheeks and tricked up and down between. Knowing what he wanted from her made Jessica more excited than she could remember.

'Don't stop –' she told him.

He moved his mouth away long enough to whisper, 'Not until you come –'

Resuming his actions, Kelly continued to kiss and nip her clit, to lightly tug on her pussy lips beneath his teeth. In contrast, that light lazy way his fingertips spiralled over her skin had her straining to behave herself. If she wanted him to let her come, she had to stay still. She knew that. But taking it, as the tickling intensified, made Jessica groan out loud. This was the only release she could get, giving into the pleasure of letting Kelly know exactly how aroused she was.

'You're close,' he murmured against her skin. 'I can always tell by your taste.'

He was right. She was seconds away from coming, but the thought of what he wanted her to do kept the climax away. She'd never played like this before, and suddenly she wasn't sure whether or not she could keep to her end of the deal. Maybe the orgasm would never arrive, and she'd teeter forever on that brink of almost reaching it, desperate and yearning. Embarrassment washed over her, turning her cheeks pink, making it impossible for her to look down into her lover's face until Kelly said, 'Turns me on, Jessie. It turns me on to see you let go. Any way that you let go.' So come for me, baby. Let yourself go. It's just you and me out here. Just the two of us alone.'

At his words, she did, obeying him in every request. The climax came first, tripping through her and then spreading outward, and then the warm golden stream flowed through Kelly's fingertips like liquid foil before raining on to the sand below. Jessica, with tears in her eyes from the power of the orgasm, locked her legs and stayed upright, feeling the cool breeze flow over her like a heavenly breath.

* * *

Dashiell was into the power of three. Three women, with three glorious bodies, three highly pumped sex drives, three desires to give him pleasure.

He didn't waste time thinking about how he'd gotten to this point. He simply acted, relishing this fantasy come to life. It took a little manoeuvring. There were too many lovers in the bed to form a sandwich – except, perhaps, a Club Sandwich – so he concentrated on distributing his time and affections evenly between them. A kiss here. A stroke there. A well-placed thrust or two where it would do the most good.

'Oh, yeah,' one of the women sighed. 'Just like that.'

The women were easy to tell apart because he'd landed a blonde, a brunette and a redhead, and although each one seemed similarly determined in her goal of getting him off, they also had their own special identities. The brunette, for instance, focused on kissing him, and she had a mouth made for oral delights. Her rosy, bee-stung lips met his, and then he felt her tongue, just flicking out, a little lick against his own. He savoured the kiss, tasting the sweetness of her mouth, trailing the tip of his tongue along her bottom lip before drawing it between his teeth and biting her. He loved that. Just nipping a woman's full lower lip and making her moan.

While he kissed the dark-haired beauty, the redhead ran her fingers over his back in a tantalising massage, before coming in close to whisper secrets to him, adding her own suggestions when they seemed appropriate.

'Kiss her,' she urged. 'Kiss Marlena like that. It's what she needs –'

He followed the command, continuing to French kiss the raven-haired beauty while waiting for the next erotic direction.

'OK, now move your mouth along her throat. Slowly, slowly . . .'

And then there was the blonde, a honey-haired goddess, bent over in front of him on the mattress, so that even while he was kissing her brunette friend, he could take this one doggy-style, thrusting in deep and gripping on to her gently rounded hips to keep steady. When the three vixens had first undressed, he'd discovered that the blonde was a decorated lady. A tattooed tapestry of different colours was hidden beneath her short red dress. A pair of detailed white wings beat upon her back. A lush flowered ring circled her waist. He tried to imagine what she'd looked like in the tattoo artist's chair. Obviously, she'd been at least partially naked for the experience, and the image of the angelic-looking blonde, stripped bare while being inked up made him groan and thrust even harder inside her.

Most people wouldn't have tried to analyse the situation, to choose favourites. But Dashiell couldn't help himself. Enjoying the situation as a whole, he couldn't quiet the running dialogue within his mind. The blonde captivated him with her inked masterpiece of a body. The redhead, with her filthy mouth, teased his sensibilities. But it was the brunette, with hair the colour of Jessica's, that made him last. His cock stayed hard as he patiently planned the way that he'd fuck her. Not from behind, like with the blonde. He wanted to look into her face, to push her dark hair out of her eyes, to imagine that it was Jessica whose pussy he was probing. *There* was a girl to go for – one who seemed, as yet, untouched by the wicked ways of Hollyweird.

Fantasising about Jessica didn't stop him appreciating this evening's erotic exploits. Experiences like this were what secured his place in the world. He'd been at his friend's club, Dream Maker, bantering with the bevy of beauties stepping up to the bar. He'd chatted with a few promising ladies, but hadn't seen anyone that particularly suited his mood. None that rivalled the trio of Amazon bartenders working behind the counter. Throughout the evening, he'd teased them, tipped well, kept up a flirtatious conversation that included all three. And when the bar had closed, he'd invited the bartenders to join him for a drink at his favourite hotel.

From there, it had been a short, though memorable, elevator ride to a penthouse suite. And to all the sweets that awaited the foursome behind closed doors.

6

On Tuesday morning, Alex rolled over in his kingsize bed, momentarily surprised to find a warm, female form at his side. *Jessica.* His hand roamed tentatively over the body hidden beneath his black sheet, tracing along the woman's hip and up her spine. Was it really the nubile young intern, current star of his daytime fantasies and his nighttime wet dreams?

The elation that he'd felt was short-lived as his fingers got quickly lost in a mess of shoulder-length, curly hair. Already knowing what he would find, he couldn't help but look over to confirm his suspicions. A sense of resigned acceptance filled him when he saw that the woman sharing his bed had white-blonde hair and crisply tanned skin, the type of clichéd California beauty whose look couldn't have differed more from Jessica's dark, delicately drawn features.

Oh, fucking Christ.

Marina. Again. He felt her body shift on the mattress, and he quickly shut his eyelids tight, faking sleep while trying to remember the events that had brought him to this unfortunate wake-up call. Monday's staff meeting hadn't gone on unusually late, but he'd stayed in the office afterwards, playing several games of darts with Pete and Todd before driving home –

No, *not* driving home.

He rewound the memory like a movie on an old-fashioned reel and tried over. Before driving to Lucy's Lagoon, which was just down the street from his apartment on the cusp of Hollywood and Los Feliz, he'd sat, at the corner of his favourite bar, a dim and smoky dive filled with old-timers who didn't care if their bar wasn't the type of trendy watering hole that made the papers. All they wanted was a place to drink. A place where, if the bartender might not actually know your name, at least he or she would pretend to like you. And like you more if you tipped well. For several hours, Alex had listened to music on the jukebox and thought about Jessica. Thought the same things he'd pondered since first laying eyes on her.

He couldn't date his intern. It would be too awkward, too unprofessional. Not that messing around with someone on the staff was actually against any written rules. *Zebra* wasn't the type of company to have a corporate policy on how to behave. But Alex was too smart to get involved in the trouble that always went with dating a co-worker. In the past, he'd watched from a distance when other staff members had played that dangerous game. Look at Dashiell, the way he trysted his way through any secretary he found even remotely attractive, then left them one by one, so dramatically that you could almost hear the sound of their hearts breaking.

Yes, dating Jessica was out of the question.

But fucking her – that's what he honestly wanted to do. Every time he looked at her, his overworked libido rewarded him with a new vision: Jessica on his bed, her hands in his as he brought them above her head, watching her eyes as they both listened to the sweet musical sound of handcuffs locking.

Or Jessica bent before him on her knees, pretty mouth opened, hungry and ready. He saw her as a girl who liked to suck cock. She had a way of licking her bottom lip when she worked, of drawing it into her mouth and worrying it between her teeth. Sucking it in, then releasing it, the lower lip slick and wet, before going through the same actions all over again. What she might do to a man's tool made his mind spin out with possibilities. He imagined her making love to his rock-hard rod between those plump wet lips. Using her tongue, the very edges of her teeth. Being gentle but firm.

This mental picture led him to another of the sultry beauty, post-climax, with her heavily lidded eyes lowered in a look of extreme pleasure ...

The whisky hadn't dulled his desire, it had simply dampened the way he felt about dating her. Maybe he *could* make it work, if the girl was even interested. He was taking that part for granted. But hadn't she shot him some serious, cock-stiffening looks during the week that they'd worked together? And then there was the way she'd flirted with him at the Halloween party before Mozart had stepped in. Her teasing question had made him want to put her over his lap right there in front of Mrs Claus and everyone. This was his favourite fantasy of all, spanking Jessica's beautiful bare bottom until it turned a rosy hue, until he couldn't wait to fuck her, when the pleasure that she won from his cock would supersede the intense spark of pain he inflicted with his sturdy hand.

It had been so long since he'd found a girl who liked to play like that. Marina wasn't into kink. Yes, she was orally gifted, and she liked fucking outdoors, or at the movies, giving into what she thought was edgy behaviour. But she'd baulked when he proposed a spanking session, and he'd never asked her again.

Jessica seemed completely comfortable with that scenario. How he'd like to make sure, to ask her seriously if she was a naughty girl. To punish her in the most excruciatingly delicious ways. These were the thoughts that had consumed him at the bar. When he'd gotten home, pleasantly buzzed but not too drunk, Marina had already been in his bedroom, sprawled naked under his sheets. Although shocked for a moment to find her there, the sight of her in his bed wasn't any life-altering surprise. She'd never given back his key after their last big blow-out. Besides, how many times had he found himself at her place, doing the same thing? Arriving after midnight in the hopes of engaging in familiar and soothing sex with someone he knew well and once had loved.

Ah, but that was the main point, wasn't it? *Once* had loved. No longer did.

They weren't going to do this any more. He made a mental note of that, just as Marina slid under the sheets, parted her lips around his throbbing cock, and introduced him to her warm, wet mouth with one fuck of a good-morning blow job.

Yeah, they had to stop.

But maybe not right this minute.

As Alex lost his good intentions in a bit of morning delight, Jessica woke up to the vibrating sound of a car engine revving. Magnified. There was something heavy and fur-covered on her chest, and her chin was all wet. She opened her eyes and found herself face to face with the purring Wacko, her butterscotch-coloured tabby cat, who continued to animatedly lick her chin until she picked him up and set him by her bed on the hardwood floor.

Why was he up so early? Jessica looked at the alarm clock. The neon green numbers read 5:15, which was an indecent time for anyone, even a cat, to be awake. She could hear the sound of someone swearing, and she quickly pictured the crazy man who walked up and down Wilshire Boulevard with his purloined shopping cart. But within seconds, she realised that the expletives were coming from inside her apartment, not the street outside.

'I can't fucking believe it!'

Reluctantly, Jessica got out of bed and padded barefoot

down the hall to the kitchen with Wacko at her heels. Her roommate stood by the tall silver garbage pail, despondently pulling yesterday's coffee grounds out of the trash.

'Damn it all to hell!'

Wacko ran in circles around her feet, making the happy miaowing sounds that indicated he knew food was coming. Sasha glanced towards the doorway without stopping her search. 'I'm filming at the beach in half an hour and we're out of coffee.' Her green eyes were huge and manic.

'You're never going to make it,' Jessica said, grabbing Wacko's kibble from the top of the refrigerator and filling his dish.

'You can get anywhere in LA in twenty minutes,' Sasha told her. Again. This was the Los Angeles promise, but Los Angeles had been known to lie.

'Buy some on the way. There's a cafe on every block.'

'I need it now. Before I drive the fucking car. Before I can make my fucking hair start. Now.' Sasha's cheeks were flushed a bright pink beneath millions of tiny star-like freckles. It looked as if she were about to explode.

'I like your hair,' Jessica said. Her roommate's flaming red curls would, after some major coaxing, defrizz and hang down her back like a model in a Pre-Raphaelite painting. But right now, her riot of corkscrew curls shot out around her head as if she were trying to pick up signals from another planet.

'Not helping,' Sasha said. Her hands were buried to the wrist in leftovers, and she grimaced as she searched for her precious java grounds. Jessica admired the skill with which Sasha picked out each tiny bit of coffee. After observing for another moment, she helpfully started to rummage through the cabinet over the stove, searching for the secret stash.

'Gone,' Sasha announced without looking up. 'Finished it yesterday.'

Jessica opened the freezer.

'Ditto,' Sasha said, straining the used grounds for eggshells and cucumber peels. She had discovered a cigarette butt in the garbage, and had the damp thing wedged between her lips, fiercely sucking on it as if some vice, any vice, would do in this extreme situation.

Jessica pulled out a can from the far rear of the freezer. It was labelled 'chicken fat', and she grinned as she passed it over. 'Extra secret,' she said, 'for true emergencies.'

Sasha let the cigarette butt fall. Her smile brought all of the idiosyncrasies of her features together, making her appear stunning instead of out of control. 'You're a life saver,' she said to Jessica, filling Mr Coffee and standing right next to it, breathing in the aroma as the brewing process began.

'I'm a Mentos,' Jessica corrected her, picking up the petulant Wacko and returning to her room. She didn't have to be at work until nine, but once back in bed, nestled in a cocoon of still-warm white sheets, she couldn't fall asleep. It wasn't only the sound of Sasha moving at warp speed around the apartment as she drank her coffee, dressed and showered in record time, and flew out the door, calling to Jessica that she'd be home late. Insecurities nagged at her. Kelly had managed to fuck those unwanted thoughts from her mind the night before. Now she couldn't keep them out of her head. What was most troubling her?

She closed her eyes and made herself confront her newly complicated love life. She remembered how Alex had looked at her the evening before – whenever he'd thought she wasn't paying attention. Was there something between them? Already? What would he think if he knew that she'd fantasised about him while making love to her boyfriend? Would that turn him on? Or was she making stories up in her head, needing excitement in her life? She'd done that before, and it had always gotten her into trouble, creating problems where none existed.

Sighing, she stood up and slipped into her running clothes, which were hanging on the back of her rattan chair. Pounding the pavement would help shake her fears away. Stomp them right into the cement ground. Quickly, she slid a band around her dark ponytail, grabbed her bracelet key, and left the apartment.

Jessica lived on the border of Westwood and Beverly Hills. Wilshire Boulevard slipped languorously through the two cities, winding all the way like an oily black snake from the shimmering Santa Monica beach to the dirty heart of downtown Los Angeles. At this part of the city, the famous street was lined with expensive, towering condominiums. Nestled in among the monsters were several little apartments from the fifties, buildings that hadn't yet been bought and demolished by some contractor with a lot of money and an ugly plan. Thankful for this, Jessica admired her apartment as she tied the laces of her white sneakers. Then she started down the concrete steps and began to run.

LA in the early morning had a dreamy effect, like an unfinished picture. The sky, lit in stripes of pinkish orange and baby blue, calmed Jessica's psyche. People who hated the City of Angels never bothered to look at the beauty of it. At this early hour, Wilshire Boulevard was almost deserted, and the lack of expensive, foreign automobiles motoring by gave the neighbourhood a quaint, almost friendly air.

Her normal route took Jessica past the condos, past the exclusive golf course where the movie stars played against studio executives. She generally ran to the intersection of Wilshire and Santa Monica, where the world-renowned Trader Vic's restaurant was situated, a haven for mostly ageing celebs who liked tropical fruity drinks and a matching Tiki-style atmosphere.

Pushing herself, Jessica jogged down Santa Monica Boulevard, towards Westwood. Normally, she'd turn right at this busy intersection, heading back in a large loop to her apartment and a well-deserved shower. Instead, she continued to run on Santa Monica as it entered the flatlands of west LA, where cheaper rents made it easier for working-class people to find a home. Bartenders and waitresses, all with stars in their eyes and future hopes of dazzling audiences from the silver screen.

People like Kelly.

Now, she was heading to his apartment. Kelly wouldn't mind being woken up at this early hour, would trade sleep for sex any day. And what Jessica really needed to calm her nerves was a good, old-fashioned wake-up fuck.

'Sweet Jesus, yes,' Alex sighed. He was on the receiving end of some of the best oral action he'd ever experienced. Marina's tender tongue tricked up and down his pulsing rod, and then she drew the length of his prick into her mouth and sucked him. Hard. The way she might suck on a sweet candy, draining the syrupy juices hidden inside. Before he could think of what he might possibly want next, she brought one hand forward, carefully cupping his balls, then lightly dragging her short mani-cured nails against that soft, most sensitive skin. Slowly, she bobbed her head up and down, her bouncy, bed-tousled curls tickling the skin on his thighs like thousands of tiny down feathers. Then she let the shaft free from her mouth and just worked the head. Oh, she was an expert at this.

For several minutes he simply enjoyed the way she took care of him. But then, as he approached climax, he began to give directions. 'Harder,' he murmured, wanting to feel it, wanting her to drain him. Instantly, she responded as he'd asked, giving him the exact pressure he craved. Knowing just what he wanted.

This was one of the main dilemmas he and Marina experienced. Whenever they broke up and then got back together for a bit of casual sex, their erotic connection intensified. Transforming from a perfectly satisfying bedroom relationship, their bond suddenly possessed a dangerous, edgy quality, because they never knew if this session would be the last they'd share. Now, as Marina ran her tongue in a line from the base of Alex's cock up to the straining, purplish tip, he groaned and arched his hips, yearning for release.

With ease, Marina shifted her slim dancer's body on the mattress so that her pretty, nude pussy was poised over his waiting lips. She'd recently gone in for the total wax job called 'The Sphinx'. It left her completely hairless between her legs, and was a look that Alex found some-what fascinating. The way her bare skin felt against him always gave him an extra charge.

With grace, she brought her mouth back to his cock and bestowed upon him one long, firm suck. Alex couldn't take much more of this. In moments he would thrust down her throat and come, shooting his load and knowing that she would swallow every last drop. But he understood the ground rules. If he was going to get off, then she wanted to as well. Eagerly, he reached for her hips and brought her pussy closer to his face, where he could flick out his tongue and gently tease her pussy lips, ease them slowly apart, touch between them, find her throbbing clit and kiss it.

Maybe this actually would be the last time they'd be

together. So let us go out with a bang, Alex thought as he made a purposeful ring with his lips around Marina's swollen clit and sucked.

Sasha sucked hard, too, swallowing the gritty dregs of cooling coffee from a large white paper cup. Caffeine was her all-time favourite drug now that she'd given up speed, and she returned her gaze with a re-animated focus to the activity unfolding before her. People bustled around chaotically, but she knew where each was supposed to be. They were already in the middle of principal photography, and this morning was an important scene. It had taken weeks to get a permit, and once they'd had that, they'd needed to wait for ideal weather. Today, the parts had finally come together. Now, the only thing that was left was for the actors to get their fucking lines right. Hadn't happened yet, but they'd only been filming for an hour.

With luck, the small but determined company would be able to wrap up the shot before the beach grew over-crowded with the normal population of surfers and sunbathers who flocked to the ocean every day of the week.

'Need to talk to you, Sash,' her line producer said, coming forward with a brightly coloured clipboard in one hand and an unhappy expression on her face.

'Later,' she said to Mica, ignoring the woman's instant frown. She knew exactly what the meeting would be about. Money. That's what it was always about. In Los Angeles, that's what everything was about. 'OK, people,' Sasha called loudly, her voice ringing out in the early morning air, 'let's do one more try before we take a break.'

'Mmmm,' was all Kelly said as he opened the door. His grey eyes were blurred with sleep, but he was happy to see Jessica standing on his 'Welcome' mat. Very happy, in fact, because his morning wood was obvious beneath the pair of striped red and blue boxers he wore low on his slim hips. 'Baby,' he said next, ushering Jessica into the apartment. 'You smell like fresh air.'

It was true. Jessica had brought the scent of morning with her, and the fragrance was enticing to the sleep-rumpled Kelly. It made his lover seem pure and untouched, which he found absolutely sexy, even though he knew that what she probably was in the mood for was a quick and dirty romp. This was despite the fact that they'd screwed twice at the beach before he'd taken Jessica, at her insistence, back to her place. She'd claimed that she wanted to catch up on her sleep in her own bed, alone. That she had to get up early. Yet here she was looking as if she wanted to fuck him right where he stood.

He watched appreciatively as Jessica began to strip out of her clothes, undressing as she walked, as if she couldn't wait to get naked. Quickly, she kicked off her sneakers, then dropped her violet T-shirt, pink jogging bra and black leggings in a trail along the hallway. By the time they'd entered Kelly's bedroom, she was completely nude, and now it was his turn to take off the one item of clothing he still had on and meet her in the tangled mess of blankets on his bed.

As he kicked off his boxers, he considered the different ways they played together. There were stern and serious bondage and dominance games; light-hearted exhibitionism and making-love-in-public games; and one of his favourite games, spanking her beautiful bare ass until it turned a blushing rose. But sometimes, Jessica just wanted to fuck. Plain and simple. Hard and raw. On all fours or on her back, spread-legged and ready.

Kelly sensed the mood she was in, and he captured her wrists and held them over her head. 'I like the way you look when you've just finished a run,' he said, stroking his free hand along her body, touching the rise of her breasts before dipping his fingers into the basin of her flat belly. He spent a moment kissing her, following his fingers with his mouth, just touching his lips to her erect nipples. Then, climbing on to the mattress with her, he tested to make sure that she was as ready as he thought. His fingertips found a pool of nectar awaiting him between her legs.

Now, Kelly simply sat up between her parted legs and got busy. His cock slid forcefully between the plump lips of her pussy, and he sighed out loud when he felt her wetness envelop him. It was, to Kelly, like coming home. Dripping, slick juices coated his rod as soon as he slid the length of it inside her. There was no better feeling. That first thrust transformed him, as he slipped in, held still for a beat, and sighed at the connection.

Jessica closed her eyes and arched her back, driving him in even deeper with the delicious, near-desperate movements of her body. Kelly had a fleeting thought of the way that she'd looked on Halloween, momentarily giving herself over to some nameless stranger for a probing kiss, but then he stared down at the real, living woman in his bed and pushed the image from his mind.

'You coming, babe?' Marina asked.

As he just had, fucking her mouth like a powerful locomotive and then sealing himself between her full lips as he climaxed in a white river down her throat, the question momentarily confused Alex. That wasn't surprising. After coming, it generally took him a few minutes to regain both his sensibilities and his mastery of the English language, which Marina knew full well from their years together. Looking up at her, he raised one dark eyebrow in a classic arch and waited for clarification. Marina stood at the foot of the bed, searching the room for the clothes she'd discarded hastily the evening before.

'Tonight,' she continued casually, but Alex understood that the blasé tone of her voice was completely manufactured. She might have climaxed for real, but now she was faking it. 'The show.'

The way she said those two words made Alex's stomach tense: *The show*. Marina was always starring in some production, and even when the two were not officially dating, he tried to be supportive of her 'craft'. But modern dance was difficult for him to either understand or enjoy. Her current revue was something that Alex had accidentally, and unfortunately, caught once in the rehearsal stage during one of their 'on again' dating weeks. A sparsely designed piece, it consisted of Marina and six other anorexic-looking dancers holding poses for long periods of time to the background music of whistling tea kettles. At least, that was Alex's unschooled opinion. In two words, he'd told Josh, it sucked.

'Meeting,' Alex said, saving himself with a sudden and unexpected brainwave. 'We hired a new writer last week, and I have to go over some of the basics with her. Sorry.' He tried to make it sound like he meant it. 'I'll catch it during the run.'

'But tonight's the preview,' Marina said, and the immediate nasal-pitched whine in her voice let Alex know for a fact why she'd been in his bed. Not for break-up sex, but as a guilt move to coerce him into doing something he didn't want to. This was one of the main reasons he'd ended things. Repeatedly. At this point in his life, Alex was tired of people trying to control him. He had enough trouble controlling himself. Look at the way he was fantasising about Jessica. Just the picture of her in his mind now made his thoughts take an instant detour in her direction. No, she wasn't ready for him. Too sweet. Too innocent. Pete was right. He'd ruin her.

Suddenly, he realised that Marina was staring at him, holding her faded blue jeans in one hand and a stretchy fuchsia T-shirt in the other. Although still naked, there was no longer anything sexually exciting about her. Alex understood full well that the look of hurt on her face was as much an act as the emotion he put into his voice. All she really wanted was to have a boyfriend on hand to display to her buddies at the after-show party. She hated going to these events alone. It made her feel like a loser.

'Really, baby,' he said sadly in his own manufactured display of faux-emotion. 'I'd love to make it. But I just can't.'

'I can't,' Kelly murmured. 'Oh, god, I can't wait.'

'For me,' Jessica urged. 'Hold on.'

Kelly was pumping hard into Jessica, trying to keep himself from coming until she was ready. Every so often, they climaxed together in synchronicity, and those experiences were amazing. Their bodies shook with simultaneous orgasms, and the vibrations that moved from her to him were almost enough to make him come again. Now that Jessica was almost there, he used one hand between her legs, stroking her clit as he fucked her. A tickle to her clit as he plunged in, and then a little squeeze between his thumb and forefinger as he slipped back out again. Tickle and squeeze, tickle and squeeze, until she was literally breathless.

Sometimes, Jessica would come solely from the way he moved his cock within her. This generally happened when she was on top and could manipulate her body, pressing forward with her hips to get the contact against her clit that she needed. But this morning, Kelly's slippery-fingered method worked, and soon Jessica was biting hard into her full bottom lip, throwing her head back against the pillow, her whole body trembling with the promise of what was about to happen.

Watching her, Kelly let himself go, and the release was overpowering. He kept his eyes open the whole time, staring at his bedmate. He adored the untamed way Jessica looked when she came, her cheeks flushing, her eyelids fluttering. Mostly, he loved the fact that something he did made her look that way.

'You're beautiful,' Kelly sighed as he came. 'Jessie, you're fucking amazing.'

Afterwards, they stayed joined together for several minutes, their bodies alive with the powerful post-climax shudderings. Kelly always thought the after-effects were like ripples of pleasure spreading outwards, radiating from the core. He let himself bask in the moment, and then watched as Jessica pulled away from him in the bed and gave him one of her most radiant smiles.

LA was Dashiell's all-time favourite location. Sure, he knew what the detractors had to say. The dirt, the smog, and the phoney quality of the majority of the population turned a lot of people off, and for a reason: everyone wanted to be your best friend. When you had money or power, anyway.

But he loved the city, regardless of its flaws. Or maybe because of them. There was a thin, greasy sheen of modern life that overlaid the old-world style, but he could see beyond it. What he wouldn't have given to have lived in Los Angeles during its heyday. Peeling back the grime and slipping right into the world of Bette Davis and Joan Crawford. Of early movie-making. That's what he saw when he looked at LA. He saw magic.

Although what he saw out of his window could have been described in less attractive terms. Graffiti covered the entire garage door of an apartment building across the way. Even that appealed to Dashiell. The colourful sprawling designs weren't of the gangland style, but artistic creations that suited Dashiell's LA frame of mind. That's because in Los Angeles, Dashiell chose to live in a more subdued style than he did when he was in Europe. There were no fancy stretch limos parked outside. No custom-made Bentley tucked away in his garage.

His top-floor apartment was small, tasteful, nothing in your face. He'd searched a long time before finding something that suited him so well. This was it, with the built-in mouldings from the 1940s, the iron railings on the balcony, the subtle touches from a time in the past that people today chose to live without. And the best part to Dashiell was that several scenes from the classic movie *Sunset Boulevard* had been filmed in his building. What could be cooler than that?

Lots of things, according to his ex-girlfriend, who had insisted that he could have afforded a place in Bel Air. Something designed by an avant-garde architect whose name appeared in all the right columns. She was correct, of course. But his ex hadn't understood, no matter how many times he tried to explain, that living in luxury meant giving up a very real part of himself. By keeping things under wraps, he had a shot at deciphering what was truly on the mind of a friend or a new lover. Was the person with him because of who he was or what was in his bank account? Thinking this, he remembered a brilliant T-shirt he'd once seen hanging in a window near UCLA: *It's not who you are, it's what you wear. Because when it all comes down to it, nobody really cares who you are.*

He loved that shirt, even if it left out an important factoid. They *did* care if you had money, and Dashiell was tired of playing the money-go-round, weary of engaging in that tiresome tango of 'do you have it or don't you?' Sure, he could get off the rollercoaster any time he chose. He was the same person with or without the bank roll, wasn't he? Quickly he pushed that question from his mind.

It was the only query he never honestly cared to ponder.

'That's one way of saying good morning,' Jessica said as she brushed the hair out of her eyes. Sometimes morning sex made Jessica want to sleep away the day, lazing between sheets still warm from Kelly's body. But now she simply felt energised. And she could thank Kelly for that. As she slipped on one of his old white T-shirts, which fell almost to her knees, she looked on the end table by his bed. Pages of a script were fanned out on the surface, and she could see that one role had been highlighted in yellow.

'Audition?' she asked as he tossed her a pair of clean boxer shorts, plaid ones that he knew she liked. He'd drive her home where she could shower and change into work clothes, but she didn't want to put her sweaty jogging outfit back on. When she flipped to the first page, she saw that the title of the script had been blacked out.

'Why the secrecy?' she asked.

'You know Hollywood,' Kelly said. 'Everything's hush-hush.'

'Do you have a good shot at the part?'

Kelly shrugged as he reached for the keys. Over the four years he'd lived in Los Angeles, he'd been cast in several movies, then wound up with most or all of his part on the cutting-room floor. Jessica knew that hurt each time, even if he had made the most of every success. One movie role had bought him his Harley. Another had paid for his Jeep.

There was no masking the excitement in his voice as he said, 'It's big, Jessie. If I land this –' He shook his head, obviously trying to regain his aloof sense again, but failing. 'I'm up for a good role. Not the lead, but I wouldn't have expected that. Doesn't matter. My part would be important. I'd get noticed.'

'When's the audition?' Jessica asked as the two left Kelly's apartment and headed down the wooden stairs to his Jeep.

'This afternoon. I'm going to read the scene again, then hit the gym just to work out my nerves. Pump myself up literally and figuratively. At two o'clock, I'll drive over to the studio.' He held the car door for Jessica and then climbed into the Jeep and started the engine. Jessica could sense how excited he was. Nervous energy made him drive too fast to her place, but she didn't say anything. It was almost eight now and the morning commute was in full gear, forcing him to rein in the automobile.

'I haven't even told you the best part,' Kelly said as he pulled up in front of her apartment. 'The director's huge,' he told her. 'I mean, giant.'

'Who?' Jessica asked, turning to look at him.

'Can't say yet,' he said, winking as she climbed out of the car. When Jessica gave him a questioning stare, Kelly added, 'Chalk it up to superstition. If I tell you now, it'll jinx it. Just wish me luck, and I'll talk to you afterwards.' He hesitated and gave her a sexy smile. 'If I'm lucky we'll celebrate together, later.'

It took a minute for Avalon to figure out where she was. The ceiling wasn't immediately familiar to her half-shut eyes. Besides the fact that she didn't recognise the colour, she thought the space above her was covered in a plush, beige carpet. How totally odd to carpet a ceiling –

And then she realised that she wasn't looking at a ceiling, but at the floor. Head over the edge of a bed that wasn't her own, she was staring down at an expensive, creamy wall-to-wall carpet. OK, so that explained the first query. The ceiling wasn't carpeted; the floor was. But even though she'd solved mystery number one of the morning, she still had no clue to the answer of the second question, which was this: Where the fuck was she?

Sitting up too quickly, she caught her breath from the head rush. Oh, dear God, she'd been drinking, that was for sure, from the way the room suddenly shifted nauseatingly to the left and then rotated with sickening slowness back to normal. But there was more to her lousy sense of balance than an overindulgence of alcohol, wasn't there? She leaned her head back and waited for the sound of the blood pounding in her head to lessen a bit. Every single move she made had disastrous repercussions. Sighing, she realised the worst of it. She'd been doing some sort of party drug, hadn't she? The euphoria was long gone, but the craving lingered.

Her eyes locked on a polished piece of wood furniture as she continued to search for clues to her current whereabouts. Then she heard a voice that explained exactly where she was, as clearly as if the location had been broadcast on a loudspeaker in her mind.

'Baby doll, I didn't think you'd ever wake up.'

She was at Josh's sprawling beach house on the lip of Malibu, clear across town from her Brentwood apartment. Why did staff meetings always make her feel lonely? And why did feeling lonely always make her climb into bed with the nearest attractive man? Because Josh definitely was attractive. He had a hard body, which he was flashing for her now as he entered the bedroom from the master bath, moving the white towel aside and drying himself off in an exaggeratedly slow manner. With a grin on his face, he performed a strip-tease in reverse. Slipping into his perfectly pressed boxers, adding a pair of chinos, a light blue shirt, a tie.

'Got a meeting this morning with the big boys over in

Culver City, Ava,' he said, before naming a studio that occasionally placed full-page ads with the paper. Then he moved closer to the bed to give her a kiss redolent of minty mouthwash. As if the kiss awakened something in him, he pushed the striped sheets away from her body and worked his way down her throat, along the valley between her breasts, across the flat of her stomach, to her pussy. Avalon sighed and closed her eyes as Josh parted her kitty lips and gave an equally welcoming good-morning kiss to her clit. Here, the added zing of the mouthwash sent a shocking tingle throughout her entire cunt. She shuddered but didn't move away, knowing that Josh would never leave a job half-finished.

She was right. Slowly, Josh kissed softly up and down her pussy lips. He lingered, teasing her, using his fingers in a deliciously light manner to hold on to her lips, then touching her waiting clit with his tongue. That felt amazing, and Avalon sighed and murmured her lover's name. He blew his minty breath directly on to her pussy, giving her a cold rush of air that made her moan out loud. What a way to wake up. Josh always knew how to make her feel unbelievably sexy. Right now, he kept at her, slicking his tongue deep inside her pussy, then running the tip of it in circles over and around her vibrating clit.

Shifting her hips on the bed, Avalon lifted her body, pressing forward. Josh rewarded her by sliding his hands beneath her firm, round ass, cradling her bottom gently as he continued to feed. Even in the state of her slow-waking haze, she felt bliss breaking through. His mouth was so delicious against her cunt. Tongue driving hard, then lapping slowly. He caressed her with every touch, teasing and pleasing her in the most perfect way.

'You like that?'

'Oh, yes,' Avalon whispered. She loved it when Josh fucked her with his mouth. There was nobody more adept at making her come from those heavenly circles, spiralling to infinity, getting smaller and more precise as he ringed her pulsing clit.

'Tell me,' he urged, and she remembered how much Josh liked dirty talking. X-rated words made him wildly excited, especially when someone as lovely as Avalon was doing the speaking. Yet even though she liked to fulfil his fantasies, this morning she found it difficult to do as he asked. Her brain was jumbled. What words could she possibly manage? Still, she couldn't let him down.

'Lick me,' she started with, and Josh did as she asked, liking the directions. 'Oh, yes,' she told him, then, 'Harder. Deeper.'

Still half-dazed with sleep, Avalon felt the climax approaching quickly from a distance, and she gripped on to Josh's strong body with her legs. He responded exactly as she needed, licking more seriously now. Pressing the flat of his tongue against her clit before lapping at it over and over again. He danced his tongue against her, dipping it between the lips of her pussy to trace deep inside before resuming the sweet circles and steady strokes that would always make her come. He never seemed to tire, actually moving more and more forcefully as time passed, and Avalon made a satisfied humming sound from deep within her chest, holding his body in place as she came against his freshly shaved face.

Moving back from her, he licked his lips, his cheeks and chin glistening with her fragrant juices. 'Gotta run, Ava,' he murmured, smiling as if there was no better taste in the world than the flavour of her pussy. 'But you can lounge around here as long as you want. You know that.'

She did know that. For some reason, she connected with the slick ad man. They fitted together, their fantasies blending, their desire for a quick fuck and nothing more was something that each could appreciate. He wouldn't have to call her later, or worry that she'd think this was going to lead to something it wouldn't. Something like a stroll down the aisle. At work, he could tease her about her sex life, and nobody would guess that he was occasionally the star between her sheets – or vice versa. The more you talked about an event openly and in public, the less people believed it would ever happen. She'd learned that rule from working as a gossip columnist.

Looking around Josh's bachelor pad while he continued to get ready for his day of selling, Avalon understood once again that he'd never have room in his life for a permanent partner. Of course, she'd known that already. Hadn't he ended things with his once-serious girlfriend, Tiffany, when she'd given him an ultimatum? Marry me, or –

Josh had chosen the 'or' immediately, and after that, he and Avalon had found themselves perfectly suited for the occasional fling. All the previous night had meant was a melding of bodies. A harmonious melding, if she remembered correctly, her back up against the wall, his large cock sliding deep inside her as she bit into his shoulder to stifle the moans. He was well hung and surprisingly considerate as a lover. After fucking her hard, he had spread her out on the bedroom floor and eaten her pussy until she'd wrapped her legs around his neck and come, her body shaking, her heart racing.

For someone who seemed cynical about women, he knew how to please. A generous lover, he'd made sure that she'd climaxed not once or even twice, but three times, before reintroducing her to the pleasures of his cock. Coke, a rare indulgence, made him hard like nothing else. He had ridden her until he'd finally come as well, then brought them both on to the bed, where they'd slept off the loneliness together.

Watching Josh now, she wondered how he always seemed on top of his game. Why did he look as if he were revved up and ready for eighteen holes at the nearest golf course, while the only thing she could think about was making a Bloody Mary and sipping it carefully through a straw out on the balcony? She wanted to slide on her shades and wrap herself in one of Josh's plush terry-cloth robes. That was the type of man he was – always had an extra robe in the closet, and a pair of slippers much smaller than his own feet to accommodate the occasional unexpected female guest.

She listened to him call out his goodbyes, then headed slowly to the kitchen to fix herself a bit of hair of the dog. As she poured in the crimson tomato juice and added a generous helping of ice-cold vodka, she wondered how many mornings like this she would go through before she stopped wanting to bite the dog back.

7

Josh moved into the downstairs office while his was being painted. He set up his work on a desk next to Alex's, placed his electronic organiser in the centre and a phone at the right, and started making calls.

'Please,' Alex said desperately, staring at his own computerised schedule, crammed with items that had to be completed by the end of the day. 'I can't listen to you shmooze all day. I'm not kidding. I fucking can't do it.'

'Come on, Alex, chill.' 'Chill' was Josh's favourite one-word line from the cult-classic film *Showgirls*. 'You won't even know that I'm here.'

That was next to impossible, but Alex sighed and began with his own roster. On Tuesdays, he returned calls to the studios, booking time to send his writers out for reviews. Most screenings were done at private theatres located in Hollywood or in the Valley. Often a reviewer would be alone, or with only one or two other writers, in a large, plush room. It was a pretty cushy way to spend an afternoon.

As he dialled the first number, he heard Josh start in on his work, 'Hey,' Josh crooned, 'you're harder to get in touch with than my wife's boyfriend. And I'm not even married. Give me a call. This is Josh at *Zebra*. You know, black and white and READ all over. We're having a special on full-page ads. Call me by noon if you wanna talk.'

He grinned at Alex and nodded enthusiastically, mouthing the words, 'See? Not a bother at all.' Then he punched in another number and began a new spiel.

'Dude, it's the big J. Got a deal for you.' There was a slight hesitation, and Alex watched Josh's face. It was as if he could see the man mentally regrouping based on whatever the customer had just said to him, instantly changing tactics. 'You're not buying this week? Why, that's a travesty! It's more than that. It's a travesty of a mockery of a sham...' As he delivered another movie quote, he raised his eyebrows at Alex, nodding. 'See?' See? No bother. No worries.

Alex wasn't worried. He was annoyed. Resigned, he continued to dial numbers, talking first to his media connection at one of the big studios and then to the lady at an independent film company. A dart flew by his head and he looked up, angry, expecting to see Josh fucking around again. Instead, it was Avalon.

'You had sex,' she announced happily, moving to sit on the one uncluttered edge of Alex's desk in the cross-legged Lotus pose. After spending most of the morning at Josh's place, swimming in the turquoise water of a pool that had a view of the ocean, she felt resurrected. With her head finally clear, she'd showered beneath the two-headed nozzle in his sumptuous bathroom, reassessing her life. So she'd been with Josh – again – but at least he wasn't just another one-night-stand loser she'd picked up at a bar. He was a friend. That counted for something, didn't it?

'Oh, yes,' Avalon continued now, enjoying Alex's shocked expression, 'you had *amazing* sex.'

A yoga practitioner for years, Avalon could bend her flexible body into an assortment of difficult positions. She did so now, contorting herself into a pretzel-like shape as a way of giving Alex a moment to gather his wits. Josh, gathering his belongings on his way out to a meeting, gave her a hungry look. As he quickly made his way through the office, it was easy to decipher the message in his eyes: want to bend you over again,

Avalon. You name the place. You name the time. She ignored the stare. Leaning her head back, she sniffed the air, as if trying to determine which direction the wind was blowing. 'You fucked Marina.'

'You're crazy,' Alex said, refusing to glance up from his computer. He acted as if he were deeply involved in the story he was editing on the screen, a hastily written review that slammed a new teen comedy. It took only a fraction of his brain power to make the necessary changes to the copy. The rest of his mind was kept busy as he tried to figure out how the hell Avalon always knew things like this. Sure, she was the paper's gossip columnist. But the role didn't need to bleed into the lives of the staff members, did it?

'Last night,' Avalon continued, arms outstretched to feel Alex's sexual aura. 'And again this morning. Dirty dog. I thought you two had broken up for real this time. Isn't that what you swore to us? "No more," you said after Halloween.' Avalon did a passable impression of Alex's deep voice. '"No more emotional fucking blackmail."'

'We *did* break up.' Now, Alex's normally steady tone of voice held a wavering quality, as if he weren't altogether sure of the statement.

'Then why was she in your bed last night?' Avalon ran one of her hands along the back of Alex's neck beneath his hair, giving him instant goosebumps. 'Why didn't you kick her to the kerb, like you said you would if you found her beneath your sheets again? Don't you remember, Alex? You told us that the best sex in the world wasn't worth the pain of sitting through another one of her dance recitals.' Avalon's eyes gleamed brightly as she told Alex off. 'You're weak, man. Weak, weak, weak.'

'Christ, she called, didn't she?' he asked, finally catching on. If he hadn't been so annoyed at Josh, he'd have picked up on the clues sooner. Avalon's scarlet-slicked lips curved into a sexy half-smile as she waved a little pink piece of paper in front of Alex's eyes. On it was a message that she had taken in the upstairs office moments before. Yes, she was a damn good gossip columnist. But she wasn't a fucking psychic.

'She said to be at her opening tonight if you ever want to feel her warm, wet lips around your cock again.' She dragged out the word 'cock' for extra emphasis, winning a broad smile from Pete, who took the time to look over from his laptop.

Savouring the victory of the moment, Avalon grinned at Alex, and he fought for inner control, not wanting to get drawn into a discussion about his love life. 'For such a tame-looking creature, that girl has a filthy mouth on her, doesn't she? I bet I could learn a thing or two from her.' Avalon laughed lightly as she let the paper flutter from her fingers and then stood and walked out of the room without looking back.

Kelly sat in a room filled with three other hopefuls, but it was a room that felt particularly hopeless to him. He recognised two of the other actors easily. One was currently featured on a long-running daytime soap. The other was starring in a prime-time cable series that had his name in the title.

So what chance in hell did Kelly have? None, as far as he could tell. Yes, he knew the stories that rotated through Hollywood to give young actors hope. Many actors paid their dues by winding up as clips in a circular file. Even so, Kelly wished he had something more to offer when he went to talk with the casting director.

The other actor in the room was someone whose face also seemed familiar. But it was more difficult to tell, because no one in the plushly decorated foyer would look at one another. It was as if making small talk would ruin their chances of being the chosen one. Tapping his foot on the floor, Kelly caught the glare of the man at his side and he instantly recognised the actor from his furrowed brow. Ah, so that's where he was from. A play Kelly had caught downtown. A good production, one that had gleaned raves in the papers, which was undoubtedly why this actor was here. On his way up from the stage to the silver screen.

Theatre people were different from screen actors. This man had an air about him that seemed to say he was better than the rest of the crew in the room. Kelly ignored his displeased expression and continued tapping his foot. He didn't care if it annoyed the man. It was one way to let out a bit of his own wired energy. How long would they all be kept in the room together?

Finally, the casting director's door opened, and a woman with artsy red glasses and upswept blonde hair motioned for all four of the men to join her in the room.

What was going on?

Usually, the men would have come in for her singly and read one at a time. It was obvious that the other actors were surprised as well, but only Kelly appeared truly calm. Here was his main talent. When the moment arrived, he would relax every time. It was exactly the same way that he felt when surfing out in Santa Monica, moving his body on the waves, giving in to the feeling of being weightless.

He followed the last actor into the office, chose a chair, and found himself staring into the eyes of one of the most famous directors of his era.

By late afternoon, Alex and Josh were not having a good time.

'Big ad dropped out,' Josh sighed, digging his right fist into the palm of his left hand in what Alex recognised as his most nervous habit, the one that came directly after chain-smoking Marlboros down to the filter and drumming on the edge of any surface with the two gold pens that he carried everywhere in the breast pocket of his baby-blue shirt.

Alex hated dealing with the financial portion of the paper. He knew they were small compared to the *LA Times* or even the more established alternative papers like *The Weekly*, but they had a following. And their diminutive size allowed them to break barriers, which was what Alex most enjoyed. He liked asking shocking questions in interviews, broaching subjects that nobody else dared to ask. Being small didn't hurt their chances of winning superstars for their covers, either. Press, any press, was considered worthwhile in the industry. They were invited to every junket, given passes to even the most star-studded Hollywood opening.

'Another ad will take its place, right?' Alex asked.

Josh raised his blond eyebrows. 'I took a meeting at my favourite studio this afternoon. I was hoping for a big, four-colour for the back page, but the ad guy weaselled out. Said they'd blown the budget on some insane building-sized billboard up on Sunset.' He groaned. 'Jesus, I miss Dashiell sometimes. The man can talk anyone into anything.'

'He's coming back to work soon. He promised,' Alex said, flipping through his files to see what other openings were coming up, then handing Josh a list of movies and studios to try. As he looked over his calendar, he felt the same way Josh did. When Dashiell came back to work, the worries would be over. They always were.

Kelly listened carefully to the stone-eyed woman behind the desk, trying his best to process the information she was giving. It was difficult to concentrate because she was so intensely pretty. Before entering the office, he'd forgotten exactly what she looked like. A loner to the extreme, this director was a Hollywood oddity. She didn't believe in the rules of the game. He'd rarely seen a photograph of her walking down a red carpet, and looking in her eyes, Kelly understood why. Like some wild creature, she was untameable. Living that unforgiving lifestyle hadn't hurt her success in any way. Nobody put out the type of instant hits that she did. When she decided to make a movie, it was a blockbuster. But better than that, it was unexpected.

Everything she did seemed to annoy someone. Like the fact that she had been chain-smoking since the start of the meeting, puffing perfectly executed smoke rings towards the ceiling, where they dispersed into a silvery cloud. The other actors in the room seemed disturbed to see this. California was known for being a smoke-free environment. Strangers actually dared to tell smokers to put out their butts in public, where the air was supposed to be free.

But Kelly liked her attitude, and he found himself captivated. The director was at least twenty years his senior, which put her in her early forties, with rich dark hair that she wore pulled back in a loose ponytail. Her chestnut-coloured mane had started to go silver in only one place, a clean streak at the very front. It made her look even more interesting. With her striking bone structure, and apparently no make-up on at all, she looked like a majestic work of art. Chilled. Unflinching.

Locking into what the director was saying, Kelly found himself even more intrigued by her demeanour. This had to be the most bizarre casting call he'd ever been on, had ever even heard of.

The director didn't want to listen to the four men read. They'd been given the script sections only to let them know what they were in for. Because the part, although not a lead role, was both key and demanding. Would they feel comfortable doing a whole scene without clothes on? Not a sex scene, precisely, but a scenario that reminded Kelly of another casting call he'd read about – a young actress was required to barge into a male locker room and confront one of the naked men inside. Because the actress had only played innocents before, she'd had to do the audition five times before being given the role, just to be sure she could handle it. The girl had aced the audition and landed the job, and in the movie she'd been both startling and impressive.

Kelly cued back into the conversation just as the director turned her piercing stare on him. She was asking him a direct question, and Kelly focused on each word. 'Would you mind doing a nude scene, one in which you were the only character without clothes?' Her voice was low and husky. The tone of it let him know that she was daring him.

'No,' he said automatically.

'Have you ever done something like that before?'

He looked around the room and realised that the stage actor had recently been in a production that had started with him streaking across the stage completely naked. That's why this man was here. The others had done nudity, as well, were famous for baring their butts whenever necessary. So it was up to Kelly to prove that he was in their league.

He'd do just about anything to work with the powerful woman who sat at the desk in front of him. He'd humiliate himself in front of cast and crew. And he'd take off all his clothes right now to prove it –

8

'This is where we stand,' Mica said, brushing a wayward lock of birch-blonde hair away from her earnest face and then pointing to a large number situated at the bottom of a long list of smaller numbers. For emphasis, the five-digit numeral was circled twice in dark red ink, but it needn't have been. The figure was shocking enough without the added double ring of colour.

'That's what's left in the account?' Sasha asked hopefully.

'It's what we owe.'

'Poor fucking us,' Sasha sighed. This wasn't what she wanted to hear. Not after ten hours of filming, baking her brain out beneath the strident Santa Monica sun. Fresh from a long, hot shower, with her robe wrapped around her naked body, all she wanted to do was relax. Listen to *Led Zeppelin II* blasting loudly on her headset. Forget her problems until tomorrow. Unfortunately, from the way Mica was looking at her, she knew this wasn't going to happen. She should never have agreed to meet with her producer after work, should have scheduled a breakfast sit-down when she was fresh and rested. Too late now.

Mica had a high-impact personality that made Sasha, normally the most energised person in a room, actually appear calm. While she watched, Mica paced back and forth from one side of the minuscule room to the other. Since there were only several steps to go, it looked as if Mica were a human racquetball, bounding and rebounding from one blue-painted wall to another. She made

Sasha dizzy, and the redhead closed her eyes, seeking peace behind her shut lids.

The final cash infusion was due in several weeks, promised long before by one of her most trusted investors. But until the money showed up, the film was virtually on hold. This meant that all of her actors and techies would be at loose ends. She might lose some before the finances got straightened out. That was, unless Sasha wanted to do something about it.

'Credit cards?' Mica asked. Now, she was the one to sound hopeful. There were famous stories in LA of entire movies being funded by cash advances provided by Visa.

Sprawling on her bed in her vintage silk robe, Sasha shook her head. Even wet, her corkscrew curls bounced each time she moved. 'Maxed,' Sasha said, eyes still shut.

'Relatives?'

'Maxed as well,' Sasha told her. She was no longer in contact with most of her family members. They didn't understand her art, let alone support her. She was better off without them; she knew that. But wouldn't it have been nice to have someone to call in case of emergencies? Someone aside from Jessica, her best friend since high school. While Jessica was always willing to help out in a tight spot, she did not have the financial means to bail Sasha out now.

'Secretly holding a winning lottery ticket?' Mica finally suggested, trying her best to lighten the situation. Sasha didn't even smile. In her personal bank account was exactly enough money to get her through the next two weeks. And she needed it to last for at least a month. If she'd done the film digitally, it would have cost a fraction of what the current tab was. You could make a movie in four months for four grand. But this was her big push – her goal to finally get noticed, and she'd wanted to do it right, with real film not video.

'So what are we going to do?' Mica asked, serious

again, perching on the edge of Sasha's bed. Mica seemed uncomfortable to be sitting, even half-sitting, and her frantic mood forced Sasha to open her eyes and deal with the situation.

'I'll do what I have to do.'

'You can't go to that party,' Mica told Sasha. 'You fucking can't.'

'Of course, I can. I've done things like this a million times and it's never hurt anyone. Including me,' she said, sensing Mica's next argument. Where would Sasha be when her soul was all gone? Now, when Sasha moved, her curls seemed to bounce up and down in agreement, adding emphasis to every word. 'Charlie said that there will be someone there I have to meet,' she explained, attempting to sound patient. 'Someone who has money, Mica, who has the ability to help –'

'If you have the ability to fuck him.'

'It's not like that,' Sasha said, but the look in her shining green eyes let Mica know she was lying. It was *always* about what you could do for someone else. The trade-off. And there wasn't a whole lot Sasha could offer aside from the seduction of her own body. She personally knew several successful film makers who had literally screwed their way to the top. Making connections, bonding with the right sort of people. Sasha had manipulated relationships to her advantage in the past, and she was smart enough to know that she wouldn't always be mired at this level. If the film gained her notice in any way that she thought it might, this part of her life would be a dim memory as she climbed the ladder to the level of success currently found only in her dreams.

'You don't have an invitation. It's a private party.' That was Mica's last excuse.

'You don't need an invitation,' Sasha said matter-of-factly. 'Not if you're part of the entertainment.' In a gesture that showed how completely she understood the give and take of the industry, she nodded her head up and down. Like a game-show hostess, she indicated her flawless figure still wrapped in the gold silk robe. Then, sighing, Sasha picked up her drink and retreated to the bathroom.

Once by herself, she stared at her reflection in the mirror, seeing not the face she'd presented to Mica, but one of fear. Yes, fear had brought her to this point. Fear and lack of funds. But once she got to the club, she knew that she'd relax, turn on, and make her plans come true. In the larger picture, it was only a little bit more money that she needed to finish the film and get it to the next big festival. Then she would be able to take a breather. The talent was there. She had that much faith in herself. Someone would notice her soon and her penny-pinching days of independent movie making would be over.

As she gave herself a mental pep talk, she could hear Mica begin to pace again. Back and forth; back and forth.

Dashiell was a city boy. In order to unwind at the end of the day, he craved a bit of excitement, the flash and glitz that Los Angeles was famous for. OK, 'unwind' might be exaggerating slightly, and he knew it. What did he need to relax from? He didn't actually do anything strenuous with his life. He'd been purposefully avoiding the paper, because he couldn't stand the daily routine of it. What he spent filling his days with instead would hardly cause most people stress. Worked out. Ran errands. Met up with friends for lunch. Got a drink at a favourite bar.

But what he really liked at the end of the day was sexual intrigue. Flirting with some striking woman, testing to see whether he still had 'it', that nameless quality that made women like him. Women who didn't know who he was.

He'd received a small taste of what he was looking for

at the Halloween party, and a larger swallow with the bartenders at Dream Maker, but now he wanted more. Sorting through the mail, he discovered an invitation to a private party at one of the hippest clubs in Hollywood. Finding the elegant invitation tucked in with junk mail and bills made him smile. The party was exactly what he was looking for.

He didn't waste time dressing up for the event, choosing a pair of casual slacks, a dark blue shirt and a black tie. He slid his favourite leather jacket on to complete the ensemble, then caught his reflection in the bedroom mirror. He looked good, but not as if he were trying. Unlike the rest of the wannabes desperate to talk their way through the doors, he didn't have to worry about getting in. Just another perk that went with being Dashiell Cooper.

Or, rather, Dashiell Jonathan Cooper the Second.

Omission in Jessica's mind wasn't the same thing as lying, not as devious, not as naughty. It just meant that she still hadn't told Kelly about the Halloween party. What could she say? 'I let some stranger touch me under the table while his date shot daggers through my heart with her cold-as-ice green eyes?'

So why did she feel so bad?

'Forgot to tell you that I ended up bartending Friday night,' Kelly said when they met at his apartment after work. 'You should have been at the party. It was a zoo. People always get a bit crazy in costume.'

It was as if he were trying to help her spill the details that nagged at her. But she found that she couldn't. Instead, she simply said, 'There was this meeting at work anyway,' inwardly wincing at the description of the wild party as a 'meeting'. A meeting of people with alcohol, music and highly tuned sex drives. Now, she spread herself on his cotton sheets. 'So, you know, I wasn't free.'

'You're not going to be free now,' Kelly told her, coming back to the bed with something silvery concealed in one hand. Jessica heard the metal chain clink, and she let the sensations flood through her, as if this was the first time Kelly was using his handcuffs on her, binding her to the bed by threading the chain through the top of his headboard.

'Been a bad girl, baby doll?' Kelly murmured.

She nodded automatically. 'Yes' was the expected answer for this particular sexual drama, because 'yes' would always get her what she wanted where Kelly was concerned.

'Now's the time to come clean with me,' he said, again offering her the perfect moment to confess. 'Come on, Jessie. You can tell me. You can tell me anything.'

She thought about the words before responding. Could she tell him anything? No. Could she tell *anyone* anything? She didn't think so. There were secrets that she knew would never make their way to the surface. Desires that unless some smart lover figured out on his own, she would have to be content with fantasising about in her head. Still, Kelly allowed her more freedom than most of her previous lovers. And, lowering her elegant lashes, she started to tell him what he wanted to hear.

'I *have* been bad, Kelly,' she whispered, refusing to meet his eyes. Besides the events at the party, she also hadn't told him about the flowers that had arrived at the office, twice now, with notes from her admirer. That was bad, wasn't it?

As she spoke, he continued to gently manoeuvre her on the bed, his hands straightening her lean legs. She was stretched out by this move, her body elongated further as he leaned down to pick up her discarded nylons and used those to bind her ankles together. He didn't speak as he worked, waiting for her to continue.

She thought about what she'd like to have said: 'I let

a man finger my pussy, Kelly. He put his hand up my thigh, touched me slowly until he reached my cunt. He brought me so close to climaxing in public that I almost cried from the delayed gratification.' But she couldn't make herself tell him the truth. Instead, she started off with something much safer.

'You wouldn't believe the fantasies I've had lately.'

'Try me,' he said.

'You and me and –'

'Oh,' he said, grinning. 'You want to play like that? You are a bad girl, aren't you, baby?'

This time, the word 'yes' was almost a hiss as Jessica realised he was going to take care of her. The trust between them was for real, even if she hadn't revealed her secret to him. Maybe it didn't matter. Maybe there were things better left hidden in any relationship. She knew that anything Kelly had in mind between the sheets would make her feel good. He got off seeing her come, and as she watched him reach into the drawer on his bedside table, she realised he was going to get off in a big way this evening. Because the toy he held in his hand was one of her all-time favourites.

'Hey, baby,' Ian whispered, walking into Avalon's bedroom and striking a provocative pose in the doorway. 'What do you have on the burner tonight?'

Wasn't it obvious? Avalon was seated at her pink wooden desk, typing furiously on her laptop, pages of handwritten notes spread out all around her. The tiny tape recorder that she took everywhere was on 'pause' while she wrote up a descriptive passage from memory. Now, her eyes took in her roommate's suggestive behaviour, then flicked to look over at the clock on her bedside table.

When the column was going well for her, the rest of the world disappeared. She no longer heard the rumbling sounds of the traffic outside the Brentwood apartment, didn't notice the noises emanating from her roommate's bedroom. But she tuned in now. P Funk. Ian was in the mood to get down. Or, more likely, to get *her* to go down.

'Working,' she said, nodding towards her screen where tiny multi-coloured fish from her screensaver swam in mass across a dark violet sea.

'Fucking,' Ian responded, following her one-word sentence structure. Avalon looked up again and noticed that her handsome roommate had placed one hand on the crotch of his ripped jeans and was ever so casually stroking his fingertips up and down the bulge poorly concealed there.

Best friends. Roommates. Sometime fuck-partners. That's what the two were. Years before, they'd met at a job interview, both competing for the same personal assistant position, and both losing to someone with more experience, meaning any experience at all. They'd felt a connection at the interview, consoled themselves later over tequila body shots, and had been best friends ever since.

Ian made enough money now that he could easily afford his own place, some fancy penthouse up in the hills. But he liked the comfort of living with Avalon. Always having someone to talk with, get drunk with, to fuck. Never having to be alone, which was the scariest thought of all for an actor. Living in a place without an audience. The horror, the horror.

Besides, what they had together was nearly impossible to replicate. There wasn't one thing in Avalon's closet – either her real walk-in wardrobe or her cluttered mental cupboards – that Ian wasn't privy to. He knew what turned her on, how to make her wet, how to make her beg. And she could do the same for him. How comforting was that, for both of them?

* * *

'Need this, do you?' Kelly asked, correctly reading the excitement in Jessica's vibrant blue eyes. 'A double-cock evening,' he continued further, starting the fun off by running the large, powerful vibrator along the side of her ribs. The best feeling ever to Jessica was being tied down, relinquishing her will to him so that she was at his disposal for whatever he had in mind. She put herself in his capable hands and let him set the scenario from start to finish. Kelly generally surpassed any fantasies that she'd previously had. Best of all, he kept her in a state of wonderment. What would he do next? How would he touch her? And where?

She could feel the wetness spreading between her thighs, and she arched her hips uselessly on the firm mattress, knowing that it was going to be a good long time before Kelly brought the toy to the split between her legs. The place where she most wanted to feel those rumbling vibrations.

He was going to make her wait. Running the tip of the flesh-coloured cock up under her sharply defined chin, between her breasts, down her concave belly. Skipping her slippery-wet pussy and going right to the insides of her slender thighs, back and forth all the way to the very bottoms of her feet. She felt energised by the massage of the motorised sex toy, as if all of her nerve endings were on the verge of climaxing. Not simply the hot zone between her legs, but every part of her entire body.

'I like the way you move,' Kelly said softly, and she realised that she'd been shimmying her hips on the sheet, sliding back and forth in time to the rhythm of his creation. 'I'd like you to move like that on my cock,' he continued, and now he was suddenly between her spread thighs, slipping the head of his steel-like pole into her lush, wet pussy.

'God, yes,' Jessica sighed, unable to keep quiet. 'That is so good.'

She said the words before Kelly made things even better. With the vibrator still in hand, he brought the toy to the ridge of her pubic bone and rested it there. Just let it sit in place for a moment without moving the shaft. She felt the magic motor humming on her, as the vibrator sent sparkling shivers shooting through her. Shudders that not only felt amazing to her, but obviously felt transcendent to Kelly. She watched as he sighed and bucked harder inside her. His rock-hard cock brought her right up to the threshold of her pleasure – where the climax was on the other side, waiting. She could feel his tool swelling within her, driving in deep, so forcefully that she sucked in her breath at the powerful tremors that shook her.

The ride was going to take a long time. She sensed it from the way Kelly worked to control himself. He was breathing slowly, moving his hips in time with hers, pushing hard and deep. Melding himself to her and letting her feel the entire length of his cock pulsing within her, the vibrating sex toy now up in his hand again.

Where would the magic wand land next?

It was also what Sasha was wondering. Not a magic wand, precisely, but the magical welcoming motion of a bouncer's curved finger as he thoughtfully regarded the sultry vixens waiting outside the door. It was up to him to choose which of the night owls he would next allow into the club. What power he held in the wave of his finger. His dark eyes flickered once in her direction, and Sasha tilted her head and lowered her long, mascara-enhanced lashes. She needed to be one of the chosen.

Did she ever.

Slowly, she hiked her short ice-blue skirt up a little further, revealing her long legs, toned and perfectly displayed in a pair of strappy sandals encrusted with crystals. Then she looked suggestively over at the bouncer again. He winked in approval and motioned with that magic finger, bringing her forward into the private party and one seductive step closer to a happy ending.

After letting Avalon listen for a moment to the background soundtrack he'd selected, Ian walked towards her desk. Standing behind her, he ran his strong fingers along the ridge of her collarbone, then moved his palms back to massage the angel-like wings of her shoulder blades.

'You're tight back here,' he said, and at the sexy tone of his voice she started laughing. Although sometimes he put on the air of a world-renowned seducer, this evening Ian wasn't being subtle in the slightest. He might as well have come right out and said, 'Fuck me, baby. I have a hard-on. You should use it.'

'Tight back where?' she asked through her giggles.

'You know, Ava,' he whispered. 'You know just where you're tight.'

'And I know just what you want to do about it.'

'Do you, oh cocky one?' Ian asked. 'Are you sure?'

'Mmm, hmmm,' Avalon purred. Ian was hitting all the right spots, rubbing in deep circles with his thumbs. She could feel her tension start to slip away.

'Then tell me,' Ian insisted. 'Tell me exactly what *I* want to do.'

'You want to lift me up in your big, muscled arms and carry me to the bed,' Avalon said, and as she spoke, Ian made the statement come true, hoisting her easily in his embrace and bringing her to the canopy bed that filled the majority of her room. Large mattress, burgundy velvet draped over the top and below, like something out of a fairy tale. The bed was the first thing Avalon had purchased when she'd sold a story to a glossy national magazine. 'And then you want to take off all of my clothes –'

'This little fluff of a nightie?' Ian asked as he slid the material up Avalon's slender body. 'I want to take *this* off?'

'Yes, you do,' Avalon answered, 'because you want to take off your own clothes and feel me all over with your naked body.'

'Are you sure?' Ian asked, even though he was stripping out of his jeans and black T-shirt as he spoke. 'Are you sure that's what I want to do?'

Avalon nodded because Ian hadn't been wearing boxers, and now that she could view his unhindered erection, she could tell that what she was saying was true. 'You want to climb up here and lie down,' she told him, moving aside to give him room. 'And then you want me to lie on top of you, to make sure that our bodies are completely joined together.'

'That's what I want, huh?' Ian asked. 'You're pretty psychic this evening, aren't you, kid?' he continued as his roommate lay her body perfectly aligned with his, and she rubbed back and forth, so that his cock pressed between the lips of her pussy, getting the length of it nice and wet before she helped him slide it inside of her.

'But what is it that you want, Ava?' Ian asked, and as he said the words, Avalon found that if she were honest with herself, she really didn't know.

Inside the party, Sasha took a moment to let her eyes focus. The mood lighting was dim to create a more personal ambience, but after a few seconds, her oval-shaped green eyes had grown accustomed to the atmosphere. She recognised several big shots right away, and she was headed in the direction of one she'd met previously. The trick was to talk to these people before they got too drunk. She could share information about herself, her movie, drop the names of her most well-known backers. Just as she was gearing herself up to glow and charm, someone rudely jostled her arm. Turning, she saw a handsome although casually dressed man at her side, and she instantly wondered how he'd gained access into the club. Look at what he was wearing. How could he have gotten by the bouncer? But she pushed that snobby thought out of her mind just as another thought replaced it. Maybe he was somebody who didn't need to dress up –

The man interrupted her mental conversation by politely apologising for nudging her and offering to make it up to her with a drink. 'Please,' he said, herding her gallantly towards the bar. 'It's the very least I can do.'

In actuality, Sasha thought, the very least he could do was let her the fuck alone, so that she could try to hustle up some interest in her project. But after watching her hesitate for a moment, the man spoke again. 'One drink,' he said, 'and then I'll let you free. If that's really what you want.'

She had to admit that she liked the way he looked, and the way he was looking at her. It had been a long time since Sasha had relaxed and enjoyed a man's company. More than that, she was tired of faking it, of always considering her agenda, which was the budget of her movie. With this new prospect looking at her expectantly, she smiled and decided to let the attractive man buy her a drink. When he pulled a bill from a battered wallet to pay, Sasha felt guilty for noticing how old and worn the brown leather of his wallet was, and for subsequently thinking again that he didn't belong in the club. It was apparent to her that the man didn't have the kind of money that the rest of the crew did. As if reading her mind, he said, 'I'm here with a friend.'

He motioned towards the main room, but although Sasha looked, she couldn't tell who he was indicating with his head nod.

'The people here are a bit –' He raised his dark eyebrows, to indicate that they were out of his league, and Sasha sighed and felt herself growing more comfortable. If she didn't have to be 'on', then at least she could be herself.

'I know what you mean,' she said, taking the drink and bringing it to her lips for the first sip.

'What do you do?'

Sasha considered the question for a moment. She had her spiel down pat, all the memorised words about being an independent film maker, following the course of her artistic endeavours, blah, blah, fucking blah. Within her mind were the little buzz words to make the people who could pay interested in investing. Instead, she shook her head and said, 'I've been talking so much about myself lately that I'm bored to death with the subject. Why don't you tell me what you do instead?'

The man grinned at her and took her hand in his. He seemed to like her answer, and the touch of his fingers against hers changed her feeling of sad desperation to something entirely different.

'Let's split,' he said after she'd had the time to down half of her drink. 'I've got another place we can go that's much more our speed.' Sasha hesitated for one more moment, then followed the man out of the bar and into the night.

In the parking lot, his pick-up truck waited for them. It was Sasha's favourite truck of all time, a classic cherry-red Ford, in mint condition. She was thrilled with this sign of the man's personality. No generic Japanese import. No German sports car. Climbing inside the cab, she felt herself further relax. Enough so that when he casually undid the tie from around his neck and asked if he might blindfold her, she actually heard herself agreeing.

'You do like movies, right?' the man asked.

'Of course.' That went without saying, didn't it? They were in Hollywood, after all. It was like asking if she was into air, or food. Who didn't like movies in this part of the world?

'I mean, that's what you told me on the ride,' he prompted her.

'I do,' she assured him. 'You have no idea.'

'OK, so you can take off the blindfold now.'

Quickly Sasha slipped off the tie that he'd used to cover her eyes. She hadn't known what to expect, but now that she saw the stairs, she couldn't help but laugh. The man had taken her to one of the most famous movie locations in Hollywood, a staircase that ran up to nowhere, but had originally been used as a prop in a classic Laurel and Hardy film.

'You know it, don't you?' he asked, and she nodded as she opened the door to his shiny red truck and climbed out. She'd been here once before, in the daytime, but at night, the stairs had a completely different feel. Not eerie, but interesting. She put one hand on the cool railing and held on. As soon as she touched the cold metal, the man put his arms around her waist.

They were going to do it on a piece of Hollywood history. She felt herself growing excited. When focused on a film, as she'd been for the past few months, it was impossible for her to have any type of fulfilling social life. Occasionally, she'd hook up with someone simply to savour the feeling of human contact, the pleasure of skin on skin. The last movie she worked on, she'd wound up fucking the lead actor, which turned out to be a tragic mistake. When they'd broken up mid-shooting, his performance on the film had changed. Whenever she made an honest directing comment, he'd flip her off, if not actually physically, then emotionally. Going for the opposite of what she'd requested. That had been a nightmare, and the film had suffered for it. All for the sake of several so-so orgasms.

Now, she'd been living like a hermit. Filming. Sleeping. Eating when she remembered to. Mainlining coffee. Not caring about anything other than her movie. And, oh fuck, she'd forgotten how good a man could feel. This man knew what he was doing, slipping her dress up to reveal the pearl-grey stockings she'd borrowed from Jessica's room. His fingers lingered on the tops of her bare thighs, and she trembled at his touch. Would he slide his hand between her legs, sense out her wetness?

No, he was taking his time. The crisply refreshing night air met her skin and she trembled again, but this time the man held her firmly in his arms, letting her feel his strength, *and* his length. Sometimes, it was good to give in, wasn't it? To bend over and have a stranger undress you, quickly stripping off your clothes. Fingers learning the curves and valleys of your body for the first time. Nothing, in her opinion, was more thrilling than being touched by a new lover. For Sasha, it was the same indescribable feeling as sitting in a darkened theatre right before the movie started, an uncontrolled wave of anticipation. This was why she'd gone into making movies. She prayed someday that other people would get that charge right before one of her films rolled on the screen. Anticipation before sex came close to capturing the hushed hopeful quality that she found herself addicted to in movie making.

Take me, she thought. Surprise me.

Her new partner seemed to understand exactly what she wanted. He lifted her hands so that she was holding on to the railing at a higher point, so that her arms ached slightly from being stretched to their limits. Then he pushed her glacier-blue skirt up to her waist, bending behind her and sliding her peach-coloured panties down over her stockings with his mouth. His tongue trailed along the split of her ass and Sasha sighed.

She loved the feeling of being touched back there. Tricking it in a circle around her hole before sliding his tongue up inside her. It was a pleasure she could never find it in herself to ask for, not even with a long-term beau. But every once in a while, a lover took a risk and made the move, and oh, did it ever pay off. Shuddering, Sasha felt a fresh flood of wetness between her legs. Her pussy felt alive as it hadn't been in months. It was as if her cunt was reminding her of what it needed and what it had been lacking.

Standing again, her lover pressed his own body against hers. She could feel his still-clothed erection pressing into her from behind, and she squirmed against him to let him know she was ready. More than ready, she was desperate to feel his skin on hers. All she wanted was for him to unzip his slacks, bring out his cock, and enter her. Thrust inside her pussy hard and fast, letting her really feel him. She could imagine just what it would feel like. Naked skin on naked skin.

Excitement made it difficult for her to breathe, and she worked to force herself to calm down. But that was useless. There was no way to still the ragged quality of her breath, no way to rein in her raging heartbeat. This moment was too powerful, and all she could do was give in to every sensation. A wondrous feeling pulsed through her as the man finally did exactly as she hoped. Pulling open his fly, he released his hard-on and slipped it deep inside of her.

And that changed everything.

While focusing on her work, Sasha had been denying

herself the gratification of male companionship for too long, hadn't she? Way too long. Now was the time to let go of the stress of work and enjoy the rush of being young, good-looking, and in LA.

Where, literally, everything goes.

Book Two:
A Spanking New Year

My love is strong,
And you're so sweet.
And someday, baby,
We've got to meet.

– The Rolling Stones

9

Dishing the Dirt with Avalon Granger

Can't say who, precisely, but if you've been following the undercover (and on the airplane, behind the bar, and beneath the pier) romance of a certain dark-eyed, well-built Italian movie stud and his nubile young personal trainer, then it won't surprise you in the slightest to hear that a little acrobat is on the way. No confirmation from either source, of course. (It's never that easy, is it?) And a raging silence emanates from both of their PR agencies, but how long can one hide that sort of news? Check back here in a month or two as the tummy swells, and listen to me say, 'Ha, I told you so!'

In from the 'rubbing the right way' department, here's a tale about the head of one of the movie studios – and we mean one of the big boys. A married exec with a secret condominium located high in the Hollywood Hills requested a massage from an exclusive Beverly Hills salon. Not some sleazy massage parlour, you understand, but a stellar skincare centre frequented by the stars. He greeted the stunned masseuse totally naked at the door, led by a part of his anatomy that could in no way be described as a 'little me'.

Did she saddle that horse and ride it?

Well, let's just say that she left with more than a tip in her pocket.

And turning our beady eyes on ourselves, we have news of the dirty variety that only yours truly could dig up. Back from a recent tour of Europe, Zebra's own editor-in-chief was spotted at a Hollywood club, making eyes with not one, not two, but three different pin-up girls ... and wouldn't you know they covered the gamut in hair colours: one blonde, one redhead, one brunette. Couldn't have been more picture-perfect if Klimt had painted the scene as a mural or if Hefner had requested the clinch for a photo shoot –

'You can't put it in, Granger.'

Avalon sighed as she reached into her slick patent leather clutch, searching restlessly for a cigarette. 'The readers love this stuff,' she said without looking up. 'You're just a fucking prude.'

'I'm not a prude.'

'An old woman, then. A stick in the mud.'

'Not a stick,' Alex corrected her patiently. 'A friend. There's a big difference between censoring your column and saving your ass.' He watched as Avalon finally found the cigarette, and then toyed with it, refusing to light the mentholated Kool in his presence. 'You know exactly what Dashiell's like and how he feels when people pry into his private life.'

'Yeah, I know him.' Avalon let that sentence hang, her striking green eyes intent on Alex's. A silent message passed between them that was readable only to people who had a specific piece of knowledge about Avalon's past. Pete, seated in his usual spot on the sofa, looked over, but as he couldn't decipher the nuance of the statement, he turned back towards his laptop and continued to ignore the discussion. 'Anyway, I know that he'll love it. This column is pure bragging fodder. He can laminate the thing and show it to his buddies down at Star Fucker.'

'Dream Maker,' Alex corrected her automatically. Always the editor.

'Come on, Harris,' Avalon said softly, and her voice

took on the slippery edge of a sultry sexual proposal. Although they'd never done it, he knew simply from the way she spoke what it would be like to be in bed with her. Raw. Hard. Unbelievably intense. But wasn't every aspect of Avalon's nature dripping with come-ons? 'What man wouldn't want to be called on the fact that he was fucking three different beautiful women at the same time?'

'Dashiell. Dashiell is the man who wouldn't want it.'

'Then he should drag his sorry ass to work and read the copy himself. If he doesn't like it, he can use his own diamond-studded red pencil to cross it out.'

This was a fair comment, and Alex didn't have any reply that would diffuse the truth in what she'd said. No, it wasn't Dashiell's job to be a copy editor, and it was widely known that he rarely paid much attention to the content of his own paper. But since returning from his European jaunt, Dashiell had visited the office infrequently. Instead, he'd spent his time taking meetings in posh restaurants, dating young starlets who were easily dazzled by his wallet, if not his good looks, and having a wild time, which apparently included fucking in trio. For some reason, Dashiell didn't seem to notice that when he was gone, the paper seemed anchorless. Drifting.

Alex wished he had the guts to confront Dashiell about the situation, to tell him that all parts of the newspaper worked better with Cooper at the helm. There was no sane explanation for it. The editor-in-chief simply had the kind of personality that made everything seem easy. When Josh had failed to pull in ads, Dashiell was often able to change things around with a phone call. At the same time, Alex was glad that his boss had been making himself scarce, and this is why he didn't respond to Avalon's comment. He had a personal reason for wanting to keep his boss away from the office: young Jessica.

'It's staying in,' Avalon said, pouting prettily when Alex, lost in his thoughts, hadn't responded to her demand. That got his attention, and while she watched, he walked the few steps over to her laptop computer, highlighted the paragraph, and deleted it with a single violent keystroke.

'Out,' he said, and his tone of voice was dead serious. 'I'm calling rank,' he said now. 'Find something else.'

'Something like the fact that Dash did this totally hot redheaded bombshell after a private party two weeks ago and nobody knows who she was? I mean nobody. I've scoured, I've begged. I've offered cash money, as well as a few more private services. I can find nothing more.' She was pushing her luck, but Alex refused to bite.

'Write something that's not about Dashiell,' Alex said, moving back to sit in his plush leather chair and pretend to be deeply involved in a file on his screen as Jessica walked into the room.

For Jessica, November seemed to fly by. She worked at the paper, doing her very best to learn how to be a necessary component of the staff. Although she'd told Alex that she was taking only two classes, easing her way back into the regiment of schoolwork after her two-year hiatus, this was a lie. In reality, she'd dropped out after the first week. She saw no point in sitting in a stuffy classroom, listening to long-winded lectures delivered by boring professors. The real world called to Jessica, and she focused hard on what she could learn from her new teachers.

Within a month of being hired, she had become indispensable to several of her higher-ups. Josh used her to calm any irate customers with her soothing manner. Avalon asked her to schedule appointments, arranging meetings with celebrity PR firms and personal assistants.

And then there was Alex.

Alex gave her the chance to watch him work. Position-ing her at the desk closest to his, he let Jessica spend all her free time learning his methods of controlling the motley crew who made up the paper's staff. Some of the writers needed coddling in order to turn in their pieces on time. Others demanded a heavier hand. Alex was able to behave in either manner required, growing hard-edged or mild-mannered, as the situation called for.

This was all interesting to Jessica, but she found that what she really was learning had nothing to do with her goal of being a big-time journalist. That wouldn't happen until Alex finally gave her a real assignment instead of having her write the little advertising column. Instead, she spent her days deciphering the intimate dance that went on between the people involved with running the paper.

This afternoon, when Jessica came in from the upstairs office, she sensed tension in the room between Avalon and Alex. But although she turned her head from one to the other, trying to gauge where the energy was coming from, she found that she was in the dark. As always. She wished that *Zebra*'s staff would open up to her, would let her in on the secrets behind the relation-ships. As she sat back at her desk and began to type, she promised herself that she'd pay closer attention. Work harder at learning more.

Power, and the way it was played with – that was what intrigued her the most.

'Edit this, if you'd like,' Avalon said, pushing a hard red plastic disk into Jessica's hands and giving her a quick smile, white teeth flashing between crimson-slicked lips.

'Your column?'

'Give it the once-over, but don't change anything,'

Avalon told her, narrowing her green eyes slightly and letting Jessica see a look of danger swirling deep within them. 'Not a word. Not a comma. Just let me know what you think.'

The gossip columnist shot Alex a look over the intern's head that Jessica missed – it was a 'Fuck you, Harris' look, and he won it from time to time for cutting items from her column. Avalon could never truly accept that Alex had the final say when it came to her writing. But he did. That was a fact.

While Jessica watched, Avalon slid into her snakeskin-printed leather trench coat and took a peek at the heavy gold man's watch that dangled loosely from her wrist like a bracelet. 'Got an important meeting,' she said, speaking to the room at large rather than anyone in particular. 'I wouldn't want to be late.' Josh, who had wandered by the open doorway, laughed softly as he walked by. Then, with a wink over her shoulder towards Jessica, Avalon slipped out of the door.

The first part of the column was identical to the one that Alex had read. But the last item was something that Avalon had chosen to put in just for the hell of it. Alex would cut this piece as well, which was fine. Screw him. It wasn't for his eyes that she'd written it.

File this one in the mysterious admirer department. Not secret admirer, because some of us know the name of the man behind that mask. But under anonymously enamoured, we have found one of the Sun Kings of Hollywood. And he is smitten.

White roses have arrived three times now for a young writer at Zebra. As she searches to find the identity of her high-end gardener, will she discover her true love, or will she uncover only thorns?

More to come, my Kewpie dolls, I'm sure. Where

there are long-stemmed white roses there is ... oh,
maybe not fire, but definitely thorns.
And remember who had the news first.

Jessica read the item twice. She wished she could talk to
the columnist, but Avalon was long gone, off to her next
appointment. After staring for several moments at her
computer screen without seeing anything before her, she
thought she understood what the woman was doing.
Avalon wanted to let Jessica know.

To know that she was paying attention.

'How does that feel?' Josh murmured.

Avalon couldn't immediately answer. Not verbally,
anyway. In her mind, she imagined that her body had
suddenly been transformed into the material used in one
of those mood rings from the 1970s, beaming out a range
of colours that clearly showed her lover exactly how
excited she was, and how close she was to climax. Josh
wouldn't have had to ask if this were the case. He'd have
seen the beams of pulsing red light shot through with
hot violet flickers, and he'd have understood what total
dream-like pleasure Avalon was experiencing.

'Tell me, baby,' he insisted, obviously wanting her to
say the words out loud.

But what were the words?

Josh had this way of dining on her pussy that made
Avalon dripping wet from the moment he approached
the task. Just the sweet memory of what he could do
with his tongue turned her on, and she often stroked
herself to mental playbacks of being with him. Part of
the excitement was the earnestness with which he
approached the job. Josh couldn't seem to wait to get in
between her thighs and start lapping at her. There was
no sense that he was doing it only to get her to recipro-
cate. In fact, he was one of the few men she'd been with

who rarely seemed interested in 69ing. When Josh was nuzzling, he wanted to concentrate on what he was doing. To do it right. To get her off.

And, oh, did he ever.

'Come on, Ava,' he urged now, 'talk to me and I'll talk to you.'

What did that mean? Avalon looked down at him, glancing at the intersection between her thighs where Josh was comfortably situated. Rather than make him explain, she did as he asked. 'I love it when your tongue flicks lightly against my clit,' she said, pushing up on her arms so that she could watch every little detail. 'Lightly, like a cat's –'

'Like this?' he asked. His tongue tickled her pussy lips, nudging them apart gently, and then tapped softly against the pulsing oval of her clit. Avalon sighed and closed her eyes, steeling herself for the ride. When she held on and forced herself to wait, the climax always became so much more intense. 'Or like this?' he murmured, and this time he spoke against her body, so that she could feel the vibrations of the words directly against her skin. *That's* what he meant. He'd talk to her – into her – against her pussy so that the words themselves became part of the pleasure.

'Just like that,' she told him, feeling his soft hair brushing against her inner thighs. He was doing exactly as she'd asked, touching her clit so lightly that it was almost like a long, soft feather stroking her up and down. They'd played that way once before, at a staff Halloween party two years prior, right after the end of his relationship with Tiffany. Avalon had dressed as an exotic flapper from the twenties, with a fringed black dress that barely covered her thighs and a fantasy-inducing feather boa around her neck. Ideas had instantly blossomed in Josh's mind when he'd caught sight of the boa. He'd wanted to tie her up with it. To tickle her all over with the very tips of those midnight-black feathers. Ultimately, they'd spent most of the early morning at his house, where he'd run the deliciously decadent feathers along her belly, her breasts and erect nipples, and between her plump pussy lips. The boa had been destroyed, while the memory of the night lived for ever.

Avalon relished the feather flashback, but suddenly, she wanted something else. Something harder. And she knew Josh well enough to know exactly how to get what she wanted. With one hand, she reached between her legs and got a handful of his thick blond hair, pulling him up fiercely so that she could look directly into his eyes.

Since they worked together in such close quarters, occasionally she actually forgot how good-looking he was. She took him for granted. He was Josh. Her co-worker. Her buddy. But the hard, unbreakable shell of the advertising executive seemed to disappear when they were in bed, leaving his striking face open and almost innocent. His blond hair was mussed now, and his jaw had the baby-soft shadow that light-haired men often get. Not a rough beard, but something fine and downy, like peach fuzz against her skin.

Avalon took a moment to stare into his waiting gaze before she spoke. She wanted him to appreciate each word that she said. 'Tongue-fuck me,' she told him when she was ready. 'Drive it into my pussy hard. Make me really feel it.'

He didn't ask any more questions. Didn't query her as to how much pressure she wanted, how deep she desired him to go. He simply obeyed. The power shifted quickly and fluidly between them as she arched her hips and worked back against him. But that was acceptable. The best part of their relationship was the balance. Sometimes Josh was in charge. Other times she took hold of the control. The power.

This thought made her smile. She understood that the young intern was on a quest to learn about power. To decipher who had it and, more importantly, how she could get it. Avalon found Jessica's innocence fetching, yet her aspirations were infinitely simple to read. The girl's thoughts were right there, shining in her large blue eyes. Yet for some reason, Avalon had decided to like her. To help her, mould her, show her the way. What she wouldn't have given for someone to have done the same for her ten years earlier, when she was starting out. But there was no need to dwell on the past. Avalon had made her way on her own.

Some day, during a round of drinks, she'd explain to Jessica all about the real source of power, because Avalon and Josh played with this erotic substance all the time. Josh telling her what to do for him. Demanding action and growing aroused when she followed his commands. His cock hardening as he made Avalon crawl before him across the floor. Completely nude, her body glistening with a thin sheen of sweat, her entire being focused on pleasing him. On obeying. Or Avalon, clad in some black PVC dress that she'd bought in the wilds of Hollywood, long legs encased in thigh-high boots and black fishnet stockings, telling Josh exactly what he'd better do if he didn't want to test her wrath.

For now, she wrapped her legs around her lover's back and held on.

Taking what she wanted until she wanted nothing more.

Despite the fact that Alex never made it to Marina's dance recital, she hadn't kept true to her ultimatum. Whenever he came home from work, there she was, waiting. Of course, she never actually *looked* as if she were waiting for him. She'd be doing dance moves in the living room, the stereo cranked to some Björk tune that he'd never heard and instantly didn't like. Or she'd be soaking in the bathtub, rose petals scattered in the scented bubbly water as if she thought she were the star of some romance novel.

From the appearance of things, Marina had decided that she could keep their relationship going simply by refusing to believe it was over. She talked to him about inconsequential daily happenings that real couples would discuss: the recent rent increase on his apartment, the lack of a cable modem. To Alex's dismay, she actually moved more of her belongings into his closet, and each time he opened the bathroom cabinet, several of her cosmetics would fall out and roll along the counter. In the past, he'd often found women's personal items disconcertingly charming. The mystery intrigued him. How exactly did one use all the little pots of coloured creams and rectangular cases of powder? Within himself, he knew that if these had been Jessica's belongings strewn through his apartment, he'd have been instantly turned on.

With Marina, he was simply overwhelmed.

He had to end it. Stage the finale to the long-running production with her. Didn't matter if she was a hellcat between the sheets, she was destroying his mind. He knew the why and the where. The only problem he had now was how.

So when Marina picked a fight with him early on a Sunday morning, he remained surprisingly calm, listening to her arguments and nodding the way a therapist would to an overly animated patient. Maybe he'd been waiting for a situation like this, knowing that she couldn't keep up the good-girl charade indefinitely. Previously, his voice would have risen to match hers in pitch as he fought back. Today, he simply refused to get involved in her nastiness and then be forced into the psychotic little make-up dance/post-fight sex scenario that had plagued their entire relationship. No more. He didn't have the energy to relive this particular drama.

'You're fucking awful to me,' Marina said in a self-pitying tone. 'You use me when I please you. Discard me when it suits you. Then take me back again, playing head games with my mind.'

Maybe he behaved in the manner that she described, but she was guilty of the same actions herself. It was as if she brought out the worst in him, because he'd never been this way with another woman. During a discussion with Pete and Avalon, after they'd witnessed a bit of Marina's over-acted drama and asked why the fuck he put up with it, he'd spent hours making up excuses. His favourite statement was that the rocks in his head fit the holes in hers. The sick joke didn't make him laugh any more.

Now, the quieter he got, the louder she became. Her cheeks grew almost as red as the velvety Mrs Claus suit she'd worn on Halloween, and Alex let her yell. Taking the abuse. Finally, when she'd let it all out, he said, 'You make a lot of sense, Marina. And I realise something now that I didn't understand before.'

Marina waited expectantly, a look of success already glistening in her leaf-green eyes. He could tell from her body language that she thought he was going to apologise, maybe get down on his knees before her as he'd done so many times in the past, slide her gauzy night-gown up her lean thighs and press his lips to her cunt through her panties. Whisper how sorry he was and beg her to take him back before pleasuring her, sliding his tongue up inside her pussy. Satisfying her with his mouth to let him repent for his irrational behaviour. Making those sensuous circles that spun around her clit before tapping the point of his tongue against the button of pleasure.

He didn't.

'I can't make you happy,' he said. 'It's not your fault. It's mine.'

She stayed where she was, head cocked to one side like a curious parakeet, obviously waiting for the rest of the apology. There was none forthcoming. Quietly, Alex handed her the clothes she'd discarded the previous evening and motioned for her to get dressed. She moved like a sleepwalker, and he had to dress her himself, guiding her into her capri pants, putting her own hands on the buttons and watching as she automatically did up the fly. Her shoes were mules, and he put them in front of her to step in. Then he helped her with her cropped denim coat, handed over her purse, and led her, still somewhat stunned, to the door.

'I need my key back,' he said, searching within the impossible depths of her black leather bag until he found the sterling silver heart-shaped ring and pulling the correct key off of it. 'I don't think we should talk to each other for a while,' he added as an afterthought. 'No calls. No visits. Trust me, it will be easier.'

Then, ushering her out into the hallway of the condominium, he shut the door between them and returned to his bedroom to lounge alone on his mattress, relishing a sense of inner peace that he hadn't felt for a long time.

10

Dishing the Dirt with Avalon Granger

It doesn't always fall into your lap. Sometimes, you have to call in favours. Offer tricks for treats. Do those enticing little erotic dance steps that make everything run smoothly in the wicked weird world of Hollywood. You know what I'm talking about. Whispering, cajoling, making all sorts of compromising promises: 'I'll stroke you, if you stroke me.'

But every once in a while, a tip – a glorious, lip-licking tip – presents itself naked and ready in your doorway. And all you have to do is lead it to the bed and spread it out on the satin sheets. Make love to it slowly, carefully, and it will tell you all the secrets it knows.

If I say that I spent the last week ensconced in my luxurious queen-sized bed, will you, dear readers, understand the size of the tip I have for you? The sweetness that lingers afterwards at such a find is still clouding my head and making me feel lazy, giddy, like a blushing new bride.

Ah, but you know me too well, don't you? Avalon Granger no longer blushes.

Alex started to laugh. Sometimes, Avalon wrote columns that were chock full of Hollywood dirt. This generally happened when public relations teams agreed, either verbally or through press releases, to reveal something sizeable about the private life of a movie star, like the birth of a new baby or the landing of a great job. Avalon hated those columns. When a celebrity's PR team was willing to go public with news, by the time *Zebra* heard about it, most everyone else had as well.

But if Avalon snagged herself a really good bit of gossip, something she could not only sink her teeth into, but drag her long fingernails down the back of, she generally bragged about her skill for a little while. That's what she was doing here.

New film on the horizon. A DD Production. That's Deleen DeMarco for those of you who missed Paradise Lounge *and* Twisted. *(And if you did miss those movies, you might as well turn in your passport and move back to whatever hole you came from. You simply don't belong here.)*

The set is closed. The gates are locked. The lips are sealed. Ha. Ha. Aren't they? Isn't that how it always is on a DD production? Ah, not when Avalon gets her mind fixated on a distant prize. I have news, my pretties. I have secrets to spill. Pull up a chair, pull down your panties, and get ready to hear what I have to say –

'Alex,' Jessica interrupted.

He looked up, startled, as if she had caught him reading a dirty magazine while playing with himself. Without seeming to notice, the blue-eyed intern reduced him to a stuttering schoolboy, yet there was no reason for this transformation. She wasn't in your face like Avalon or game-playing like Marina. All Jessica seemed to expect from him was guidance. He should have been able to give her that without being flustered.

'I want a real assignment,' she said, and he leaned back in his chair and adopted what he hoped was a patient, listening expression and not a 'I want to jump your bones' look. 'You said yourself that what I've been turning in is good.'

'It is,' he agreed, nodding. 'You're doing an awesome job.' Christ, he sounded like a teenybopper.

'So give me something else.'

While listening to her talk, he saw in her eyes that she was hungry. Not jaded. Not trying to get something from him that she didn't deserve. Just hungry for work and filled with a desire to prove her abilities, not only to him, but to herself. He found that clean, sweet quality pulled hard at him inside.

'Let me look in my files,' he promised her. 'I'll see what I have.'

When Jessica returned from working upstairs in the ad room, Alex said, 'You told me once that you'd heard Todd's band, right?'

Jessica nodded, wondering where her boss was going with the question.

'We'd like to put a review of the next show into the paper, your standard concert write-up. But we're all so close here, it's difficult to get someone to write something impartial.' He hesitated, trying to explain what he wanted from her without making it seem deceptive. 'Not that I'd ever want you to slam him, but at least you can give your honest opinion without being afraid of –'

'Breaking my heart,' Todd cut in, entering the office and seeing the press pass to his concert dangling from Alex's fingers. He batted his long eyelashes at Jessica, and she suddenly recognised him as Elvis from the Halloween party, where his gold shades had hidden the greater part of his face and extra padding had distorted his lean physique. 'Love me tender,' Todd sang to her, 'love me true, all my dreams fulfil. Don't diss me in your review, or you, I'll have to kill.' When Jessica laughed, he looked as if he were ready to continue singing, now getting even more into character.

Avalon, perking up from her desk, interrupted him. 'If he were that good, he wouldn't still be working here.'

Todd looked momentarily hurt at the comment, but then seemed to shake it off. 'And what about you?' he asked. 'If I'm some sort of hack, what does that make you, sweetheart?' he purred, as if giving her a compliment.

'A pro,' Avalon said.

So Dashiell hadn't gotten back into the daily grind of working at the paper. So what? He wasn't actually needed there in person, was he? The staff members knew well enough how to run things without him. They didn't need him breathing over their shoulders. Hell, that's what Alex was there for. Dashiell could peruse the final lay-outs late on a Thursday night, stopping in after an evening spent drinking at Dream Maker or dancing at The Queen of Hearts. Make minor edits or suggestions, just for the heck of it, and then wait a whole week before he had to do it again.

With an embarrassed pang, he remembered the fact that while in Europe he'd actually been excited about coming back to the paper. Obviously, he had forgotten how boring he found the work. Others in the office seemed to thrive on it. When he did stop by, he saw Alex intent on the phone, Avalon reading emails at a furious pace, Josh convincing someone to place a larger ad than the person had intended. And although the staff were all working, they also seemed to be enjoying what they were doing.

In truth, Dashiell was enjoying himself as well. Enjoying the sweet way his cock fitted inside the nubile young dancer he'd picked up the night before. Usually, he would go to a fancy Beverly Hills hotel with a girl, or occasionally back to her place, not interested in letting people know where he lived. But this was different. Because this girl already knew where he lived and who he was.

That's because she was Marina.

All right, so fucking his managing editor's very recent ex-girlfriend might not have been the smartest thing in the world, but it honestly wasn't Dashiell's fault. He hadn't recognised her in the dim light of Sammy's Mango Hut, and when he'd finally figured out who she was – the realisation dawning on him that she didn't simply have a *familiar* face, she had a face that he had been introduced to countless times – it had been too late. She'd already been bouncing on his cock in the front seat of his truck.

And, oh, did she know how to bounce.

With her thighs parted, she'd rocked back and forth, letting the shaft of his cock almost all the way out of her pussy, pulsating her muscles on the rounded head and making him groan. Tighten and release, squeeze and hold. There was no better feeling than that, those welcoming embrace-like grasps of her cunt muscles as she contracted. He could have done that all night, just fuck and fuck, coasting in that delirious place of almost-coming. Making it last.

Yes, once he'd recognised her, he found that he had a few issues with the situation. Dashiell might be over-sexed and under-conscienced, but he was not stupid. Somewhere in the back of his mind he'd wondered what she was up to. The girl definitely had an ulterior motive for being with him, aside from a simple desire to get off. She had to have known exactly who he was when she'd approached him at the bar, shaking her shimmering curls out of her comely green eyes and daring him to do a Zanatini with her.

'A what?' he'd asked, intrigued not only by the name of the drink, but by the way she was pressing her gorgeous hips up against him in the crowded throng congregating at the bar. Even with the crush of customers around them, she didn't have to be quite that close. He could feel the heat of her body through the thin little skirt she was wearing, and it made him want to slide one hand into the split of fabric at her thigh and touch her naked skin above the visible band of her stockings.

'Zanatini,' she'd repeated. 'It's a Martini with a Xanax stuffed inside of the olive instead of a pimento. I know the bartender. She'll make one for each of us if I ask.'

A Xanax was a prescription pill used for panic attacks and nervous disorders. It calmed users down right away. Dashiell had no need for this sort of medication, but he'd done the drink with Marina for the hell of it, because he hated to back away from a dare. That was also probably why he'd ended up fucking her, feeling no pain, no sense of morals. Once he'd realised who she was and understood that they'd crossed that sexually dangerous bridge there was no reason not to have a little fun. After a quick yet satisfying sexual ride in the parking lot, he'd driven her to the apartment where they'd spent the rest of the night in various unusual clinches.

Now he reached one hand up, twirling his fingertips through her jumble of curly blonde hair, and she tilted her head and played coy with him. With her pale green eyes and flushed pink lips, she had a doll-like innocence to her that Dashiell found extremely appealing. Especially since it was obvious from the way that she moved that she wasn't the least bit innocent at all.

Then she did one of his all-time favourite tricks that made him stop thinking of anything except the outrageous fuck they were sharing. Lifting his hand in hers, she daintily drew two of his fingers into her warm mouth and sucked on them. The wetness and the pressure felt exquisite, mimicking the way her pussy squeezed and released his cock. Heat, wet heat, caressed him. Fuck, but she was good. Was this why Alex always had those dark circles under his eyes? From nights spent doing it like this? And, if so, why in the world had the two broken up? The girl was too talented to discard over emotional matters, wasn't she?

'A Zanatini,' the lithe brunette bartender told Avalon. 'That's what he had.'

Avalon shook her head as she took notes. Whatever Dashiell was getting himself into would never make it in the final edition of her column. She knew that. If Alex wouldn't let her write about the trio of sexually adventurous bartenders, there was no way in hell that he'd put in this new bit of gossip about Dashiell doing drugged drinks. But she still couldn't help herself from keeping tabs on him ... and on the other staff members. If there was information to know about, then Avalon felt it was her duty to hear the scoop first. Besides, it always paid to have a bit of dirt on people. You never knew when information would come in handy.

'Have you tried one?' Lily asked Avalon next, moving quickly behind the bar as she spoke.

'Not my style,' Avalon said. 'A downer drug mixed with alcohol. Why would you ever come up for air? I'm a tequila sort of girl, myself.'

'I know that's what you drink,' Lily murmured, quickly sliding Avalon a shot in a salt-crusted glass with a floating wedge of lime. 'But what is your style?'

It was in Avalon's head to say, 'You are,' slipping her hand on to the stunning bartender's and letting her feel the weight there. The light pressure. No, she didn't need to trade sexual favours for the tidbits she was receiving, as long as she kept the flirtation on high. But she did occasionally sleep with her sources, when the mood struck her. Today, Avalon said, 'You tell me what you think the answer is next time I stop by. If you're right –'

She let the sentence hang there, unfinished, so that the bisexual bartender could fill in the rest of the statement however she wanted to. Always leave people wanting more. That was Avalon's favourite way to play the game.

But sometimes, something happened to change the situation. Sometimes, the other player had a few tricks of his own. Or, in this case, *her* own. Lily wasn't ready to let Avalon leave so quickly. Moving around the bar, she took the shot glass from Avalon's hand and had a small sip herself. Then, licking her lips, she pushed up on the barstool and locked eyes with Avalon, waiting.

Maybe Avalon didn't want to play a game right now. Maybe what she wanted to do was kiss this pretty girl. Stranger longings had filled her before, and she'd always taken care of them.

'There's more to tell,' Lily said softly, offering up the one bit of power that she had. For Avalon, secrets were the best foreplay of all.

'Then tell,' Avalon whispered, coming to stand between Lily's spread thighs and kiss the girl's lovely white skin at the base of her neck. Oh, she smelled sweet. Some exotic perfume that had faded to a final musky note. Avalon licked and then nuzzled her mouth against the bartender's skin, waiting for the girl to keep talking, but there were several moments when the two women were totally silent. Enjoying the pressure of each other's bodies, paying attention to the sounds and the scents and the warmth of one another.

'She wasn't just a dancer,' Lily final murmured. 'Some fluttering waif in a show downtown. She was somebody you know.'

Now Avalon started to undo the buttons along the front of Lily's black leather vest. Since the bar wouldn't be officially open for another hour, there was no need to worry about being caught, and the two knew they could take their time. Avalon easily unhooked the last button and slid open the leather vest, revealing Lily's amazing breasts captured in a fuchsia lace bra. Another sleight of hand and the bra was open, and Lily was waiting.

Quickly, Avalon bent and kissed one breast and then the other, trailing her fingertips across Lily's nipples so that they stood up hard. She pinched Lily's nipples lightly and then a bit more forcefully, and the girl made a husky sounding 'yes' to let her know that's what she wanted. But Avalon knew. She always knew. Lily was someone she could read with ease. Start with a little kissing, a bit of teasing fingerplay, then get down to business.

On a familiar route, she tricked her tongue along Lily's collarbone, tracing along the delicate beauty's skin until she reached the hollow of her throat. She kissed Lily here, then nipped lightly at her skin, understanding that soon she'd be leaving marks. She wouldn't be able to help herself. Once they started really going at it, Avalon was going to lose control. Tonight, Lily would be sporting an array of lovebites while she worked.

'Oh, that feels good, Avalon,' Lily murmured, shifting her hips on the barstool as her clothes suddenly felt constraining. 'It's been too long.'

Weeks. Several weeks. Not an eternity in most people's schedules, but the way Avalon and Lily connected was special. They had a perfect sense of timing. Lily knew the exact point to stop playing the receiver and start acting, her own hands undoing the zipper at the side of Avalon's dress, helping the columnist out of her clothes.

'So tell me,' Avalon purred when she was down to her matching bra and panty set, her mouth making a wet trail from Lily's breastbone towards the waistband of the bartender's painted-on jeans. She undid the row of buttons on the 501s and pulled them open, revealing no panties beneath. Such a naughty girl.

'Tell me who . . .'

11

Some days, Sasha enjoyed a relaxing drink at the end of shooting. Other days, she needed one. There was a big fucking difference. Today, for instance, she needed two, one right after the other. According to her drinking schedule, reality was a long way off.

She didn't even taste the first gin and tonic; drained it as if she were a desert wanderer and it was a glass of ice water. The second drink was far more pleasurable. G and Ts were her favourite concoction, served in a chilled glass, imbibed while sitting on the outdoor balcony of the hipster restaurant 'Bougainvillaea By The Shore'. It was a place habited by people who were as beautiful as the surroundings. A place where Avalon Granger went weekly to gather information for her column, paying off the maître d' for insider information, such as who received a blow job beneath the most private table in the restaurant and what that particular decadence had cost him.

Honestly, Sasha couldn't afford the exorbitant prices of the elegant restaurant, but it was where she most wanted to be. There was nobody to stop her from blowing her last little bit of cash on a night of drinking. She stared out at the beach, watching the lights twinkling, the sand and surf glistening brilliantly beneath the crescent moon. And all the pretty scenery made her think of was money.

That's because she had run out of it. To her dismay, her last investor had dropped out, leaving a gaping hole in her budget, and she'd found nobody to take his financial place. Low-budget movies were a specialty of LA's youngsters, people like Sasha who hoped to market their films at festivals, to win a contract, or at least gain notice. But Sasha didn't even have enough cash any more for low-budget. Hers was now officially classified as a 'no budget', and as she drank her second G and T, she wondered what the fuck she was going to do.

She wouldn't go back to stripping.

Yes, she would.

No, she wouldn't. Not even for this. Sure, the money was good. Amazing, sometimes. At the place where she'd worked in the past, a high-end strip bar up on Sunset, there were men who thought nothing of slipping twenty dollars at a time beneath her glittery G-string. She'd receive the occasional 50 or 100 when a celebrity was in the crowd and his posse insisted on showing off by flashing the green.

Ladies went to strip bars now, too, as if to show how cool they were. Blasé about the fact that another woman was standing inches from them, displaying her body. The women were generally even better tippers than the men, out to prove something, and there was something sexy to Sasha about the feel of a lady's fingertips against her thigh as she slid the money down.

A waitress interrupted her thoughts by asking if she was ready for another, and Sasha nodded.

Once, when doing a private bachelor party, she'd brought home three grand in less than four hours. The thought of making money like that gave her a momentary pause. How many nights would she have to work to get her film back on track?

She shoved the idea out of her head. What if Mica found out, or her cast and crew or, God forbid, Jessica.

A third drink. That's what she needed. And then a phone call to Jessica, because what she'd really need after her third strong gin wasn't money at all.

It was a ride.

* * *

During dinner, which was a picnic meal out on his fire escape, Kelly shared his big news. 'I landed the part, baby,' he said. 'My agent called this afternoon. It's mine.' He was beaming. 'I mean, it's really fucking mine. All mine.'

Jessica leaned over to kiss him. They were seated on a soft, quilted blanket on the metal grid floor, spread out beneath the stars. From where they sat, they could see the Santa Monica pier, the lit-up Ferris wheel going round and round. Squeals of laughter from the kids on the rides created a happy noise, far enough away to set a background mood.

'What's the role like?' Jessica asked, leaning back on the quilt. With one hand, she lazily traced her fingers along the back of his tanned arm.

'A dangerous guy. Someone who isn't at all what he seems on the surface. Like I told you before, it's not the biggest role in the film. But it's meaty. I'll definitely get noticed.' He actually lowered his voice then, even though nobody was anywhere near by them. 'The director's Deleen DeMarco.'

'You're on the set with her?'

Kelly nodded, and Jessica could see in his eyes how pleased and excited he was. There would be no more nights spent at acting classes or voice classes or fencing classes or tap-dancing classes. Honing his skills, any skills, in hopes that someday they would come in handy. Kelly was going to make it.

'When does the shooting start?'

'It's *been* shooting. I'm the last principal to be cast. They actually hired someone else, one of the other guys with me at the audition, but after a few takes, the director decided she didn't like the chemistry between him and the lead. Bad luck for him, poor bastard, but good fucking luck for me.'

'Where will it be filmed?'

'Here.' His smile broadened. 'It's futuristic, but mostly done in sets on the lot. My scenes start right after Christmas, but I don't have to go to some godforsaken desert in the outback or some rain forest in Ecuador. I can stay right here. With you.'

As he said the words, Kelly reached into the picnic basket and pulled out a long, thin package. Jessica flushed as he handed over the box. Her guilt at what she'd done at the party with Mozart was compounded by the fact that she hadn't told Kelly about the flowers she was still receiving.

'Open it, Jessie.'

At Kelly's insistence, Jessica undid the box, revealing the thin, red leather collar coiled inside. The gift instantly made her smile. Kelly hadn't bought her an elaborate piece of jewellery, something that she wouldn't be ready to accept. No, he was giving her a bit of a fantasy, and now she handed it back over to him and lifted up her hair.

Without a word, Kelly fastened the collar around her neck, and the feel of the cool leather against her skin made Jessica's breath catch. Next, he pulled a matching leash out of his pocket. It was tightly wound, and Jessica watched, eyes wide, as he slowly began to unroll the leather. Oh, God, he was going to attach it to the leash. She could easily visualise him making her bow down, making her beg. Sometimes begging was a very good thing. Begging him to fuck her, to put his cock inside her, to let her come.

But he didn't do any of the actions she imagined. He simply slid the leash back and forth between his fingers, stroking it, playing with it. Was he going to use it on her like a belt? Slide her white jeans and lemon yellow thong down past the curve of her ass and let her feel the cool leather heat up against her naked skin? Or did he have other plans? She wasn't sure where Kelly was going with the toy, but she knew that she was going to like it. Knew because of the sensations throbbing inside her.

Not just inside *her*, but inside her pocket. Her cellphone, switched to vibrate, was ringing. Damn, who would call her now? Right when she and Kelly were about to embark on something destined to be erotically memorable?

'Let it ring,' Kelly said urgently, his fingers stroking the underside of her chin. The look in his eyes was filled with a promise that Jessica hated to put on hold. Imminent pleasure was what she read in his expression. Yes, that pleasure would undoubtedly be tinged with pain, but that was the way she liked it. She'd heard so many songs that captured her desires, lyrics spilled through her head as she fingered the collar around her neck.

Take your baby by the ears, play upon her darkest fears.

But what if it was an emergency? Pulling the miniature, high-tech phone from her inside pocket, she answered tersely.

'Jessie, it's me.' The voice was slurred, but Jessica easily recognised her roommate's despondent drawl, and she understood instantly that Sasha was drunk.

'I need –' Sasha started.

'A ride,' Jessica finished for her, shaking her head exasperatedly as she said it. They'd played out this little act before. Too many times, in Jessica's opinion. The scene was starting to get old.

'Seventy-six thousand dollars,' Sasha finished. And then she started to cry.

After dropping Sasha back at home, tucking her into her tiny bed with a full bag of ice for her head and, at her desperate request, a half-empty fifth of vodka for her soul, Jessica dragged Kelly to the concert.

'I had other ideas,' he told her, stroking his fingers along the collar still attached to her slender throat. She'd forgotten about it during their rescue of Sasha, and the feel of his fingers on either side of the thin strip of leather had her excited in an instant. Her pussy responded to his action as if he had touched her clit with his thumb, brushed against it forcefully, instead of simply stroking the collar around her throat. 'If you hadn't understood that before,' he added gruffly, 'the collar was only the start.' Now, he slid one finger beneath the leather band and tugged gently, then a little less gently, letting her feel the pull of it against her neck.

'This is work.'

'No.' He shook his head, and his eyes gleamed at her with subtle humour. 'It won't be work at all. It will be fun. Dirty, filthy fun. Exactly your type of fun, Jess. Blow off the concert.'

She could hear the rest of the statement in her head. 'Blow off the concert and blow me instead. I will treat you right, baby. Spank that pretty ass. Colour it up a nice, blushing pink. I'll stand you before the mirror and make you watch over your shoulder as I thrash you. Maybe I'll get my wooden paddle. The special one we reserve for the most serious evenings. Really tan your hide while you stare at your punished reflection. You like that, don't you, Jessie? You like to watch.' Yes, she did. She liked all of the different ways they played together. Now, Kelly urged her on. 'I'll make you cream, baby,' he said. 'Make you come like never before.'

She insisted that they do what she wanted, heading towards the venue. The 11.30 show was the one to be at. With her press pass in hand, she pulled Kelly after her into the starkly decorated main room of Sammy's Mango Hut. It was like all other Hollywood clubs of its type. If you turned on the lights, it would lose all of its magic. But in the hazy glow, a pulse could be felt. The heartbeat of both good music and perhaps impending stardom. That's what everyone hoped for, wasn't it?

Kelly sulked only until Jessica pulled him after her on to the dance floor. She wanted Todd to see that she was there in support of him, and she wanted Kelly to move with her, to understand that if he was paying attention, he would realise that she hadn't actually told him 'no'. She'd only told him 'later'. There was a big difference. If he kept himself under control, then what they might do after the show could be even more spectacular.

They rocked as part of a sea of dancers, long-time fans of Third Leg who seemed to know every lyric, every beat. Jessica felt as if she were part of a wave of heat, and she closed her eyes as Kelly held her close, as he once again slid one finger, then two, beneath the leather collar and tugged.

Writer's block was the worst illness that Alex had ever succumbed to. Staring fixedly at his computer screen, he tried to get the words to flow by sheer force. Tried and failed. This was the final draft, the polishing process, yet nothing seemed to make him want to stay put and get the job done.

Re-read the fucking thing from the start. That's what he would do. Force himself back into the movement of the screenplay by utter determination. Without feeling immodest, he knew the writing was fantastic. His agent had told him that, and Sam never had a good word to say about anything. He was the most difficult-to-please man in the world, which also made him the most craved agent in the city.

Rubbing one hand along the scruff of his evening shadow, Alex finally cancelled the idea of spending the night stuck at the terminal. Terminally stuck. As he reached for his leather jacket, he decided that he'd go to the concert after all. Run into Jessica, maybe. If she'd gone, as he'd requested, then it might be a place for him to finally talk to her. And he had to talk to her. Eventually.

What Alex had meant to do was ask Jessica to go to the concert with him, but when handing over the assignment, he'd found himself floundering in Avalon's presence. And in the presence of his own impending hard-on, he had given Jessica a press pass and told her to turn in a review as soon as she could.

'Be creative,' he'd said. 'We like to play things a little differently.'

But he had more reason to go to the concert than to watch her scribble notes in a pad. He was hoping that if he saw her out of the office, he'd be able to speak to her unhindered. Not worrying about what Avalon would say or how she'd mess with him later. Not biting his tongue because Josh or Pete was sitting there, listening.

Deep down, Alex was still disturbed by the Halloween party. Disturbed by what he'd seen but not stopped. Dashiell, secretly back from Europe, had already succeeded in making the moves on Jessica. What could Alex do about that? Nothing. Warning the kid off didn't make any sense. Why? So that he could tear off a piece for himself? That's what Dash would think – and that would be a bad place to enter. A fight for a woman would damage the balance of power in the paper's staffroom.

No, Alex wouldn't get involved. That was the best position to take. A weak position, though. That was his problem. He couldn't finish his screenplay for the same reason that he couldn't approach Jessica.

He simply didn't have the balls, did he?

Marina went to the club where she'd spotted Dashiell before. This evening, she was decked out in her favourite 'fuck me' outfit: a micro mini pink suede skirt, magenta high-heeled sandals and a black and pink striped top that fitted her perfectly. She was proud of her body and liked to show it off, and to Marina that meant as little clothes and as much skin as possible. Although she won the approving glances of the bartender, who sent over a free drink, she didn't see Dashiell anywhere.

What to do? She had to manoeuvre herself back into Alex's stratosphere somehow. It wasn't that she wanted to get him back. No, that would be too normal. In truth, she wanted to get back *at* him. There was a big and twisted difference. As she downed the free Flirtini, she spotted someone else she recognised from the paper. Todd X, guitar in hand, performing with his band.

Todd might work into her plans, she thought, moving so that he wouldn't be able to miss her when she started dancing in front of the stage.

The pressure against Jessica's throat made her pussy wet. Dangerously wet. As always, Kelly sensed her desires intimately, knew to keep running his fingertips under the leather band, to press two of his fingers against the pulse point at the hollow of her throat. The feel of his hand there brought forth a series of images. She pictured the two of them in bed together, the collar now clipped on to a silver chain running to a hook on his headboard. She'd be caught, pinned down, and he would straddle her high up on her chest, part her lips with the head of his cock, thrust in deep.

With her eyes covered behind a velvet blindfold, she'd suck on him. Darkness enveloping her senses, she would focus only on the way Kelly's cock tasted, the heat of his body, the slight saltiness of his skin. Pleasing him, she would take her time. Use her lips to caress his rod, use her tongue to stimulate that centre of nerves right under the head.

There was something undeniably sexy to her about giving up control. And she was one of the people who thought, deep down inside, that the person submitting actually had more power than the one dominating. The sub got to choose how far to go. That was real power.

From the way Kelly played with her in public this evening, she understood the give and take, the way that he wanted her both to obey him and rebel against him. But when she opened her eyes, she saw behind him, standing against the wall, that her managing editor was at the show. And that he was watching her.

Suddenly, things changed within Jessica. She remembered the way she'd felt when she'd first seen Alex. Those haunted circles, the smudges of fatigue beneath his eyes, had called to her. The way he'd worked his way into all of her fantasies. While Kelly had fucked her at her apartment, she'd visualised Alex's face in her mind as she'd come. At Read My Lips, she'd imagined him watching her get a spanking over Kelly's lap. Now, as he stared at her, she had a different fantasy, and this one didn't involve Kelly at all. She pictured Alex striding through the club, cutting in.

Nobody did that sort of thing any more, because dancing styles had changed from the time when someone could tap a man on his shoulder and whisk away his lady. Now, dancers pressed their bodies together in a tight fit, or not touching at all, not even seeming to be moving to the same song. But in her head, she still saw Alex cutting in. Kelly fading back into the throng of Third Leg's audience.

And then what?

Her boss pulling her after him out of the club, roughly removing a collar he hadn't chosen for her, discarding it as he hurried her to his car. Claiming her with actions rather than objects. That's the way it would work with Alex. She understood that much from the look in his eyes. He wouldn't need accessories.

Jessica found herself growing more aroused as she

continued to add details. It was all there for her, unfolding in her head at a decadently slow pace. With a whispered excuse to Kelly, she started to make her way to the edge of the dance floor. She would talk to Alex, finally. Outside of the office, it would be easier. They'd connect without anyone else paying attention. But when she finally reached the corner of the room where she'd spotted him, Alex was gone. Oh, God, she was losing it. Had he been in the room at all, or was he a figment of her X-rated imagination? Was she really at the point where she was creating imaginary sexual playthings?

With her back pressed up against the wall, she waited out the next song, and the one after. From where she stood, she scanned the dance floor, looking for her boss. He simply wasn't there. But Kelly was, now dancing closely with a tall girl sporting short red hair. As Jessica watched, Kelly pulled the girl in tight against him, hip to hip. His hands roamed over his partner's waist, fingertips trailed along her sleek body. Jessica paid attention to the way he looked as he moved with this other woman, and when the girl leaned in and kissed him, she wondered why she felt no jealousy at all.

'You OK, baby?' Kelly asked, when the song was over and he found his way back to her side.

'I'm fine,' she murmured, her eyes on him. But as Jessica reached up to wipe a peony-coloured smear of the other girl's lipstick from his face, a wave of sorrow crested through her. This was the end, or the beginning of the end. When Kelly met her gaze with his, she thought she saw understanding there.

Back on the dance floor together, they danced hard, their bodies in tune. He slid both hands into the back pockets of her white jeans and pulled her to him, so that she could feel his erection pressed against her. As always, the promise of what awaited her made her knees feel as if they could no longer keep her upright. The physical connection remained as powerful as always, even if her inner feelings had changed. She let herself semi-collapse into his embrace, and he quickly lifted her in his arms and walked her out through the throng and to the parking lot.

Avalon had eyes everywhere. That's the way it had to be. When she wasn't able to get to a place in person, her sources looked out for her. One of them saw Alex watching Jessica, saw Jessica with Kelly, and he knew enough to pay attention. The newspaper staff hung out at the bar often enough to have become familiar faces. Didn't Avalon always like to know what was going on in the world of *Zebra*?

The bartender followed Jessica and Kelly out to the parking lot, and later he told Avalon exactly what had happened after the show. The handsome blond boy had walked the dark-haired girl to the edge of the lot, where his Harley was parked. There, Jessica had bent over the seat, staying still as Kelly unbuttoned her jeans and slid them down her thighs. Her yellow panties were next, pulled down below her knees, revealing naked skin that had a pearly glow to it beneath the moonlight.

After what appeared to be a moment's hesitation, Kelly had thrashed her. Seriously and lovingly. Using the red leather leash, he'd striped her pale skin over and over, but after every few lashes, he'd stopped to kiss her. To lick along the stripes he left with his belt. To tongue between the lovely cheeks of her ass, making her toss her hair like a wild horse, that tremendous mane spilling free of her ponytail.

The source, a bartender named Chester, had described the scene in detail to Avalon. Each stroke. Each line. The look on Jessica's face when she'd turned her head to the side, eyes closed as she'd taken it. And she'd taken it all.

Everything the boy had in him to give. When he was finished whipping her, he'd fucked her, still pressed against his bike, his own jeans undone, cock out, driving in deep. Jessica had moaned as she'd come, loud enough to be heard over the traffic.

This was how they said goodbye. Jessica let Kelly do what he wanted to her; what he needed to. Punishing her for her indiscretions on Halloween. He might not know that's what he was punishing her for, but she did. And she took each stroke against her skin, that fiery pain pulsing all the way to her core.

It would be their last time together. She knew it. And she thought that he knew it. When he fucked her, she slid one hand beneath her waist and strummed her fingers against her clit, coming with him at the end in a finale like none other.

12

On the days when he did come to the paper, Dashiell moved through the office without seeming to notice Jessica. Yes, he'd shaken her hand when initially introduced to her, warmly welcoming the youngster to the staff, but he kept his distance. Most of the days he spent behind the closed door to his office, scheduling catch-up meetings with Alex and Josh and sorting through the pile-up of papers that had grown in his absence and continued to grow since he'd arrived home.

Jessica tried to get a feel for the man's personality but couldn't. Who was this Dashiell Cooper that people grew all flustered around? He didn't seem worth the big build-up. Yes, he was attractive, and Jessica's fixation with old-time movies made her run an instant cast list in her mind – prospective actors to play the part of Dashiell in the movie of her life. A young William Holden? Too clean-cut. Cary Grant ... hmmm, that was the closest. But Grant always had a bit of self-deprecating charm to soften the edge of his striking good looks. Dashiell seemed to take himself very seriously.

His light-brown hair was grey-streaked at the temples, and looked to her as if he'd spent time each morning styling it. To Jessica, there was something unappealingly feminine about a man who fell into the same beauty trappings that women did. That was why she appreciated Alex's look so much. He appeared not to have the inclination to care about silly products like mousse or gel. His long hair suited him perfectly, framing his soulful tired eyes.

Still, Jessica found herself interested in Mr Cooper, the sole owner of *Zebra*. Whenever she went to the upstairs office, her eyes continued to roam restlessly to his closed door. On the few times he did appear in the main downstairs room, she paid attention to how he walked, to the outfit he had on, to the way he spoke. He didn't seem nearly as interested in her, and that was fine. She wasn't looking for his scrutiny. As a neophyte journalist, what she wanted was to observe on her own, to make her own judgements without anyone watching her.

In reality, Dashiell kept careful tabs on Jessica. He could sneak a peek into her computer easily, because of the office's expensive network system which connected all of the different computers to one main electronic brain. While she was at lunch, he read through her files, opening and closing items that caught his eye. He wanted to know all about her. Was she a good writer? Did she spend time fucking around on the Internet like so many of the rest of his staff writers, checking stock reports, listening to free music downloads, shopping and surfing for porn?

It interested him immensely to learn that Alex had given Jessica her first real assignment. Dashiell had found that out by reading through the log book. Her official job was to write up small pieces for their regular advertisers, a throwaway bit of fluff writing. But then, as a little bonus, Alex had sent her out to do a music review.

Dashiell read the first draft with keen anticipation. He hoped that she was at least a fair writer, and he found himself almost giddy about how much of a thrill he felt at the prospect of reading the review. When had he last been so excited about something so small?

Third Leg Throbs at Sammy's Mango Hut

He kissed me. Kissed me hard, fast, making my head
spin. I needed water, air, something. Something to
steady me. And I found it at Sammy's Mango Hut.

What was this? Dashiell re-read the opening and then
pushed on.

My date had suggested the show at Third Leg as a way
to end our night. But, in actuality, the concert turned
out to be the beginning. The music, pounding, raucous,
re-energised us. We spent the whole set on the dance
floor, buffeted by the die-hard fans who sang every
word along with Todd X. Their excitement was infec-
tious, spreading throughout the club, and by the time
the drummer ejaculated his sticks into the audience at
the end of the final song, the fans were ready to lick
that stuff up.

She'd written it like a column rather than a review, not
offering a critique of Todd's work but giving an overall
feel of how the concert seemed to her. Unusable? Dashiell
wasn't sure, and he wasn't the one who would decide.
Those sorts of choices were up to Alex, thank God.
Dashiell rarely got involved in the content decisions of
the paper.

But still, Dashiell found himself wondering who the
fuck her date was and what he meant to her.

Yes, Alex was going to run the review. It was exactly
what he'd requested of her. A different type of piece
than what you'd find in *The Times*, as if they'd ever
waste their space sending a reviewer to a Third Leg
show. The review read more like a story than a flat-out
description of a concert. Jessica hadn't even listed the
songs played, and he added them for her, sliding them
into the sentences without damaging her style.

He worked on her article last, after everything else

was done for the paper, because he wanted to take his time. To do a good job for her. It was late on Thursday night, getting dangerously close to press deadline, but he drove on. Since he'd been present for part of the show, he remembered the set list. As he typed, he saw her in his head, saw the way she'd looked dancing with her boyfriend, and he clenched his teeth. When her handsome boyfriend had pulled Jessica in tight for a kiss, the band had been playing 'Diamond Diva'. When her blond beau had stroked his fingertips along the red leather collar around Jessica's neck, Todd had launched into his big finale, 'Just My Type'.

By the time he'd finished editing, Alex had a headache from grinding his back molars against each other. Avalon didn't seem to notice the mood he was in as she entered the office and tossed a neon green disk in his direction. It landed on the top of one of Alex's paper mountains and then skidded to the edge of his desk.

It was the wrong day to turn in her column late.

Dishing the Dirt with Avalon Granger

Yes, lovely ones, I have news for you. News of the whispered variety. Third Leg, one of the upstart rockabilly bands on the Hollywood circuit, has snagged a film role. At least, their hit song, 'Just My Type', has. Chosen to play over the credits during a new Claude LeBay film, one can sense that they are destined for greatness.

And Todd X, lead singer extraordinaire, has snagged a little bit of seaside bliss himself. Marina Cheshire, a performer in this fall's unbearably incomprehensible Nutcracker Sweet *(not to be confused with the classic ballet) has been seen canoodling with the Elvis lookalike at several downtown clubs. A little nutcracking of the personal variety for Zebra's own managing editor,*

> *who had an off-again, on-again relationship with the*
> *witchy woman for several years.*
>
> *How do we know this?*
>
> *Oh, my pretties, don't worry your little heads about*
> *where I get my news. Just understand that I get it first.*

'Out,' Alex said. 'Out. Fucking out.'

Pete turned to look at him from the depths of the sofa. 'Who are you tonight? Lady Macbeth?'

Alex ignored the comment, staring angrily at the computer screen. Avalon could go too far sometimes. This was one of them. Yes, he already knew about Marina and Todd. He'd seen his ex showing off at the Third Leg show, and it was why he'd gotten out of the place as fast as he had. But there was no reason for the information to appear in Avalon's column. No reason except that she was testing him.

Well, fuck her. Avalon had turned the piece in three hours past the final, extra-final, no more excuses, cut-off deadline, anyway. It was well within his rights as managing editor to replace the column with something he had on hand as a back-up.

Curious, Pete pushed himself up from the sofa and wandered behind his boss to read over Alex's shoulder.

'The tidbit? You're going to cut the blurb about Todd?'

'I'm cutting the whole column,' he said. 'The whole fucking piece.'

Pete snorted. 'She's going to be pissed, you know?'

'Not as pissed as I am.'

Josh had gone to Tiffany.

The store. Not the person. At least, he hadn't gone to the person yet. Not according to Avalon's gossip channels. But he *had* gone shopping.

Without consulting any of his buddies, he'd strode right in and bought something worth several pay cheques, just like the advertisements suggested. 'How can two months' salary last for ever?' or some such shit. Avalon had learned this from one of her most reliable sources, actually hanging up the phone before she'd heard all of the minute details. Completely numb, all she could think of was the fact that Josh had managed to reunite with his ex-flame, Tiffany, and that he was obviously going to propose. Too clichéd for words, wasn't it?

And, fuck, fuck, fuck, she couldn't do anything about it.

For once, Avalon felt as if her normally organised world was spinning out of control. Ian was away on a shoot, which meant that there was nobody to go home to. Nobody to collapse against at the end of the day and tell what was bothering her. But how could she even have told Ian if he'd been there? What would she say? 'My other fuck-partner is going to get married and then I'll only have you.' That would sound really sweet. He'd like that a lot.

This was the reason why she'd messed with Alex in her column, lashing out at him because he was there. A standard Avalon Granger move. Fuck with someone, anyone, when she felt cornered. Now, she truly felt guilty for letting that slip – but too bad. They'd clear the air soon, probably before Monday's staff meeting. They always did.

On top of everything else, her interview was late. Avalon hated to be kept waiting. Hated to be left alone with thoughts she'd rather not be contemplating. She glared angrily at the heavy man's watch that dangled from her slender wrist, a gift, if you could call it that, from a former lover. OK, honesty here, Avalon, she mentally chided herself. Always be honest at least with yourself. The watch had not actually been an intentional gift, just something a man had left on her bedside table after a raw and hungry night between her blush-coloured satin sheets. Since he hadn't ever bothered to call her again, she'd never bothered to return it. But she hadn't gotten rid of it either, because this was an expensive watch left by a rich man.

Rich, attractive, powerful. Those were the three little keys that opened the locks on her heart. Or between her legs. Now, on Friday evening, as she glanced at the glass pane of the watch face, she saw her own ghostly reflection. She looked good. At 28, she believed that she could easily pass for eight or nine years younger. This must be true, because the bartender had carded her when she'd ordered her drink. Either he'd been fooled or he was simply flirting. She looked over in his direction again and saw the blond boy smile at her.

Mmm, yes, she'd like some of that. She enjoyed the way that his eyes kept dancing over her body, then back to her face. A small smile of approval on his lips. But it didn't matter how appealing he might be. She'd had her fill of struggling actors. Models. Musicians. People who hadn't made it yet but by God they would soon. No, Avalon was ready for the ones who had *already* made it. Who owned the cars she liked to ride in and possessed the bank accounts to buy the items that equalled the good life in her mind. Vacations to exotic places, fancy designer clothes ... and occasionally even fancier designer drugs.

She could bed the men who had this type of money. No problem. With her stunning looks and her quick wit, lovers flocked to her door. They just never stayed very long.

That was the problem.

Kelly had mixed feelings about the separation. Not separation, but announcement that he and Jessica were open to see other people. She claimed that it would give them time to tell whether they were meant for each other. If they felt bad about being with others, then that was a sign that they should make a commitment to one another.

To Kelly, it sounded an awful lot like an ending. Even though Jessica had promised that they would still hang out, still go out, still stay in. Hadn't he heard that before? Sure he had. He'd been the one to say it, breaking some poor young girl's heart as he swore to her that being apart for a while didn't mean things were over. That space would be a good thing, would let them grow. All of that was bullshit, the things you said to make someone else feel better when what you wanted was your freedom.

Now, he was forced to play out the stupid scenario he'd agreed to. Maybe he'd dally with someone like the lean blonde goddess at his station, and see if that would melt Jessica's heart. Make her jealous for once. The same reason he'd kissed that girl at Sammy's Mango Hut, wanting Jessica to see what it was like, what he'd felt at the Halloween party.

Would it work this time? He didn't know. But he had to give it a shot.

Todd spread Marina out on the floor of the studio between two large speakers. The naked blonde looked up at him, trusting, as he moved to the control board and began to adjust the instruments.

'It's the latest song,' he told her.

She nodded, waiting. This was thrilling to her, an artist showing her his craft. Alex had never bothered to share his writing with her, insisting that his words weren't ready for another set of eyes. But Todd was different. This was a man who asked to see her latest routine, sat patiently while she did the dance steps for him. Encouraging and admiring.

Yes, they'd only been together a short time, but they'd spent every single day together since the show at Sammy's. Even in this brief period, she was able to see his true personality. Todd wanted to share, to let her see what was in his head, and that softened her somehow, altered her plans, if only for the moment. When he'd told her where he was taking her this evening, she'd found it difficult to respond, overwhelmed by the emotion.

But even better than all of that, he was into something that she had to offer.

'The song's called "Sublime Skin",' Todd said, smiling as he came back and tore off his rock concert T-shirt and then peeled out of his jeans, his metal wallet chain clinking as the pants hit the floor. 'A homage to you,' he added, indicating with a look how much he adored her beautiful body. Nude, she was stunning. So smooth and soft. He came forward as the music began to play, making love to her while they could actually feel the bass line of his song throbbing through the floor and into their bodies. Raucous and hard, like all of Third Leg's music, this one had a beat that she felt echoing within her body, and within her cunt.

'Please tell me you aren't being stood up,' Kelly said as he came over to Avalon's table with a fresh drink.

The columnist, momentarily broken free from her miserable contemplation of her love life, smiled up at him. 'It's not a date.'

'Should be a date,' Kelly said. 'Friday night. Pretty, pretty girl...' He let the sentence trail off at the end as he waited for her to interrupt.

'You're always this forward?'

'My last shift here. Got a big break,' he said, smiling both self-consciously and charmingly. 'I only came in as a favour to the owner because he's always been good to me. So, really, I don't have much to lose.'

'A tip,' she said. 'If you annoy me.'

He shrugged. 'Worth the risk. I don't really need the five bucks.'

Avalon looked at her watch again. Maybe the rock star she was supposed to interview was going to leave her hanging. It had happened before. Hard to trust people who made their living by playing loud music for a swarm of screaming female fans. They had no concept of time. Of other people's time. Of what it felt like to wait.

'How late do you have to be here?' she asked the bartender. Smiling, Kelly looked over at her watch, and he pointed with his finger to the witching hour.

'If my appointment doesn't show,' Avalon said, 'then you're on.'

'On for what?' Kelly drawled.

'Whatever you have in mind.'

Yes, she could bend her rules for someone this stunning, couldn't she? Sure she could. That was rule number three, after all: Always be prepared to break the rules, even your own.

With Marina really gone – and it seemed as if she'd finally understood what 'end' meant in regards to their relationship – Alex found himself with more time on his hands than he'd had in the four years that they'd dated. Time to wander, to worry, to think and to drink. He spent most of his nights out on his deck, a cigar in one hand, a glass of good whisky in the other, seeing if he could obliterate the stars with the hazy brownish-grey smoke from his Cuban. What Avalon didn't know wouldn't hurt her.

But after several evenings spent in this useless, unproductive way, he found himself wandering once again through his nondescript apartment until he came to sit at his home computer, tinkering with a script that had been untouched since . . . since he'd sent it out and gotten slammed.

Had he really thought he'd make it first time out? Was he that egotistical? He considered the question seriously. No, he wasn't an ego maniac. He simply hadn't had the nerve to face a serious bout of rejection. That's why he'd kept going back to Marina as well. Never willing to concede defeat, to admit that he was wrong in such a life-altering situation.

Turn that around, he told himself. Fix the script the way he knew that it should be fixed. He was older now. He was an editor who could always see what was wrong in other people's work. It was time to turn that unflinching eye on his own writing. Then he would be ready to play the game Hollywood-style. At the very least, he'd find out for himself if he was a good enough writer to go further. At the best, well, he couldn't think that far ahead. So on the nights that visions of Jessica plagued him, he pushed the nymphet's image from his mind and got down to work.

Back at her apartment, Avalon found herself alone. Not a good place to be when she was in this sort of mood. If her roommate had been here, life would have been different. Ian's best skill was sensing her moods. No, she rarely needed a shoulder to cry on, but she definitely could have used a good, solid put-me-to-sleep fuck. A body-shaking orgasm would have made her forget her problems.

But Ian wasn't around. Didn't even call to check in.

On a rampage, Avalon tore through the jewellery scattered on her dresser. The presents from ex-lovers. She saw them for what they were now. Exchanges for sex. Gifts for blow jobs or amazing tricks between the sheets. She might as well have been a prostitute.

No, that wasn't fair. At least, prostitutes were up front about what they did. Avalon lied all the time. She lied to herself, to her friends, to anyone she met. There was no reason to tell the truth when she could come up with a believable fib. It was what protected her. The wall of lies she'd built around her until she was fully hidden.

This evening, she found that the wall was crumbling around her. She'd passed on the bartender, because thoughts of Josh wouldn't leave her alone. Now the watch stood out as the most obvious display of lost affection, and she pulled it off and slammed it hard against the black lacquered wooden top of the dresser. Nothing. The piece was too expensive to break so easily. Looking around, she caught sight of a pair of high-heeled shoes with pointy tips encased in metal. She used one to slam into the face of the watch and, this time, instantly and gratifyingly, the glass shattered, sending tiny diamond-like shards everywhere. Even that wasn't good enough for Avalon. On a quest for total destruction, she reached for the heavy wooden jewellery box, closed it, and used the box as a mallet to pulverize the watch. She hit it repeatedly, until the fine workings were demolished, no longer able to make the pleasing tick-tock sounds.

The action meant something, she thought, finally calm again as she surveyed the damage. She wasn't sure what, but it meant something big.

13

Christmas Eve brought with it mistletoe and kissing in every doorway. *Zebra* held the party in-house this time, as it was a much smaller congregation of people than the Halloween bash. Rather than 500 plus partiers, there were barely 50, but that amount still managed to crowd the office. The flirty little green mistletoe plants dangled dangerously overhead, and every step Jessica took seemed to put her in the path of someone who wanted to lock lips with her. She smooched with Todd X, with Barton, and even once with Pete, who seemed so grateful to her for actually going through with the kiss that he couldn't speak afterwards.

'Merry Christmas,' she whispered to him, watching his face turn the red of one of the shiny glass globes hanging on the tiny tree behind Alex's desk. He nodded and ducked away, on the pretence of refilling his eggnog cup. When he moved out of the way, Jessica saw Alex watching her. Just her luck – there was no mistletoe anywhere near him.

Still, she was ready now. All he had to do was give her a sign that he would be willing. But every time she looked in his direction, he was talking with someone else. Avalon. Pete. Josh. Jessica didn't rush, mingling with the staff members she'd grown to know over the past few months, paying attention to the little nuances that made this party different from others she'd been to in the past.

It seemed to Jessica that each time Alex looked over in Todd's direction, the musician grew flustered. Whenever Josh got close to Avalon, the columnist skirted away. And whenever Alex got close to Dashiell, the editor-in-chief headed in a different direction. What a weird celebration, where everyone apparently was trying to avoid someone, all in a fairly tiny space.

Finally, Jessica decided she'd had enough. Making her way through the crowd to Alex, she was going to get her first kiss with him if she had to grab him by his long hair and force him to pay attention to her.

It was a tense spot for Dashiell. He didn't know if Alex was aware of the one-night stand he'd had with Marina. At first, he'd pushed the thought from his mind, but he'd heard through the office grapevine that one of Avalon's columns had been cut. And that Alex had been incensed. Was it over Marina? Did the gossip hound have that bit of information yet?

Rarely did Dashiell second-guess things that he'd done. What was the point? But he actually had a flash of guilt now. How would he have felt if Alex had done the same thing to him? If he'd followed up with one of Dashiell's many ex-girlfriends?

Better to let time go by before bringing up the subject with his managing editor. For the party, he played a non-stop game of manoeuvring through the room just ahead of Alex. Never stopping too long to talk.

Yes, Josh had gone to Tiffany's. And, yes, Josh wanted to talk to Avalon. The two events were interconnected and important. But Avalon wouldn't even let him get close. Not by phone. Not in person. He left messages for her, but she never called him back. Whenever he tried to force a private conversation at work, she said she was busy and hurried away.

The party was the place, he decided. With all the people around, Avalon would have a difficult time ignoring him without being seriously rude. Taking a deep breath, he charted a path towards her, making it obvious that he was coming her way.

Avalon knew too much. For the first time ever, owning information had backfired. She couldn't even look at Josh. No, he hadn't brought his ex-girlfriend to the party, but from the way he kept staring at her, it was clear that he wanted to talk to her. To tell her that they wouldn't be able to hook up together any longer. That he was turning into one of the people that they'd made fun of all these years. A stuffy, boring married person. She wouldn't have believed that Tiffany's ultimatum had actually worked, but obviously it had.

Still, she didn't need to hear him say it.

For over a week, she'd managed to avoid him. Staying out of the office when she knew he made his morning phone calls, then sliding in later when he visited clients or took appointments.

She couldn't keep this up for ever. She knew that. But for now, the method of avoidance served her purpose. So when Josh looked as if he was finally going to force her to listen to him, she grabbed hold of the nearest person for a kiss beneath the dangling mistletoe.

That person happened to be Jessica.

The kiss floored her. Jessica didn't know how to react, but her body took over automatically when her mind stopped working. Leaning in, she felt Avalon's hands cradle her, caressing her hair, stroking her shoulders through the pale pink silk dress she'd chosen. Shutting her eyes, Jessica focused on how sweet Avalon's lips felt pressed to hers. Then those signature scarlet-glossed lips parted, and Jessica did what she would have with any lover. She met Avalon's tongue with hers, trembling all over as the kiss deepened and lengthened.

For a second, she pictured what it would be like to be in bed with Avalon. Stripped nude, she would lie still in the centre of Avalon's mattress as the more experienced woman took charge. Avalon would leave those lipstick imprints all over her skin. Kiss marks. Red like wine sliding from the hollow of her neck along her collar bone and down, lower.

Lower.

A roomful of people watched hungrily, and Jessica was aware of every set of eyes on her. This only made her more excited. How many times had Kelly told her that she was an exhibitionist? Yes, she'd agreed that she was into showing off. But for him. For him alone. And look at this. He'd been right after all, hadn't he? Because her lace-trimmed blue panties were soaked in the centre now, and as Avalon moved away from her, Jessica wondered whether the columnist could sense the sexual scent emanating from the very core of her body. Wasn't Avalon known for sniffing out the truth in any situation?

'Mistletoe,' Avalon whispered. 'Couldn't be helped.' The blonde's jewel-toned eyes flickered over her, and Avalon gave Jessica a friendly smile that seemed completely out of place. There was no speaking in the room, the only sounds a mixture of breathing and the music playing on the stereo, some old Commodores' song with the chorus, 'Oh, yeah, sweet, sweet thing.'

14

Alex poked through the disastrous terrain of Avalon's desk, looking for something that would explain what the woman was up to. He understood that she was playing head games. That went with the job, didn't it? As a gossip columnist, she fed on the excitement generated by her words. Even when she wasn't at work, she craved chaos, inventing it when there was not enough electricity humming on its own.

But what was she honestly doing playing around with Jessica? Kissing her beneath the mistletoe in front of the entire staff. That had been a cock-hardening moment for just about every male present. No one had been prepared for watching Avalon grab hold of the nubile intern, press her lips to Jessica's and wrap her in a quick, erotic embrace. Lips to lips, bodies to bodys, Avalon's fingers running through Jessica's hair, touching and caressing. When the women had parted, Avalon had appeared pleased with herself while Jessica had looked flushed and pretty. Then Todd had started a round of applause, effectively breaking the mood.

From experience, Alex believed that Avalon was up to something deeper than a simple kiss. For weeks, she'd been putting innocent-sounding tidbits about the intern in the column, knowing that Alex would cut the pieces before they hit press. It was obvious that Avalon knew something big, and that she was just waiting for him to confront her. Yet if he asked her, put it flat out on the table before them, then she'd have proof that he was interested. She'd narrow her cat-like eyes at him and know everything. He didn't want to go there with her. Didn't want to try to beat Avalon at a game that she'd invented herself.

Where Avalon was concerned it was best to tread lightly. Not a game player himself, Alex still understood and could abide by the rules. Could even change them when he put his mind to it.

On a hot tip, Avalon found herself in the bar she'd been in the week before, but not for a rescheduled meeting with Joey Angel. The rock star had deigned to meet with her earlier in the day, and the interview was complete in her tiny tape machine. This evening, she was looking into the same handsome boy's face that she'd seen the last time she was in Read My Lips. But rather than being blown off by her appointment and kindly consoled by the sexy bartender, her appointment was *with* the bartender.

Only in Los Angeles could something like this happen, and they happened on a regular basis. It was why, out of self-preservation, you should never be rude to anyone in LA. So many people seemed oblivious to this simple fact: the waiter you stiffed one week could be your boss the next. And revenge was a big part of success. Avalon had heard of celebrities who kept lists of people they refused to work with, holding grudges for years.

Now, Avalon focused on the new upcomer. Kelly was wearing a black shirt and faded jeans, and he lifted his beer in a toast to her as she sat down across from him in the deep, leather booth. This evening, Avalon had pulled her shining hair back in a loose French twist. She'd accompanied the slightly forties style with a faux-fur trimmed black sweater and black suede skirt. As always, she was wearing a pair of incredibly tall stilettoes. Avalon could have done a 10K in her high-heels. She wore them everywhere – to work, to shop, and often to bed. Oh, did she like the way it felt to trace her heels along the back of a man's thighs. To slide the soft leather of a pair of really good Italian-made shoes against naked skin –

'This time you kept *me* waiting,' Kelly said, speaking without a trace of anger. 'Was it a payback for the last time you were here? Did I go too far?'

Avalon shook her head as she set her miniature tape recorder on the table and reached into her red velvet pocketbook for her notepad and favourite silver pen. 'Time got away from me,' she told Kelly. 'It rarely happens. I'm sorry to be so late.'

As she spoke, her interview subject reached over to circle her wrist with his hand, holding the place where the watch used to be. 'My watch got away from me, too,' she said, relaxing as she looked over her notes, pages that she'd jotted down from her research on the Internet. She had rumours to confirm. Questions to ask. Work, to Avalon, was always easier than play. She knew instinctively how far she could go with her questions, having no problem pushing the limits of cordiality. Teasing, taunting, making it all seem as if the conversation was only between friends. There was a way that Avalon asked invasive questions that made the queries seem less probing and more playful.

Kelly motioned to the bartender that Avalon was ready, and when the slim-hipped, dark-haired girl approached their table, he ordered the same drink that Avalon had requested the last time she'd seen him. Good memory. She gave him points for that. Then, hitting the play and record buttons on her tiny tape machine, she started in.

'Big break,' she said, 'you told me that the last time we met.'

Instead of answering, Kelly smiled and leaned back

against the booth. Beneath the table, Avalon felt his foot meet hers. She shifted slightly, moving out of his reach, but his foot followed her, brushing against hers again.

'You're working on a film that's completely under-cover. No leaks. No press. Just like every other DeMarco production. So why did you agree to meet me for an interview?'

'Not an interview,' Kelly said, leaning forward earnestly, and again she felt something brush her leg. This time, though, it was his hand, stroking along the length of her stocking-clad thigh. Avalon instantly shifted again, trying to regain her composure. 'A rain check. Remember?'

The man was handsome. Gorgeous, really. And, although the timing had been wrong, she'd been ready to sleep with him when she'd thought he was a bar-tender. For a moment, she held her ground.

'You said you'd talk to me.'

'I will,' Kelly told her. 'I'll tell you anything you want to hear. You like dirty talk, don't you, Miss Granger? X-rated nothings whispered in your ear. I know that's what you like. I know you, Avalon.' As he said the words, Avalon got an instant picture of what he was offering. A picture with a soundtrack: Kelly whispering exactly the type of phrases that made her come. Calling her a dirty little slut. Yes, she loved that. Some of her high-strung feminist friends would have found the words offensive, but Avalon could draw a line between fiction and non-fiction, between fantasy and reality. It's what made her perfect for her job. She knew what part of the truth was important.

'Anything you want,' Kelly murmured to her just as the drink arrived. She took a sip instantly, because it gave her something to do. Then she cocked her head at him and waited. If he wasn't going to give her a scoop on the film, at least she could be sure that the night wouldn't be a total loss.

When they were alone, she hit the record and play buttons simultaneously and surreptitiously, activating the tiny device in her purse without Kelly having any idea of her secret. The thought that she was being taped was an instant turn-on, and as Kelly got on his knees in front of her and slid her skirt up past her waist, Avalon gave in to the pleasure of the moment. She sighed as she ran her fingers through the boy's fair hair, then looked down at him and gave him one of her trademark smouldering glances. Her eyelashes fluttered and her lips parted as she took a breath.

'Tell me what you want,' he said, his voice rough-edged.

She remained silent, testing him. Could he read the desires written in her eyes?

Yes, he could. The boy was good, slipping his tongue up the seam of her panties and pressing firmly against her clit through the fabric barrier. He found her pulsing gem without trying, and that feeling of warm wetness through the lace was almost more powerful than an unhindered mouth-to-pussy kiss. Avalon sighed and closed her eyes, letting herself enjoy the heady feeling of being taken care of.

They didn't have a lot of time, she knew that. Not in a location this public. But she hated to sacrifice a mood, to lose everything to speed when a few slow moves could be so much more spectacular. Kelly seemed to understand this, taking his time as he slid her black lace thong panties down her thighs. Kissing along in the wake and making her feel that much more naked for the way he was touching her.

'Such naughty panties,' Kelly whispered. 'Who would ever have guessed?' he asked as he turned her around in the small room and had her place her palms flat on the cold, white-and-blue tiled wall.

He was going to take her from behind. She liked that. The power in it. Even though she was the older one in this little tryst, the one who should have been in charge, he knew what she wanted.

'Say my name when you come,' he hissed to her. 'Say it.'

With both hands, Kelly cupped Avalon's ass cheeks and then slid them gently apart. His cock drove home, into her waiting pussy, while he used his thumbs to make alternating circles around her asshole. First one thumb, then the other, overlapping, slipping a little bit further inside with each rotation. As Avalon's pussy grew wetter, Kelly played more firmly in her back door, thrusting one thumb all the way into her ass and holding it there as his cock stroked her pussy from within. He filled her in both holes, held still for a beat, and then resumed the ride. His cock travelled in and out, while his thumbs spread her cheeks apart and tickled around the ring of her asshole.

Avalon couldn't believe how incredible it all felt. Almost unconsciously, she did as Kelly had asked, murmuring his name over and over as he played with her. She did nothing else. Let him take care of her. Let him set the mood, the rhythm, the course of their journey.

There was a pleasure in giving up that Avalon had almost forgotten.

Kelly reminded her all over again.

Midway through Alex's excavation of her messy desk, Avalon entered the office. He moved away quickly, watching as she threw her jacket on the back of her chair and pulled a crumpled package of Kools from the lower drawer of her desk.

'Five bucks,' he said loud enough for her to hear.

'This doesn't count,' she snarled without looking up. 'It's been a day.'

Alex walked to her side and put his hand out, intent on collecting the cash. He wasn't kidding when he opened his palm in front of her. 'You're supposed to be quitting,' he said. 'That was the deal. Five dollars each time you light up. Regardless of what type of day it's been. Because with you, Ava, it's always "a day".'

Scowling angrily, Avalon reached into the inside pocket on her vintage purse and pulled out a folded twenty. She handed it over and waited a beat, until Alex pulled out his own black leather wallet, preparing to make change. Then she said, 'Keep it. I'm having four. You can sit there and count, if you'd like. I'm sure you don't have anything better to do with your time.'

Now Alex looked concerned. Avalon was known to chain-smoke, lighting one cigarette with the butt of another until the whole pack was empty. It was why he'd pressured her to quit. She couldn't be a casual smoker, occasionally lighting up at a party or bar when it could be seen as an accessory more than anything else. When on a smoking binge, she needed a cigarette constantly between her lips. During tight deadlines, you could hardly see Avalon through the cloud of silver-grey smoke that surrounded her.

Alex was worried about her health – it was why he'd issued the challenge in the first place. And he'd been proud of her to this point. Hardly ever had she lapsed. The few times that she had, she'd been the one to come forward with the cash, confessing that she'd slipped up. Post-deadline. Post-sex. It was different with him and the cigars. He hardly ever set one alight; liked the feel of them between his fingers more than anything else. But he'd agreed to quit with her, to keep her company.

'What's wrong?' he asked now, and even though

they'd had a blow-out when he'd cut her column, there was genuine concern in his voice. Alex considered Avalon one of his best friends.

'I said,' she repeated, sprawling on the nearest of the two sofas, not caring that from this position he could see up the line of her dress. 'It's been a day.'

Alex sat across from her on the other couch, waiting. The view was breathtaking, staring at her black lace panties, but he and Avalon would never sleep together. They'd fight too much to ever get down to fucking. And each of them knew it.

'You're not upset at all,' Alex decided, realising the air that Avalon had about her. This wasn't a fumigate-the-world cigarette binge. It was a post-coital one. 'You just got laid.'

Avalon started to laugh, kicking her legs up on the arm of the sofa and pushing one heel off with the other. Barefoot, she relaxed further, digging into the leather cushions as she shifted her hips. 'Fooled you for a moment, though,' she said. 'Cigarettes taste so much sweeter after sex.'

'The boy didn't give you one of his?'

'Not a smoker. He's an actor – can't give in to those types of habits. Early wrinkles. Bad breath. Smoker's cough.'

Alex stood and grabbed his coat, ready to leave now that he'd discovered her charade. But then he turned back around. 'You were at Read My Lips, weren't you?'

Avalon nodded.

'The bartender was an actor?'

'Just got his big break.' She didn't look up as she spoke, already engrossed in the latest issue of *Watch Me*, their biggest competitor. Without even looking at Alex, she reached into her purse again and pulled out her notebook. She'd jotted in the tidbit while seated in her car after the 'interview'.

Four little monkeys standing on their heads. They'll do tricks for you in bed. Which one will be cast, does anybody know? The one who wins will steal the show.

It made no sense to Alex at first, but he read on.

In the moving up quickly department, we have learned about a young hotshot bartender who looks to have beaten out three big names on a DD production. And it's been said that actors will do anything – stand on their heads, do tricks in bed – in order to be cast in one of these movies. But we know who won, and we know why, and we promise more on this later. Be prepared to watch this blond James Dean lookalike knock everyone on their asses this spring.

Her tag line was the same sort of thing, as always.

And remember who had the news first.

Poor Jessica, Alex thought as he left the office.
Sweet fucking kid.

15

With her eyes closed, Sasha could pretend that she was dancing in an empty room. Shaking out her curls, swivelling her hips, moving sensuously to one of her all-time favourite rock 'n' roll songs, 'Dream On'. Aerosmith knew what they were doing, didn't they? Even after all these years.

Behind her tightly closed lids, she was in her bedroom, dancing with a fantasy partner, preparing to lead him to her tiny mattress. In reality, Sasha was gyrating up on a stage, bright lights flickering over her nearly naked body. Men sat around the stage, leaning forward over their drinks, watching her hungrily.

While she danced, Sasha thought about her movie, *New Car, Caviar*, a line stolen from another one of her favourite rock bands, Pink Floyd. The song was 'Money', and she'd chosen it because her film was about money, about people who had it and people who didn't. Unfortunately, now her life was also about money, and about how many more nights she'd do this before she had enough to start up production again.

The song ended, and she opened her eyes and lazily looked around the crowded room. The bar was always filled, but this evening she found herself surprised by the multitude of faces. These people didn't have anywhere else to go on New Year's? She was even more shocked when she locked eyes with her one-night stand from Dream Maker. What was he doing here? At her questioning glance, the handsome man gave her a half-smile and raised his hand up in a greeting.

* * *

For several days, the tape recorder had sat forgotten amidst the rest of the normal gossip-columnist clutter on Avalon's desk. There was her pair of heart-shaped, rhinestone-studded sunglasses, a gag gift from an interview junket she'd been invited to weeks before. A half-buried ashtray, evidence that she really was trying to quit smoking if only because it was so hard to reach, sat on one corner of the desk, partially obscured by several fashion magazines. A slew of paper coffee cups, each imprinted with dark lipstick kisses, jockeyed for desk space with notebooks, press releases, and glossy photographs of semi-celebrities.

Avalon glanced at the mess, spied her tape recorder, and realised she still had to transcribe the interview with Joey Angel. At the thought, she groaned loudly. There went her plans for tonight. No party for her, but then, gossip never took a break, did it? Jessica, walking by, caught Avalon's moan.

'Everything all right?' Jessica asked.

'Don't want to do my own fucking job,' Avalon said sheepishly. 'That's all.' She hadn't expected that anyone was paying attention to her. Now, she gazed up at Jessica, and saw true concern in the intern's eyes.

'What part?'

'I hate transcription. I heard enough proof of Angel's inflated ego the first time around. Besides, it takes me fucking forever. Constantly rewinding. Backtracking to lose the 'ums' and 'uhs'. I've been doing this for years, and I've never gotten any better.' She sighed dramatically and pushed a wayward strand of gleaming blonde hair away from her tired eyes.

'*Joey* Angel?' Jessica asked.

'Another starstruck fan,' Avalon said, reading the girl's look correctly. 'Believe me, you wouldn't be if you got to know what's in his head.'

Jessica picked up the tiny black recorder and popped out the tape. 'Let me.'

'No.' Avalon shook her head, her long mane swinging as she reached her hand out for her property. 'You've got enough –'

'I'm quick,' Jessica said, 'haven't you heard?' There was a beat of silence after that, and in the room, empty for once except for the two women, a charge of electricity seemed to flicker in the air.

Avalon reached out to stroke the side of Jessica's face. 'Quick when it counts, but slow when you want to be.'

'Let me,' Jessica said again as she closed her fist around the tape and slid it into her pocket. 'You can pay me back later,' she added. Without hesitating, she grabbed her bag and left the office.

Dashiell was waiting for Sasha outside the bar, and she gave him a wide grin when she saw him sitting in his truck. He watched as she made her way towards him, her body long and lean in a pair of dark denims and a shiny green satin blouse that matched the colour of her bright eyes. To his surprise, he found that he was already hard by the time she'd flung open the door and stepped inside. There was a delicious female sensation that washed over him – the smell of her body, a combination of her perfume and shampoo and lotion – and he instantly felt relaxed as he breathed in.

'Hey, Johnny,' she said, 'glad to see you.' He heard a tone of wonderment in her voice, poorly suppressed shock at the fact that they were together again when they'd both obviously chalked their first and last connection up to a one-night stand. She was too cool to comment on it, or too hardened by her years in Los Angeles, playing musical mattresses. But the way she said the words made Dashiell think that she really was glad. Not just turned on because they had some white-hot sexual connection, but that she actually was excited about the fact that he'd found her again.

'I missed you,' he said as he shifted gears and pulled away from the curve, and what was amazing to Dashiell was that he actually meant the words. Didn't have an agenda. Didn't have a real reason for even seeing her again. But once he'd caught sight of her up on the stage, he realised that he *had* missed her.

That was true.

Sasha was out again. Jessica found herself slightly concerned because her roommate had been acting so odd lately. Drinking more than she ever did during production. Going out every evening and acting suspiciously secretive about her whereabouts. How many night shoots could they be doing? But rather than dwell, and excited at the prospect of hearing a live tape with someone of this celebrity's stature, she poured herself a glass of wine, set up the tape player by her laptop computer and got to work. Her main goal was to show everyone on staff that she was worthwhile. She wanted the masthead to include her name in a larger capacity than intern, and the way to do this was to be irreplaceable.

One sip of wine, then she pressed the start button on the tape. There he was. Larger than life. A man whose guitar licks had made her wet. What woman wouldn't want those magic fingers strumming somewhere else? She closed her eyes as she listened, not even bothering to start typing. She wanted to hear what he had to say, and she wanted to learn from this experience. Paying careful attention, she noticed when Avalon nudged the musician to a different topic, stroking his ego as expertly as this star fingered the chords on his priceless guitar.

Avalon was fantastic at her job. Jessica understood this as she listened to the journalist keep the man focused. Yes, there would definitely be editing done. A few brackets here and there to explain references. But for the most part, the interview was smooth and captivating.

After listening to the entire tape, Jessica flipped the tiny cassette over, just to hear what was on the B-side. At first, she wasn't sure what she was listening to. On the first side, there'd been background noises from the bar, but this didn't sound like the ambient noises of revellers. Nor did it sound like a real interview conducted for the paper. In fact, after a moment of listening, her eyes wide open now, Jessica recognised the sounds exactly: this was fucking. She made out hands on clothing, soft sighs, deep breaths. Then she heard Avalon moaning, urgently, words that had no meaning. Those mumbled 'yeses' and 'ohhhs' – sounds you make when you can't even think straight any more.

'Tell me what you want,' the man suddenly said.

It sounded like Kelly fucking. There were noises again, kissing, the whisper of lips sliding on bare skin. Jessica backed the tape up. Was it really Kelly? She listened again. Yes, it was. Kelly saying different things than he said to her, but using that same soft voice. His voice seemed to caress when he spoke.

Her heart slammed in her chest. She felt a combination of shock and ... and what? Not anger. No. Not confusion – except about how Avalon and Kelly met and why Avalon had taped their interaction. But it was clear to her what the attraction would be between them. Avalon was stunning, with her confident swagger and her come-hither gaze. Kelly would have been a fool not to accept her invitation. So how was Jessica feeling?

Intrigued.

Just as she'd listened to the interview on the A-side of the tape, she listened to the entire sexual episode once, relaxing against the leather club chair, her feet over the edge. With her eyes shut, she imagined the entire scene, saw it for what it was. A good, quick fuck. One hand starting on her throat, she stroked her fingertips gently down her body, touching herself through the silky material of her navy and white polka-dot robe. When she reached the split of her body, she stroked herself there, listening to the heated sounds of Avalon's moans as they grew in intensity. Not louder, just sweeter. Musical.

Had Avalon meant for her to hear this?

No, she couldn't have. She'd had no idea that Jessica would offer to transcribe the tape, would bother to flip the sides. Did she even know that Jessica and Kelly had ever been an item? There was no reason for her to have that information. But then, Jessica thought, Avalon seemed to know everything about everyone.

For an instant, she wished Sasha was home. The two could discuss this, the way they'd talked about men and life and love in the past. Sasha was so busy, consumed by her movie. She no longer had the time to play Miss Lonely Hearts.

One more solid drink, and Jessica decided what to do. She spent two hours transcribing the interview with the musician, getting every word right, every nuance in parentheticals. 'Joey (laughing) reveals a bit more about his history ...' that sort of thing. She wanted Avalon to be impressed.

Then she flipped the tape back over and transcribed the B-side as well. She labelled one file: 'Joey Angel', with the date following after. The other, she simply titled: 'What Avalon Wants'.

KELLY: You like that, don't you, baby?

AVALON: Can't you tell?

KELLY (sighing): You're so wet. So fucking wet. Tell me what you want.

AVALON (with a different inflection): Can't you tell?
KELLY: I can take a guess ...

She'd give both to Avalon in two separate envelopes and see where that would take her. When the work was complete, she popped out the tape and printed the transcription for Avalon. Just as the printer finished spewing out the hard copy, her phone rang. She let the machine pick up and heard Kelly leaving a message. 'Baby, it's me. Call me, Jess. Just call me. We can talk. We don't have to ...' A pause. 'You know. We don't have to, Jessie. Just call me to talk.'

After a moment, she went to look in her address book by the phone, then lifted the handset and dialled a number.

Sasha and Dashiell sat together on the back of his pickup truck, the bed down, their feet dangling over the edge. They were parked in one of his favourite spots, a Lover's Leap type view of the city spread out before them. Lights twinkled on and off below in a random, mesmerising pattern, as if the good citizens of Los Angeles were putting on a show for Dashiell and Sasha's personal enjoyment.

'You want to talk about it?' he asked her finally. She'd been so quiet during the ride, and even though he didn't know her very well, didn't know her at all, he sensed that something was troubling her.

'Not important,' she said, shrugging and flipping her brilliant red curls out of her eyes with a well-practised shake of her head. 'Nothing I can't work out.' Then she looked over at him. 'How about you?' she asked. 'I could ask you the same question, couldn't I?'

He smiled at being so easily read, and for a flash he actually considered telling her everything. Confessing to her who he really was. Still, why bother her with that information? This was a girl who seemed to like him without knowing about his status. Who was willing to play as fiercely as he was without any discussions first. Without any plans, any rules. Fucking outdoors. Giving in to the sensations of lust without seeming to worry about repercussions or emotional ties that neither were interested in.

So here they were, two virtual strangers ringing in the New Year together. He'd passed on the staff party, and on several other star-studded invites that had found their way to his desk. And he didn't miss the other world at all.

Sammy's Mango Hut was a popular place for New Year's revellers. Strands of multi-coloured lights draped festively over the bar created a glowing, fire-fly effect in the dim atmosphere. The handsome bartender, Chester, was wearing a long-sleeved T-shirt imprinted with a tuxedo design: black sleeves, ruffly white front, red carnation in the lapel, all painted on to the shirt. This was the most dressed-up he ever got.

On stage, Third Leg prepared to blast in the New Year with their raucous, untamed sound. Most staff members from *Zebra* danced to the raging rockabilly beat, while a few gathered in a corner booth, drinking tropical mixtures in Day Glo colours. There was a sense of total abandonment, and it was abandonment in public, more fun than at a private party.

From the bar, Avalon watched Jessica carefully. She'd gotten the girl's page, a quick message that simply said Jessica wanted to talk, that she would be at the staff party. And she had heard what she could have sworn was the sound of impending tears in the girl's voice. As a gossip columnist, Avalon felt secure in judging people's emotions from the way they spoke. Often people revealed more information in how they said something than in what they said.

But now Jessica seemed the same as normal, drinking Mai-Tais in a booth with Alex. The two were talking animatedly but from across the room Avalon couldn't hear what was being said. Instead, she watched, learning as always from body language. Jessica had her dark hair up in a ponytail, and she'd sprinkled glitter liberally throughout, so that every time she moved, she sparkled. This evening, she was wearing a strapless dress made of iridescent blue satin, the colour complementing the dark cobalt of her eyes.

Avalon couldn't decide whether she should interrupt them or not. Alex seemed a study of avoidance, not making direct eye contact with anyone but Jessica. That was easy to understand. On stage, Todd was now belting out a fire-tempoed ballad to Marina. Avalon would avoid that fucking scene, too, if she were Alex. Couldn't the girl have found a new boyfriend who did not work in close proximity with her ex? That was simply asking for trouble, but then Marina had never impressed Avalon with her mental abilities.

Now, as if coming to some decision, Alex gave Jessica a kiss on the cheek – chaste, sweet, like the gentleman he truly was – and then made his way through the throng and out of the door. He didn't spare one look in Marina's direction, which was impressive, in Avalon's estimation. It was difficult not to look at the dancer, whose eyes were shooting arrows of love in Todd's direction.

More power to you, Alex, she thought. But now she wondered something else. Would Jessica follow?

Not if she could help it. Avalon made her own instant decision. Avoiding Josh, who was making his way towards her from across the room, she slapped a $50 bill on the wood counter for Chester and then grabbed hold of the neck of a bottle of good tequila from behind the bar.

Avalon wasn't going to let this opportunity get away.

Sasha was the one to make the first move. She stood up in the truck and slowly undid the tiny buttons that ran the length of her emerald-green blouse. Each time she popped open a button, Dashiell was able to see more of her naked skin. By the time she'd undone the entire shirt and pulled it off, he was so aroused he could hardly wait for the rest of the show.

It was strange because he'd already seen her up on stage this evening, peeling off her clothes for an audience of testosterone-pumping men. But this was just for him, and there was something so present about the way she moved. She wasn't lost in her private thoughts as she'd obviously been at the club. Vitally aware, she stared right at him, and the look in her eyes made him harder than anything else.

Beneath her blouse, she had on a jade-green satin bra trimmed with lace. Would her panties match? Somehow, he was sure that they would. And now he stared, mesmerised, as Sasha unzipped and then kicked off her black boots and slid her indigo-coloured jeans down her thighs. Yeah, he'd been right. Underneath she had on a pair of jade-coloured thong panties. They looked so sexy on Sasha's slim form, creating a little V-shape over her pussy. When she turned slightly, he could see her nearly nude ass, and he remembered the way he'd made love to her at their first meeting. The way her skin had tasted; how he'd parted her luscious rear cheeks with his hands and kissed her in between them.

Now that she was almost naked, she stared down at him and waited. Could he beat the fuck they'd had on the stairs that led to nowhere? Dashiell didn't even think about comparisons. He simply stood in the truck with Sasha and lifted her into his arms. She wrapped her thighs around his waist as he bent to kiss her neck, to move his mouth up against her forehead and breathe in deeply, drinking her in.

Again, it was in his head to confess. To tell her his real name and his real life situation, but then she was murmuring 'Johnny' like a mantra, and he stopped thinking about anything except slipping aside her shiny thong and thrusting his cock deep inside of her. Taking her. Fucking her. And erasing every other thought in the process.

'Your fantasy,' Avalon cooed, sitting next to Jessica in the large bed, holding her miniature tape recorder directly in front of Jessica's mouth. The girl's cherry-coloured gloss had been kissed forcibly from her mouth until it was almost all gone. Smeared slightly around the edges, the trace of lipstick made her look debauched.

'Don't you mean my resolution?'

'I hate fucking resolutions,' Avalon said. 'They only work to make you feel bad about something you can't possibly promise to. That's not what I want to do at all – I want to make you feel good. So instead of telling me some phony resolution that you'll undoubtedly break in less than a week, why don't you tell me something that I can make come true?'

For a moment, Jessica was silent, contemplating how the two had gotten to this point. After hearing the tape, she had taken stock of her emotions. Then she'd paged Avalon, saying that they needed to talk. But where? At the party, of course. Didn't all important *Zebra* interactions happen at some celebration?

At the Mango Hut, where it was difficult to have a conversation on normal days, much less New Year's,

Avalon had suggested that they retreat to her apartment in Brentwood. Then, once she'd read through Jessica's transcription, the women had faced off – in Avalon's bed.

'Come on,' Avalon whispered. 'You can tell me, Jess.'

'Which one?' Jessica slurred. She was feeling the shots the two had done at Sammy's, and her body felt languorously relaxed, as if she'd spent the day lazing away in a hammock on a sunny beach. Easily, she shifted in the bed, slipping down so that she was staring up at Avalon's deep red canopy.

'The one that's forefront in your mind. Don't think too hard. Just say it.'

'Why should I tell you?' Jessica put as much power behind the question as she could. More than anything else, she didn't want to seem like a pushover. Not in front of Avalon, the person on staff after Alex whose respect she most hoped to win.

'Because,' Avalon said easily, 'you want to.'

As her co-worker spoke the words, Jessica realised that she was right. She *did* want to confess a fantasy to Avalon. And she had no idea why. The reporter was good, wasn't she? Softening her up, loosening her reserve, her resolve, not with the liquor, but with the manner in which she approached this particularly kinky X-rated interview.

'Why on tape?'

Avalon shrugged somewhat self-consciously. Then she reached over and opened a drawer in the chest by the side of her bed. 'My number one turn-on,' she said, waving one hand over the hundreds of tapes within. 'I like to listen to people's fantasies.'

'Blackmail?' Jessica suggested, glancing over.

'I don't even write down the person's name,' Avalon insisted. 'They're anonymous. I just like to own them. To have all these different fantasies in my room. At my disposal.' The way she said the words convinced Jessica that she was telling the truth. She had an image of Avalon wearing a Walkman and listening to the tapes while she played with herself. And *that* was a turn-on to Jessica.

So all right, the young reporter thought. This was clearly some sort of test. She and Avalon had been getting along well at the paper. Better than she would have expected when the two first met. And now the reporter was asking her for proof.

Give me something to hold on to, Avalon was saying, so I can trust you. Jessica understood those types of games. Shutting her eyes, she decided to play. Because, really, what did she have to lose?

'I like being spanked,' she said, finding the words easier to get out than she'd thought they would be. The statement sounded perfectly matter-of-fact, as if anyone could say the same thing without being embarrassed. Not true, of course. Speaking that simple sentence out loud made Jessica's stomach tighten up as she waited for Avalon to make fun of her.

Avalon didn't. Her response was more of a purr than a word, a sound to help Jessica continue talking.

'And I have no problem finding people who like that, too.'

Now, Avalon nodded. Her silence, as well as the look of heat in her eyes, encouraged Jessica to continue talking.

'But I've always wanted one . . . well, two, other things that go with the fantasy.'

'Tell me.'

Could she? Why not? Because maybe, if she said the words out loud, she would be that much closer to having these fantasies come true.

'I want to watch someone else get spanked.' Jessica said the words in a rush, and she could feel her cheeks turn their usually bright pink blush as she spoke. But she didn't care. This was a test, she reminded herself, and she was determined to pass, even if she didn't fully understand Avalon's method of grading. 'And I want to be spanked while someone else watches.' As she finished talking, she had a clear image in her mind of Kelly spanking her for Alex's pleasure, an image she'd returned to again and again. The concept of it made her unbelievably wet, and now she wondered whether Avalon would be able to sense her arousal.

'Easy enough to fulfil,' Avalon told her, sounding, Jessica thought, like some kinky fairy godmother. A wave of her vibrating wand and all her naughty fantasies would come true. 'Are you up for it?'

Jessica didn't respond immediately, watching Avalon carefully. What exactly was the woman offering?

'It's a simple question,' Avalon continued. 'Are you in or are you out?'

Jessica reached for the bottle of alcohol on the night-stand, then looked into the drawer filled with tapes as she took a swallow. All those tapes were fantasies. Had Avalon made each one come to life?

'In,' Jessica said quickly, before she lost her nerve. 'I'm in.'

'Stay right there,' Avalon told her. 'Don't move.'

While Jessica watched, her co-worker left the room, leaving her alone with her thoughts. What was Avalon doing? Going to get an audience? Would she flag some-one down on the street? Within minutes Avalon had reappeared with a handsome stranger who Jessica quickly realised was the hunky Blake Daniels from the soap opera *Danger's Foe*. What was he doing here?

'My roommate,' Avalon explained with a wave towards the dark-haired man. 'And accomplice,' she added with a wink. 'He's a fan of fulfilling the fantasies of lovely young reporters.'

'Be serious,' Jessica said, not believing Avalon's intentions.

'He's game,' Avalon continued, 'if you are.'

Ian took a step closer and put his hand out to Jessica. 'Ian Sinclair,' he said, smiling, 'at your spanking service.'

The way he said the word 'spank' made Jessica instantly wet, *wetter* than she had gotten from simply confessing the fantasy to Avalon. She tried uselessly to remember which panties she had on. Were they pretty? Her pale pink satin ones? Or her favourite black lace ones? She hoped she'd chosen well, because from the way Ian was looking at her, she had an instant image of him putting her over his knees, sliding up her little dress, and then taking his time observing whatever undergarments she had on beneath.

But how were they going to get to that point? Taking the first step seemed impossible. Finally, Avalon took charge.

'He knows,' she said, indicating Ian with a head nod. 'I told him exactly what you told me. So now it's up to you to help us out.'

'How?' Jessica murmured.

'You said you wanted to be spanked for an audience, and that you wanted to watch someone else get spanked. Which do you want to happen first?'

Jessica couldn't answer. Naming a fantasy and having it come true were two completely different things. Real fears suddenly besieged her. She was going to have to see Avalon at work, and Avalon would know things about her. But didn't Avalon already seem to know her secrets? And, besides, she'd have the same dirt on Avalon, wouldn't she?

Interrupting Jessica's thoughts, Ian leaned forward and pressed his full lips to Jessica's ear. 'It doesn't really matter, does it? You're going to come either way. You're going to come from watching me spank Avalon, and you're going to come again when I spank you. It will be unreal, Jessica. You won't believe how fucking turned on you're going to be.'

His voice was soft, soothing, and stirred Jessica's excitement all over again. She agreed with him by nodding, and then felt panic flood through her. What exactly was she saying yes to?

'Then let me take over,' he whispered. 'I promise, you're going to have fun.'

Fun. What a simple way to state it. So innocent-sounding compared to what they were actually embarking on. A ménage à trois ripe with decadent sex, unlike anything Jessica had done in the past. What would Kelly say? Or the mysterious Mozart? Or Alex. Oh, God, Alex. He'd spoken to her at the party, kissed her, then left. What would Alex think?

Back in his apartment alone, Alex typed furiously. He had never been on such a roll before. Like a crazy person, there were voices in his head. He heard the characters talking to each other, screaming out words in a way that they never had before. Sure, he'd read about people having breakthroughs like this. Writers often claimed that a story had 'written itself'. But he'd never experienced the pleasure of being an instrument through which someone else told a story.

Drinking cold, hours-old coffee without tasting the bitterness, Alex fuelled himself for an all-nighter. Oh, he'd lied before. He'd cheated. He'd done all of the wrong things for all of the right reasons. He'd manipulated his characters, made them do things that they never really would have. That's why he'd been stuck for so long. They wouldn't let him make the wrong move for him again. Wouldn't let him give the movie a false ending.

His fingers tapped with a melodic rhythm on the

keyboard. He remembered this feeling from his college days at UCLA's screenwriting programme. He'd been the star, the young upstart who everyone had watched eagerly. Failed them all, hadn't he? Now, something had changed. The magic was returning. Focusing on his screen, he felt like an observer as his fingers flew across the keyboard, driving hard until the end.

Ian erased Jessica's fragmented thoughts with actions rather than words. Silently, he slid into the bed and took hold of Avalon around her slim waist. 'I'm going to give you a quick demonstration on my willing roommate. Just so you can prepare yourself. I think anticipation is the best type of emotion. You'll be able to savour what's going to happen to your own bare bottom by watching the pleasurable punishment I inflict on your girlfriend.' He hesitated, manoeuvring Avalon so that she lay properly across his sturdy lap, and then lifting her silky raspberry-coloured dress, revealing her fine hindquarters. 'Does that sound like something you want?' Ian asked.

Yes, thought Jessica. Yes, that's exactly what I want.

Sitting with her knees up under her body, Jessica watched as the man spanked his feline roommate. It was as if Ian had actually witnessed her most personal daydreams from inside of her head, the images she came to when playing with herself late at night. Avalon gave a perfect show, arching her back, tossing her hair so that the long, golden strands covered her flushed face. It was obvious to Jessica that Ian was inflicting some pain as well, because Avalon's pale skin held a glorious rosy flush to it. Jessica could make out Ian's handprints, fingers splayed, decorating Avalon's derrière from the dimples at the top of her ass to the fine curve at the bottom.

This was a dream come true. She'd always fantasised about watching someone receive a serious spanking, but she'd never been able to make the scenario a reality. Confessing the idea had seemed too bold. Too frightening. What if her lover turned her down? It had happened before. Even as she watched Ian punishing Avalon, she recalled the last time she'd come clean about her turn-ons with a beau. First, she'd gotten drunk. Seriously drunk. Working through several straight vodkas at his house before getting up the nerve. The man had seemed to understand something important was going to happen, but he hadn't been prepared for what Jessica had said.

'I want . . .' she'd slurred.

'You want what?' The way he'd said it made it sound as if he'd thought she was going to ask him for money. His tone of voice should have let her know that he wasn't the right person to confess to, but it was too late for her to stop. Still, she'd decided to start small. Even though she was drunk she could sense somehow that this night wasn't going to have a happy ending.

'I want you to tie me up.'

He hadn't even smiled. Kink seemed to bother him. Even lightweight kink. In her head, she heard the real things that she wanted to say. And, fuck it, she'd closed her eyes, leaned forward, and said it all. Straight out. As straight as the vodka she'd downed. 'I want you to put me over your lap and spank me. Use your wooden hairbrush. The back of it. Spank me hard. And then, right when I'm about to come, I want you to fuck me. Slide your cock inside me and let me come right on it. And keep on spanking me right through the ride.'

Opening her eyes slowly, she had seen the look of disgust on his face and she'd felt something in her chest tighten. She wouldn't do that again, she'd thought. But later, sober, she'd realised that she would. Because this was something she truly wanted. She simply wouldn't do it with someone like him.

Now, she could already visualise what she would feel like being over Ian's knee, and that was the thought that made her panties impossibly wet, drenched in the centre. Watching was thrilling, but doing – it was as if Ian understood exactly what her thought process was. As soon as Jessica had reached the fever point where she was actually desperate to take Avalon's place, Ian gently moved his roommate off his lap and motioned for Jessica to come forward.

'Your turn, Jessica,' Ian said.

But she couldn't make her body move. Oh, she wanted to. She wanted to drape herself over his strong lap, to feel his hands firmly slide her skirt up to her waist, to tremble all over as he revealed her underpants. She knew how frightened she'd be in the moment before he pulled her panties down. The second before he spanked her for the first time. That flash of worry, of panic even, before the initial spank made everything OK, as it always did.

'Come on, baby,' Ian said, reaching out to circle her wrist with one hand. When had she last been this excited? She couldn't remember. And it was all because of Avalon. Jessica felt her stomach do a dive, but she gave in. Allowing herself to be manipulated, she found her proper place over Ian's lap, waiting breathlessly for the first punishing blow and fantasising about how it would sting.

When his hand finally connected, everything that had been speeded up in her world seemed to slow down. Her heart rate. The ragged breathing. The way her eyelids were fluttering. All grew calm within her. Kelly had trained her that well. She knew one thing – how to take it.

'Harder?' Ian asked, and Jessica heard her own voice answer, even though she wouldn't have thought she could speak. Opening her eyes, she caught sight of her reflection in the mirror across the room. She was upended over Ian's lap, and his fingers stung each time they connected with the bare cheeks of her naked ass. It hurt, but Ian was right. She wanted it harder. She wanted to really feel the pain.

'Tell me,' her new lover urged. 'Tell me and I can give you what you want.'

'Yes,' she whispered, 'Oh, Jesus, yes, spank me harder.' She felt Avalon move off the bed, the weight shifting, and come to sit on the floor in front of her, as if she were desperate to watch the expressions change on Jessica's face. Softly, Avalon brushed Jessica's dark hair out of her eyes, cradled her chin in one hand, made her stare into her own intense face.

'That's right, Jess,' Avalon murmured. 'You take it. You take it as hard as Ian can give it to you. Because afterwards, when you come on my tongue, when I kiss each place he spanked you, the reward will be so much sweeter. I promise.'

It was. Avalon judged exactly when Jessica was ready, and she slid behind her and began to kiss the heated marks left by Ian's firm hand. She licked up and down, parted Jessica's pretty thighs, tasted between them. There was no sweeter way, in Jessica's mind, of saying goodbye to the old year and ringing in the new one.

There were flowers on the front step when Jessica got home. Reaching down for the card, she saw that it was addressed, once again, to Little Red Riding Hood, and this time it was signed, 'Happy New Year, from the Wolf.' Her tricky, costumed flirtation partner, still after her with the long-stemmed white roses. As she walked up the stairs to her apartment, three questions danced through her mind in rapid order:

Who was he?

What did he want from her?

And why did she feel so excited at the thought of having a secret admirer when all the rest of her admirers were right out there in public?

'Where were you?' Sasha wanted to know as Jessica walked into the living room with her arms full of flowers.

'At Avalon's,' Jessica said, a steady flush already starting to creep along her cheekbones. 'You know, working.'

Sasha gave her a questioning glance. 'I know what you're doing,' she said.

'At least one of us does,' Jessica told her, trying to make a joke.

'You're experimenting,' Sasha explained. 'I mean, how many lovers were you with before Kelly?'

'Before?'

She nodded.

Jessica acted as if she was thinking hard, but Sasha nudged her so she had to say, 'Two.' It was true. Maybe that's why she was on such a quest now. 'So you don't think it's odd that I keep getting myself into these situations?' Jessica asked.

'You're on a search.'

Jessica had been standing by the fireplace, staring at her reflection in the mirror over the mantel, at the heat that still lit her blue eyes from within. 'What do you mean?'

'You split from Kelly. You're hanging out with a woman who can only be described as the flirt of Los Angeles. You must be after something.'

'Love,' Jessica finally said. She hadn't found it with Kelly. They had a connection, physical, chemical, but nothing deeper than that.

'Love,' Sasha repeated, and her voice let Jessica know that the answer had pleased her. 'You're looking for love and finding sex.'

Now Jessica shrugged. 'Maybe if I look for sex, I'll find love.'

'No,' Sasha said, starting to laugh. 'You'll only get arrested.'

Book Three: Spring Fling

Love my sweet thing.

– Mick Jagger

16

'Hold up, firecracker,' Dashiell said as Jessica was leaving for the evening. 'You need a ride to the party on Friday.' He spoke the words as if making a statement, forceful and commanding. From watching him over the past few months, Jessica understood this was one of Dashiell's most attractive features to other women. He took charge from the very start, and they simply followed along after him like obedient puppies, tails positively wagging.

'Another party?' she asked, ignoring his tone. When did these people get any work done? Or how? First the Halloween bash. Then the Christmas fiesta. After New Year's, people had been sleepwalking through their jobs for almost a week. Now, only six weeks later, it was already time to celebrate Cupid's favourite holiday. And 'celebrating' to this crew meant more than simply popping open a bottle of expensive champagne. Was there any time when the staff members weren't either drinking, drunk or nursing a hangover?

'A private shindig at the Très Jolie Hotel on Sunset Boulevard. Just the staff. No riff-raff.' He paused. 'Except the staff members who are riff-raff themselves.'

Jessica thought it over. At least, she let him believe she was thinking it over. In fact, her decision to go with him was instantaneous, but she wanted to see how he would respond if she didn't act grateful that he was paying attention to her.

'Pick you up at eight,' he said into her silence, and then he walked out of the office before she could respond. Maybe it wasn't a smart move, since he was her boss's boss, but she found that she just didn't care.

That was Avalon's attitude rubbing off on her. Since their wild night together, the women had been almost inseparable. Not only in bed, but as friends. Avalon had been coaching her, helping her to toughen her outer shell, to keep her emotions in check. So far, the lessons had paid off. Maybe Alex had noticed a change in her, but it was so hard to tell with him. Hard to tell what was going on behind those dreamy eyes.

Marina was going to the Valentine's Day party. No doubt in her mind. She needed to show Alex what he was missing. And for once, she had no difficulty in figuring out how to make her plan work. Sure, the party was by invitation only, for the staff and a select few of the advertisers, but Todd had already told her he wanted her to be there. Since the night she had danced at his concert, he'd been smitten. She was pleased with herself. She wasn't playing any of the psycho emotional blackmail games she had played with Alex. With Todd, she found herself relaxing.

In fact, she actually enjoyed his company. He was a sweet guy, no big musician's ego on him. And he liked her. God, did he like her. He spent hours stroking her naked body with his fingertips. Playing her.

When Alex saw, he would go out of his head. Marina was sure about that.

She had no idea that he didn't plan on attending.

In the spirit of Valentine's Day, Jessica dressed all in red. Pairing a crimson dress with spike heels and her vintage faux leopard-print coat, she felt untameable. It was exactly the way she wanted to feel as far as Dashiell Cooper was concerned. Why he'd asked her to the party, she had no idea. But it was obvious that Alex wasn't going to; he'd been reticent to the point of rudeness with her lately.

Dashiell arrived in a simple black suit. When he handed her a bouquet of roses, she looked up at him, startled. Was he trying to tell her something? His expression was indecipherable as he led her to his truck. Although she had thought there might be other people driving with them, when she saw the red Ford, she realised they were by themselves. She wondered what Alex would say when they arrived, then pushed the thought from her mind.

At the Très Jolie Hotel, Dashiell let the valet attendant take the truck. Then he ushered Jessica into the hotel, towards the bank of mirrored elevators. She noticed women looking at him when they crossed the lobby. Turning, as if casually choreographed, to watch him walk by. Did they know who he was, or were they simply impressed with the James Bond look he exuded? Either way, she wondered if it was always like that, wherever he went.

Just then, a flash went off in her face. Blinking, Jessica turned to see what was going on. By the bank of elevators, several crouching journalists had been waiting to take a shot of someone picture-worthy. Apparently, Dashiell fitted the bill. Jessica looked at him, still seeing circles of golden light from the flash, and she noticed the line of his strong jaw was tightly set now. He hustled her into the elevator and put his back to the door, keeping her hidden by his body. In the privacy of the elevator, she thought that he was about to kiss her, but he didn't.

'I'm sorry,' he said as the doors closed. She could tell that he meant it, but she didn't understand why. 'It's a hassle,' he said next. 'You don't know when they're going to find you, so you have to be on the lookout all the time.'

Suddenly, Jessica felt a wave of pity for him. She'd never considered what it might be like to be a celebrity. Here Dashiell was one, simply because of how much money he had – and it was something he had to deal with every day. No, she never would have thought she'd feel bad for someone who was as handsome, as wealthy, and as put-together as Dashiell, but there it was. Everyone had problems, didn't they, and most were much more serious than Dash's, but she felt grateful that he had tried to protect her from prying eyes and she found herself re-evaluating her feelings for him.

That is, until they joined the rest of the party.

On the ninth floor, Jessica could hear the sounds of partying before the elevator doors even opened. People had spilled out into the red-carpeted hallway, staff members who Jessica said hello to. Dashiell didn't stop to talk to any of them. He headed straight for the bar on the pretence of getting each of them drinks, leaving Jessica alone. She spied Avalon by the bar and went to talk with her.

'You came with Dash?' Avalon whispered. Here was a tidbit of information that seemed to actually shock the columnist.

'He asked me if I wanted a ride,' Jessica explained. 'I don't think we're here together.'

'That's just the way he is,' Avalon said. 'He'll be back at your side in a few minutes, holding your hand, kissing the back of your neck until you get shivers, that sort of thing. Watch out for him, Jess.'

At those words, Josh entered the room. He shot Avalon a look, and she lowered her eyes, pretending she hadn't noticed. When she'd had enough of his phone calls, she'd finally caved in and called him back. But on her terms. Before he'd been able to say anything, she'd told him that she was sorry, but she didn't think they should hook up any longer. It was hurting her work. She'd asked him to be a gentleman, not to bring up their sex life any longer, and she'd taken the long, stunned silence on the other end of the line to mean that he'd agreed. Since then, there had been palpable tension between them, which they had both tried valiantly to ignore.

'He's trouble,' Avalon finally continued when Josh had passed.

Jessica shrugged, turning to watch Dashiell flirting openly with the attractive female bartender, a brown-eyed girl with a visible tattoo of a blue rose on her left breast. The woman batted her lashes as she poured him a shot of whisky. In order to make Dashiell pay attention to her, would she have to flirt with the equally handsome waitstaff? Or go down on one of the editors behind the bar?

Avalon lowered her voice and said, 'You know he's rich, right? So rich he doesn't know what to do with his money.'

It didn't matter to Jessica if Dashiell didn't know what to do with his money. There were advisors who could help him with that sort of situation. What was more obvious to her was that he didn't know what to do on a date. She could see him in the main room now, talking to two of the advertising executives. Occasionally, he'd look over, raise an eyebrow, nod his chin, as if that was enough to keep her content. Or as if he were simply making sure she hadn't left.

Fuck him.

Jessica decided that she was going to have a good time, regardless of how Dashiell was misbehaving. To her, this meant having the freedom to talk with any man she wanted to. Although she wanted most to talk to Alex, he was nowhere in sight.

By the party's end, she found herself out on the balcony with one of *Zebra*'s art directors, a tall young man with a short goatee. She was surprised, but not upset, when the man took her hand and placed it on his crotch. In any other situation, she would have removed it immediately and stalked away, except that she could see Dashiell watching her with renewed interest through the glass doors. The look on his face was the most intent it had been all evening.

'See what you do to me?' the art director asked.

She raised her eyebrows.

'You drive me crazy,' he continued. 'All women in red drive me crazy. Especially sleek little brunettes.'

'I'll remember that,' she said. Through the glass door, she saw that Dashiell was now heading her way. All right, she thought, leaving her hand in place. The art director pressed his body firmly against it. She could feel his erection continue to grow, and the promise of it, even if she didn't plan on playing with him, turned her on.

'You're breaking the law, you know,' he sighed.

'Am I?' she asked, laughing. What they were doing seemed mild for Hollywood.

'Not wearing a bra, and it's after Labor Day.'

'I thought that was white shoes.'

'I may have to take you away in chains.' He paused, lowering his voice. 'Would you like that? Handcuffs around those lovely wrists of yours?'

Before she could answer, Dashiell came up behind her. He bent down to whisper in her ear. 'Is this how you always act on a date, Ms Taylor?'

Now, Jessica moved her hand from the guy's jeans and turned to whisper back. 'We're not on a date.' Dashiell looked confused. She decided it was a good look for him. 'You didn't ask me on a date,' she reminded him. 'You asked if I needed a ride.'

Now he smiled. 'Do you need one home?'

The art director turned his head from one to the other. He sensed that his lady in red was about to become out of reach, but he wasn't going to fight for her, not with the man who signed his pay cheque.

'Just a ride,' Jessica said. 'That's all I'm in the mood for. Besides, I've got my chastity belt on tonight.' Dashiell nodded and took her hand in his, pulling her from the balcony. They left the party without saying a word to anyone, but when Jessica hesitated at the door, she saw that Avalon was watching and shaking her head. What did she have to worry about? He was just driving her home, right?

Wrong.

They didn't drive to her house. Instead, Dashiell sped through the Hollywood Hills, up a series of dark winding roads, until he reached the parking lot at the Griffith Observatory, made famous in one of Jessica's favourite movies, that James Dean classic *Rebel Without a Cause*.

'Avalon told me you were well off,' Jessica said when he parked, 'but I didn't realise you owned the Observatory.'

'Thought you'd like the view,' he told her, coming to her side of the truck and opening her door. She took his hand and they walked to the observation point together. As they walked through the deserted grounds, he said, 'You know, Avalon told me about you, as well.'

'The girl's got a mouth on her,' Jessica said, suddenly remembering the way Avalon's mouth felt on her pussy. That tactile memory made Jessica shiver and Dashiell quickly put his arm around her shoulder.

The lights flickered before them, reminding Jessica of why she'd moved to LA in the first place. She'd wanted to live in a city that was 'on' all the time. Dashiell's hand now wandered to rest on her ass.

'I don't feel a chastity belt,' he said.

'It's one of those lightweight types. Made out of new-age micro-fibre material.'

He squeezed her. 'Pretty lightweight. I can't feel it at all.'

'It's on,' Jessica assured him. 'And I left the key at home.'

'Like a good Little Red Riding Hood.'

She turned to look at him, startled. 'What's it matter to you? You're nobody's teacher.'

'Not my style,' he said agreeably, 'but from the way you were handling yourself on the balcony, you may be the one to teach me a thing or two.'

Now Jessica smiled. 'Not my style.' Without looking back, she turned and walked quickly to the truck, reminding herself what Sasha had said. It's a game. Play it like it doesn't matter, because it doesn't. But I want love, she'd told Sasha. More than anything, that's what I want.

'You'll get it,' Sasha had assured her, 'when you forget about it.'

It's what she told Dashiell when he tried to switch gears with his hand on her thigh instead of the stick. 'Forget about it,' she said, trying to put a smile in her voice so he knew she wasn't upset. Then, as he pulled to a stop in front of her apartment, she added, 'But thanks a lot for the ride.'

He tilted his head back to watch her, and she could feel his eyes on her body as she walked up the stairs. She knew that if she turned and looked over her shoulder at him, he would follow her. But she didn't want that. Didn't want to play a game with this man who seemed to be on an entirely different level than she was. Not only financially, since that didn't interest her. What stopped her from trysting with Dashiell was the fact that she didn't understand the rules to his game. Not yet.

Still, as she reached the door to her apartment, she took a mental survey of how she felt, and was pleased to discover that she felt just fine. The crazy man started yelling as he pushed his shopping cart past her building. Instead of joining in with him, she closed the window, put on her headsets and turned on her stereo. Loud.

The next day the enlarged photograph had made it to the front page of the entertainment section of the *Times*. Sasha got the paper first, scanning the movie reviews, as always, looking for bombs. She couldn't help the fact that she liked it when another movie did badly. Especially the multi-million-dollar productions. Failure at that level made her feel as if there was room out there for her. For her to do better.

Automatically her eyes flickered to the gossip column written by one of Avalon's foes, and she couldn't believe what she saw. There he was. Johnny. Her mystery man. He looked distinguished in black and white, and she knew that in almost any other circumstance, she'd have felt a shocking jolt of pleasure at discovering she'd been fucking a celebrity. But not today. In the picture, Johnny's arm was tight around Jessica's waist and his handsome face was an incomprehensible mask.

It took only a moment for Sasha to decipher the sticky situation. She'd been toying around with Dashiell Jonathan Cooper the Second. Son from the shortly lived union of an infamous playboy and a stunningly beautiful fashion model. He'd gotten his looks from his mother, his money from his father. Now, at 40, he was famous, truly, for being rich.

She was so stupid. She'd known he looked familiar, but there were too many celebrities to keep track of in LA. How could she have been expected to recognise him? That was easy to answer. She wasn't supposed to. He'd been playing at being an anonymous partier. Someone who was living the fringe lifestyle of a struggling artist, like all of the other actors, writers and wannabe directors in LA. Like Sasha herself, when it came down to it.

And did she blame him? Had he come clean with her at that party at Dream Maker, wouldn't she have become someone else herself? Yes. She would have turned on, explained her goals, her financial predicament. Asked whether he was interested in investing in the movies. In her movie, precisely.

Sasha was scrutinising the photo when Jessica stumbled out of her bedroom in search of coffee. She tried to put the pages of the paper back in order, to pretend that she hadn't seen the picture, but Jessica saw the photo immediately.

'That's not me –'

'Yes, it is.' Sasha put as much warm humour in her voice as she possibly could. There was no way for Jessica to have known she'd already been with this man – her boss – and there was no fucking reason for her to find out, either. It wasn't going to happen again. Not now.

'Johnny' wasn't going to tell her. That was for sure.

17

Kelly was out of his league. He had known it from the start. The way this set worked stunned him. Yes, he'd been on movies before, but a DeMarco production turned out to be completely unique. The director seemed to have the entire cast and crew in a state of high suspense. Of fear. And of respect. There was quiet on the set before she opened her mouth to demand it. Nobody questioned her total authority, and in the face of such startling power, Kelly was overawed.

He knew he wasn't the only one. It seemed to him that the cameramen grew orgasmic when DeMarco spoke to them. That everyone around was simply waiting for her eyes to glance in their direction. Kelly was different. He didn't want to gain her notice. But he did watch everything that went on, paying attention, making mental notes that he was quick to write down later.

He was deeply ensconced in a new plan to get back to Jessica. He'd tried calling her after spending the night with the beautiful blonde, but she hadn't bothered to answer. He'd left gifts. Now, he had an idea that would surely get him back into her heart.

It was risky, but worth it.

Upside-down, with her long hair dangling towards the mattress, Avalon tried and failed to catch her breath. She and Ian were doing something brand new, fucking on a swing suspended over the very centre of his bed, and she was leaning backward as far as she could go. Her cheeks were flushed a hot pink, partly from the blood rushing to her face and partly from the way that Ian was treating her. She couldn't remember ever being fucked this deeply. Each time he pumped the swing, he slid in further into her pussy.

Her roommate had brought the toy back with him from New York, installing it in the ceiling without telling Avalon about his plans. She'd heard the sounds of a power drill, had been curious as she always was about something she didn't know about, but had waited patiently until he'd come to her room and called for her.

Now Avalon felt a weightlessness flood through her, the feeling of fucking while flying, and she loved it. The thrill at being suspended in the air was intense, and she rocked back against him. Instantly, she was rewarded with a fresh tremor of pleasure.

'Hang on,' Ian said, and Avalon sitting up now, gripped into the sides of the swing, waiting for whatever was next. Ian pushed his feet against the bed, and suddenly they were moving higher in the air, back and forth as he continued to plunge her sweet depths.

Upright now, Avalon shut her eyes and aligned her body as close as possible with her roommate's. With her thighs overlapping his, she could press the juncture of her body against his, getting the pressure that she craved against her clit. As he continued to pump the swing, and to pump inside her, she felt the first taste of the impending orgasm rumble through her. Just a flicker before the full force of it washed through her.

'Oh, yes,' she murmured, resting her head on Ian's strong shoulder and sighing.

Afterwards, Ian said something to turn Avalon's world upside-down for the second time that afternoon.

'Moving,' she repeated softly. 'You're moving.'

This was too much. First, Josh had effectively left her, at least emotionally, and now Ian was going to leave her physically. Both times the news had hit her unexpectedly, and with a power that shook her entire being. That wasn't a good sign for a gossip columnist, was it? Not having had the news ahead of time. Maybe she was losing her edge.

'Why?' she asked.

He didn't answer right away. When he did, he spoke slowly and clearly, as if not wanting to test her wrath. He'd been offered a part that he couldn't turn down. He wasn't simply moving from LA to New York, he was moving up, from soap-opera star to Broadway. The sex swing was his way of going out with a bang. Of saying goodbye in a memorable, Avalon-type of way.

'Just for the run, right? Six months or so?'

Ian shook his head, and although it was obvious he wanted to say more, Avalon didn't want to hear it.

'You can't leave me,' she said, and at the words she felt the lowest she'd ever been. So weak. So clinging. 'I didn't mean that. I'm happy –' That was such a lie. Tears were streaming down her face. 'I'm happy for you. It's good news,' she choked out, wishing she were anywhere else but naked in his bedroom talking to the second man in two months who was breaking her heart. For years she'd convinced herself that she no longer had a heart to be broken. That she was too tough for love. But she'd been lying.

Ian put one hand out to touch her, but Avalon flinched away from him, scrambling to get off his bed and hurry to her room, locking the door behind her.

Dashiell stood outside the door to Jessica's apartment. For once, a girl was making him confused. Usually, he understood their games. Wasn't hard to decipher what they had in mind. He was a prize, a catch, and they would be willing to do just about anything to be with him. Sex wherever, whenever he wanted it. Not like that was a big sacrifice, of course. He was good in bed. Better than good.

In general, Dashiell had a predictable pattern with women. When he wanted a girl, he got her. Or, in the case of his tryst with the trio of bartenders, when he wanted several girls at once, he got *them*. The problem, of course, was that as soon as his interest was reciprocated, he had the urge to move on. Only two women had made him lose any sleep recently. Sasha, the pretty stripper, who had come back into his life after their first one-night stand, and Jessica, the little intern. Both were unique and interesting to him, Jessica more so at the moment. He knew that being in a relationship with Dashiell Cooper was something a lot of women wanted. It gave him the upper hand. Which he had lost, somehow, with Jessica.

Why?

Because she didn't seem to care about the money, or the power, or even the fact that he was good-looking. She liked him. There was no doubt about that. But she didn't melt every time he walked by. Her attitude at the Valentine's Day party had proven that, and the way she'd treated him since then had backed it up.

How was he going to change that? By acting completely unexpected. That was the plan, anyway. Showing up out of the blue to take her on some wild, adventurous ride that only he could give her. Where, he wasn't entirely sure yet. He trusted himself enough to know that being spontaneous meant just that. When he saw her face, he'd know where to go next. But once again, Jessica foiled his plans, because it was Sasha who opened the door. Sasha, with her wild red hair and her puffy red eyes. What was she doing at Jessica's house? He found himself at a loss, standing like an idiot on the front step, shaking his head.

'She's not here, Dashiell,' the tousle-headed beauty

said softly, choking back tears and trying to look as if she were simply suffering from some sort of hayfever. She buried her face into a hankie, refusing to meet his gaze.

So she knew somehow. Knew who he was and what that meant.

'Jessica's out,' Sasha continued, explaining the rest to him in a rush. 'She's my roommate and I don't have any idea where she is tonight.'

And even though Dashiell meant to apologise for interrupting her at what was most obviously a private time, he found that he simply didn't have the heart. Staying had nothing to do with the fact that Sasha's supple form was easily visible in the semi-sheer white robe she was wearing. At least, that's what he told himself.

'You OK?' he asked, stepping across the threshold and into the apartment. He put his arm around her and walked her over to the sofa, as if she were in his place instead of the other way around. Didn't Dashiell always act as if he owned the location? And wasn't that something that charmed most women?

'Come on, Sash. What's wrong? You can tell me.'

'Cut,' the director said sharply, and Kelly felt his face instantly turn the bright red of an overripe cherry. Not just red, but hot, so that he wished he had a tall glass of cold ice water to drink. Or to pour over his head. How many times was he going to have to do this fucking scene? The answer to that question was simple: as many times as Deleen DeMarco demanded.

He tried to act calm. He was an actor, wasn't he? He should have been able to pretend that it was normal for him to walk around with no clothes on. The director had kindly insisted upon a closed set, which meant that the only people around were the cameraman, the rest of the actors in the scene, and a few technicians. Didn't make things easier, though. He'd learned during the past few days that being naked in front of one stranger was just as difficult for him as being naked in front of twenty.

'A word with you,' the director said, nodding in his direction.

He had to approach her now? As nonchalantly as possible, he reached for the white towel on the end of the bed, but was instantly stopped by a props person who had carefully arranged the thing to match all of the previously shot scenes. Usually, there was some little PA, ready and willing with his robe in hand. But right now, when he needed it most, the robe was missing. He wished for a moment he was big enough to throw a fully fledged tantrum. A brighter star than he would have agents calling, handlers demanding better treatment.

Ah, but nobody really misbehaved with this director. Not even the top stars. Did it, possibly, have something to do with those steely eyes of hers? The way that she could slice someone off mid-sentence simply by shooting a look in the poor bastard's direction? All of these thoughts wormed through his head as he walked to her side. And all were deleted by the one thought screaming louder than all the others, throbbing in his mind as he reached her chair:

Just don't get hard.

'I'd like to speak with you privately,' DeMarco said softly to Kelly. He was instantly warmed by the tone of her voice. She wasn't yelling, wasn't angry. It seemed obvious to him that she was being kind now, asking to meet him in her private room in order to spare him from taking criticism in front of the cast. But why should she spare him, when she'd spared no one else so far?

He didn't know. All he could do was nod, his hands covering his cock which was thankfully obeying him, at least for the moment. As the director stood, he saw why he hadn't been able to find his robe. The thing was draped over the back of her chair. With an uncharacteristically impish look at him, she handed it over, as if she'd known the whole time exactly where it was. Yes, that was definitely the case. She'd been playing with him, making him tremble like a cowed pupil in front of a powerful principal. And it hadn't made him angry in the slightest. All he wanted to do was please her. There was no sense of false pride within him, or even false modesty. He would follow wherever she led, which, at this moment, was down the hall to her office.

Wrapping himself in the sumptuous blue silk robe, Kelly trailed after her. He didn't look at anyone else on the set, the rest of the crew who were taking a much-deserved break after hours of working. Some would go out and smoke, he knew. Others would call friends on their cellphones, making plans for late in the evening, wanting to chill with a beer or two and unwind from a day spent on one of the most tense sets in the industry. Nobody would rat out what had just happened. Everyone wanted to stay in DeMarco's good books.

Kelly had no such thoughts of unwinding. Slowly, he walked into DeMarco's office, watched her latch the door behind him, and then waited to hear what she'd have to say about his performance. Don't fire me, he silently begged. I'll be good. I'll do whatever you say. Whatever you want.

Deleen responded as if he'd spoken the words out loud. 'The rule on my set is that we do things my way.'

Kelly nodded anxiously, his head bobbing like one of those ridiculous toys people keep on the back shelf of their cars. Up. Down. Up. Down.

'That's the only rule,' she continued, coming towards him and undoing the tie on his robe so that it fell open. His cock was no longer listening to his brain, and he knew without looking down that he was harder than a table leg. Instead of commenting on his wood, the director simply let her cool hand graze the length of it, and Kelly's knees threatened to buckle. Her hand was soft, her short nails just tickling his skin. 'You've done well so far,' she said, and he felt a new warmth flood through him, this time of pleasure rather than embarrassment. 'But I'd like to help you go the distance. I want you to be the actor that I know you can be. Some people believe that praise works the best of all tricks, yet I have different methods that I employ with my actors.'

Deep within himself, he knew what was going to happen before he heard the words. Yet he couldn't actually believe it. Amazed, he saw her hand go to the waistband of her pale, cream-coloured slacks, saw the oily black leather belt with the pounded silver buckle as it was unfastened from her slender waist and pulled free. For over two months now, he'd watched her finger that metal buckle during meetings, had seen her stroke the leather of the belt absentmindedly. Why hadn't he understood? Since they were so similar, had he simply blocked out the recognition? Do doms ever recognise other doms?

As she made him take the position, he found himself wondering about the many times he had been on the other end of such a scene with lovers. With Jessica, in particular. Suddenly, he could appreciate how she must have felt in the moments before he punished her. Because even though his mind couldn't fully believe it, that was exactly what Deleen DeMarco was going to do to him, wasn't it?

'Count for me,' the director said. Kelly couldn't help but smile at this. He had said the exact words to Jessica so many times. Made her count. Made her think about the next number and what it would mean in the equivalence of pain against her trembling body. And made her think about how many more strokes were in store for her. You never told a submissive. Never gave them a final answer. That was the game. Pushing, teasing, testing the very edges of their boundaries.

'Yes,' Kelly said, when he realised DeMarco was waiting for his response. 'Of course.' He would do whatever she asked. He realised that as the belt found his skin for the first time. This wasn't about the movie role, about pushing himself harder. It was about the underlying intense connection he felt with this striking creature. If he had to take the part of the submissive in order to be with her, then that was what he would do. Because the prize of what lay in store was too powerful to deny. He could see it in his mind. Touching her. Making her lose that hard-eyed gaze. Melting her.

First there was the whipping to get through. The belt cut deeply into his skin and he counted out each number. His voice was low, and the words sounded harsh, as if he were biting them off. 'One, two, three –' The blows came in rapid succession as the lady lined them up on his naked skin. And each stroke against his body made his cock strain even harder in front of him. He couldn't believe how excited he was, how turned on, and he actually found that he was completely calm. Waiting for the next blow, steeling himself to take it. Every tiny detail in the room came into focus. The pictures on the wall – powerful modern art, no simple watercolours for this woman. The sound of Deleen's breathing. The breeze in the room stirring slowly from the air conditioner.

'You take it,' Deleen said, and he thought that she wasn't telling him what to do, but simply making an observation. He could take it. He could take whatever she had to give for as long as she needed him to.

In a flash, he realised what this meant. They must be done shooting the scene. He must have finally nailed it.

Because she wouldn't mark him like this and then make him do another take, would she?

What *wasn't* wrong?

For a moment, the thought of revealing her troubles made Sasha feel instantly free. She'd been wound up tightly for so long, hiding her secrets from Jessica. From everybody. And Dashiell already knew part of it. Knew how she was honestly spending her nights. He'd listen. He'd understand. She could explain that she was a film maker and that she had received an encouraging letter from a festival. Based on the script she'd sent in much earlier, they wanted to consider her movie. All she had to do was send in the final print. But currently she only possessed the trailer – they'd never take her based on four minutes, would they?

What a relief it would be to tell someone. But just as quickly, she changed her mind. This was her set of problems. She didn't need to confess to him. Not based on their history, a one-night stand that had refused to stay in the past. She knew that sexual connections like theirs were best left unrepeated, but theirs had become a multiple-night stand. After New Year's, he'd shown up a few times at the bar, rescuing her after work for a wild night of pleasure. The randomness of their connections was what made their attraction so special. You could act crazy, because you had no ties to the person who was behind you. Beneath you. Pressed up tight against you.

What a shock it had been to learn the truth, though. He'd been slumming. And she'd fallen for it. In Los Angeles, things tended to go the opposite way. A man would pretend to be wealthy, but end up working at some shoe store, or as a law clerk, or a PA on some awful movie. And while Sasha didn't think she was a snob, she hated to be lied to. Fucking hated it worse than anything else she could think of. It was why she hated lying to

Jessica about her boss, pretending and play-acting that she'd never met the man before. That would have to change at some point. As soon as Jess and Dashiell finished their little romantic dance and decided whether or not they were going to be together – then Sasha could come clean.

But Dashiell was asking her to come clean now.

'Tell me,' he said, leaving the living room only long enough to gather a bottle of wine and two glasses from the kitchen. Returning, he expertly popped the cork and poured them each a hefty serving of the chilled Chardonnay. Sasha was embarrassed for a moment at the thought that she was serving him – or being served by him – a glass of wine from a bottle that probably cost less than what he'd normally pay for fizzy water. But she couldn't help that. She didn't live by his rules or his bank account.

Still, she allowed herself to be manoeuvred on the worn, canvas sofa, feeling Dashiell lift her legs and place them over his thighs, because she was too miserable to fight it. Besides, wasn't there something between them? She knew that he had feelings for Jessica, but the feelings hadn't been returned yet, had they?

Alex was still at his desk late in the evening, fighting with Josh. The ad man had sold the back page to a studio that was paying for a four-colour process. This meant, in the unwritten rules of the newspaper business, that the client expected a positive write-up. Usually, Alex was not so easily bought. But as the evening progressed, he felt his resolve weaken.

'It's a good movie, anyway,' Josh said.

'You didn't see it.'

'Well, the trailers looked awesome.'

'You just like Nicolette Sheridan. The movie sucks.'

'It will make a lot of money,' Josh said, as if that was

some point. 'Come on, Alex. You don't have to write it. Assign the review to one of your underlings.'

For a moment, Alex considered calling one of the writers in his stable who'd do whatever he told them for the money, but he was tired of cleaning up their second-hand copy. They didn't care about the job, just the booze the job would buy them.

'What about Jessica?'

'What about her?' he asked.

'She's been begging you to let her write more. Why not give her a chance? You know she'll write something positive. They always do when they first start out.'

Josh was right. Every intern the paper had ever had believed reviews were supposed to be positive. At least, at first. Later, they got cynical. But that took sitting through twenty or thirty bad movies.

'It's a set-up,' Alex said to Josh, as if that would change his mind.

'What's with you, Alex? You develop a soul or some-thing? We need to stay in the black here. This ad does it for the week.' Josh sounded tough and defensive, and when Alex gave him a quizzical glance, he frowned harder. What had happened to the man lately, Alex wondered. Josh had always tiptoed along the tightrope between salesman and sleaze, but in the past few months he seemed to have gone over to the bad side, losing what was left of his conscience.

As Josh handed over the phone, Alex gave him a mean look, then dialled Jessica's number.

'From memory, huh?' Josh said, noticing.

Alex ignored the comment. Sasha answered the phone, and he was about to ask for Jessica when he heard Dashiell in the background – making some com-ment about wine. Where was it? Did she want more? Alex didn't wait to hear, he simply hung up the phone, instantly picturing his boss and Jessica involved in some deep conversation over a glass or two of fine Merlot.

'What's up?' Josh asked, looking concerned for once. Alex simply shook his head and left the office in a rush.

Jessica didn't know exactly how it had happened that she and the gossip columnist had become so close. Avalon was so glamorous, so worldly. Usually, anyway. Now, as she paced through the apartment, she seemed just like any other wretchedly heartbroken woman. And Jessica was doing her very best to comfort her.

'I thought –' Avalon whispered.

'I know.'

'I mean, I really thought . . .' she let the words hang there, unfinished. She'd given Jessica only the sketchiest outline of why she was so upset, calling and asking her to come over. To help. Even though 'help' was such a strange term for what she needed – which was company. Ian had fled immediately after giving Avalon the news, hurrying to catch a plane back east, leaving a note that movers would be picking up his furniture within days.

Now, while Avalon choked back a sob, Jessica nodded and laced her fingers through Avalon's and led her back to the bedroom. Here, she took the blonde in her arms and stroked her fingertips through Avalon's long, straight hair.

'You rushed over here.'

Jessica nodded. 'You sounded bad on the phone.'

'I mean, you really rushed.' Avalon touched the tips of her fingers to Jessica's hair, still wet from an evening shower. She'd taken a run after work and hadn't bothered to dry her hair after getting Avalon's desperate call. 'Were you still all wet –' Avalon took a sip of wine before finishing the sentence, 'from the shower?'

Jessica felt her body responding automatically to

Avalon's teasing. All wet. Yes, she was. All wet between her legs, and the rush of it came over her suddenly. She had been in a different mood only moments before, here to assist Avalon in a crisis, help any way that she could. But now, from the look in her friend's radiant green eyes, it seemed that what Avalon wanted was very specific. To be comforted. Sweetly. Slowly. In a manner that Jessica was perfectly adept at.

Without another word, Jessica undid the iridescent mother-of-pearl buttons running the length of Avalon's animal-print nightgown. Even in distress, the woman had dressed like a bombshell. She couldn't help it, could she? Avalon squirmed lightly, wiggling her body so that she was lying flat on the sheets. Then she waited while Jessica peeled open the nightie, spreading the soft material out around her. For a moment, both women looked at each other, and the connection of their gaze was as exciting as what Jessica did next.

No thoughts. No plans. She started at the centre. Started between Avalon's legs with a little kiss to the woman's bare pussy lips. Soft kiss. Sweet kiss. And then a more probing move of her tongue along the centre of those closed lips, tricking and tickling up the split to coax out the wetness. She moved with finesse and with fantastic restraint, making every single gesture count. When she slid her hands beneath Avalon's lovely round ass, the columnist relaxed into her embrace. Jessica could feel the tension leaving her friend, and she was gratified that it was because of something she was doing.

Now, moving a bit more forcefully, she nuzzled her face against Avalon's pussy. Using her chin, and her cheeks, moving her head back and forth, she teased her co-worker with a range of delightful sensations. Her long, still-wet hair tickled up and down Avalon's thighs as her face grew wet and shiny with the woman's juices.

'Like this,' Avalon suddenly said, and she reached

down to move Jessica. At first, the intern thought she was being corrected, that she'd done something wrong. But then she realised that Avalon wanted to 69.

Quickly Jessica slid out of her clothes, tossing them on to Avalon's bedroom floor. And just as quickly she moved so that her own waiting pussy was poised above Avalon's mouth. Then she hesitated, expecting the more experienced woman to make the next move. Avalon did, automatically reaching for Jessica's hips and drawing her in close. Now, mouth to pussy and pussy to mouth, the women truly connected. Like a dream, they moved together, sometimes rolling on to their sides to get in deeper, then moving so that Jessica was beneath and Avalon on top. They both knew exactly how to work together, like long-standing dance partners who understand when to expect a change of steps.

In the hazy afterglow, Avalon and Jessica lay entwined. Body to body. Warmth seeping from one to the other. The columnist decided to reward the intern, to give her a gift of the most important type to Avalon: information.

'You've been getting flowers still.'

Jessica nodded.

'I know who they're from.'

Her heart pounding in her chest, the intern just stared at Avalon. From the columns, she'd known Avalon knew, but here it was. Ready for her.

'Dashiell,' Jessica said at once.

Avalon shook her head.

'Kelly?'

She shook her head again, and smiled for real. 'Three's the charm,' she said.

Alex wasn't into playing games. He was too fucking old, for one thing. And he'd never really enjoyed the whole complexity of trying to manipulate someone into doing what you wanted. But that didn't mean he didn't understand the rules.

He knew Dashiell was after Jessica. He'd guessed this well before his boss had asked her to the Valentine's Day party, and now he had heard for himself that she was enjoying the attention. Wasn't that enough for him to get her out of his mind? Unfortunately, no. Knowledge that he was up against Dashiell for the affections of the intern didn't immediately turn off his fantasies. But so what? He was a big boy, he could control himself. Forget about her. Focus on his work at the paper, or even Marina –

No fucking way. That was out of the question.

She'd been in his mind lately, but that was only because she was doing Todd. Thanks to Avalon, he knew all about it. And he knew why she was behaving this way – to make him want her. It had worked, but that didn't change the fact that he and Marina were poison together. Yes, she could get him off in record time, but he was done with toxic relationships. Better to be alone, standing on his balcony, as he was now, looking over the city.

He loved Los Angeles, with the lights that were on all the time, people out having fun, or getting into trouble, fucking each other. Like Dashiell was probably fucking Jessica, slipping up her filmy skirt, stroking the insides of her supple thighs. Touching, just barely brushing, his fingertips against her clit. He was undoubtedly feeling her wetness, or tasting it by now, on his knees in front of her, mouth against the seam of her body, tongue flicking forward into her sopping slit –

Jesus fucking Christ, stop, he told himself. Just stop it. He reached into his pocket for the cellphone. He'd call. That wasn't playing a game. He liked her. That was the difference. Really liked her. Thought they might have a chance at something together. He could put that out for her to consider, let her give him an honest answer, and then move on. If she said no, then where would he be? He couldn't work with her any more, and there'd be no way not to. He'd have to leave.

Was it worth it?

He stared bleakly again at the lights of the city, as if they might hold the answers to his questions. When the phone rang inside, he let it. The machine picked up and he heard the sound of his agent leaving a message. Alex ignored it. There was nobody he wanted to talk to right now. Nobody except Jessica.

18

Avalon had disappeared.

Yes, she'd gone MIA in the past, hunkering down over a hot bit of gossip and refusing to answer her phone or her page until she'd written the final draft of her column. She considered this professional hibernation, and nobody could convince her to behave otherwise. Even when she missed important events, she didn't consider it rude. Work was her god. She obeyed the power of gossip at all costs.

But this was different. She'd flaked on turning in anything for two issues, which was completely unlike her. At her lowest points, Avalon still finished her column. During her tenure at the paper, even a ski accident hadn't stopped her from writing. She'd called her sources from her hospital bed, high on pain medication, gathering the information she needed. Now, Josh was worried. He didn't expect her to get in touch with him. Not since she'd ended things so abruptly – obviously upset with him for some unexplained reason. But two weeks had passed, and if he could trust his co-workers to be honest with him, then nobody had heard a word.

He tried to hide his feelings, paying attention to the business of the newspaper that generally captivated him. Like Avalon, work balanced Josh's life, centred him. That didn't stop him from pretending he wasn't looking at Avalon's desk every time he went into the office. Each morning, he asked Alex, as casually as possible, if the man had heard from her, but Alex just shook his head, fingering a cigar and frowning.

The entire paper seemed different without her.

But worse than that, Josh was different, too.

With Avalon gone, at least temporarily, Alex gave Jessica the assignment she had spent her life dreaming about. From the time that she'd first decided to be a writer, all she'd wanted was a chance to prove herself. Yes, she'd done well on her school papers and on the underground 'zine in Paris. But those didn't count in her mind. Now, Alex was giving her a real shot.

'It's a closed set,' the managing editor said, handing over the only material he had on the film. Just a single piece of paper in a manilla folder. 'I want you to write a piece on it. Even if the story is just about how difficult you find it to get any information whatsoever. It's crazy. In a town like this, there should be leaks, but there aren't. Even Avalon ran into a wall.'

Jessica's hands trembled on the file. She wanted to open it. To see what was inside, but she forced herself to wait and listen.

'It's no big surprise that the armour is up. That's always the case with a DeMarco production.' At the words, Jessica tried hard to keep her face serene. Kelly was on the set. That was her pass. She listened carefully as Alex continued to brief her. He wanted the inside scoop, information about what was really going on behind the gates, and Jessica had a way of getting to the very core of the production. Would Kelly help her? That was an easy answer. He still called every week, 'just to talk'.

'I don't know why,' Alex began, 'but I think you're going to succeed on this one.'

Silent Movies

A DeMarco production is a silent film. Silent in the sense that nobody speaks about what happens on the set. No leaks. No chinks in the bricks. Is that possible? Could there even be a movie where none of the players sells out, nobody plays both sides? The answer is simple: yes and no.

Yes, in the sense that until now, we have heard nearly nothing about the new DD production. And no, because a source has been found. A double agent has come to our side. And here's the news:

The genre is horror. But this is a horror flick like none other. No ghosts. No slashing killers. Nothing that you've seen before. DeMarco pushes limits. That we know. Even more interesting, however, is what we now know about the set. About the reclusive director and the way she handles, and that is manhandles, her actors —

Alex stopped reading to look over at Jessica. He had given her the assignment for several reasons. One, he thought she could handle it. Two, there wasn't anyone else he would trust with the piece. Three, he really wanted to know what was up with Jessica and Kelly. Based on the way she'd written her review of Todd's band, he knew that she'd put herself into the article, would explain, perhaps, where she was romantically without him having to ask. Yes, it was obvious to him that Kelly was spilling information. But if that was the case, then the two must still be together, right? Even after Kelly's fling with Avalon. As if sensing his questions, Jessica started talking.

'Can't tell you who,' she said. 'But my source is good.'

He nodded, then said, 'I'll read the rest. If I can print it, how do you want your name?'

Jessica thought for a moment, and then said, 'Red Riding Hood.'

* * *

Sasha was with Dashiell again. She wasn't sure exactly how it had happened. She'd spent the evening planning on confessing her situation to Jessica. State the fact that although she'd told Jessica she was doing night shoots, in actuality she'd been stripping again. Trying to slide together enough money to finish her film.

But Jessica hadn't come home, out on some hush-hush assignment, and Sasha had been left pent up, with words waiting to come out but dammed up inside her. Wanting to talk to someone, anyone, she'd found herself dialling the number Dashiell had given her the last time he'd seen her. Calling and saying her name. Just her name. Then waiting to see what he would do. Leaving the decision up to him. If he said, 'Sasha who?' she'd know not to bother him. Sasha was no psycho. She'd never stalk him, never turn into one of those women she read about in what she personally had nicknamed Avalon Granger's Misery Column.

No, she'd let Dashiell make the decision. And it was a big one. She understood easily if he didn't want to play the game that she was offering. Because there was much more involved now than simply stretching out a one-night stand.

He loved her roommate, and she loved her roommate, so why couldn't she let him alone? Simply get drunk until she couldn't see straight and pass out? That's what other people might have done in a similar situation. That's what she'd have done before meeting Dash. But not now. Having sex had reminded her of the fact that she liked sex, and had missed it. Dashiell had awakened her libido. She needed warmth, human touch, another being.

And she needed someone who didn't mind being filmed.

* * *

'Explain it to me again,' Dashiell said, smiling broadly at her, the skin at the corners of his eyes crinkling with obvious good humour. Sasha took a moment to drink in his expression. He seemed genuinely interested in what she had to say, and he also appeared excited at the prospect. His excitement fuelled her own, as well as clouded her ability to think straight, and she had to work to figure out how to make her desires clear.

'I don't know,' Sasha stuttered, finding it hard to put into words what she had in mind. 'It just turns me on.'

'Directing. That's what you do.' He laughed now, and his laughter was sweet. Not mean-spirited at all. 'But most people I know like to take a break from their job when they're in bed.' He was playing with her, teasing and pushing buttons. All right, so that was not exactly true. *She* was the one pushing the actual buttons. Playing with one of her high-tech cameras. Setting it up on the tripod, but still issuing directions to her man. She couldn't help herself. When she had the camera anywhere near her, the commands spilled freely from her subconscious and out of her lips. Directing was in the very inner workings of her mind. It was what made her tick.

'What will you do with the film?' Dashiell asked next. She saw in his eyes the cunning that had kept him safe to this point in his life. The carefulness about himself, his reputation, his ego.

'I don't care. You can keep it. We can erase it. I just like the light on –'

'You're afraid of the dark.'

'The *red* light,' she corrected him, now joining him on the mattress and pointing to the tiny light at the side of the recorder. They were in his minuscule apartment, sprawled on the pull-down bed. It was the perfect setting for what she had in mind. Not exactly seedy, but bare bones. Nothing to detract from what they were going to do or how they were going to do it.

If she couldn't focus on her film, at least she could focus on fucking.

She would be fine. Avalon knew that. She would pull herself together. Snap out of it. All those little platitudes that people said when someone was going through a break-up. Of course, she wasn't really. She'd never considered Ian or Josh her boyfriends. But that didn't make her feel any better.

Jessica had managed to console her for a short time. But once the girl had left and the moving van had arrived the next day, Avalon felt herself slipping away. Falling into a nothingness that frightened her. She was lucky, so lucky, when the phone rang. Screening her calls, she'd heard Lily leaving a message.

'Tip for you, Avalon,' the woman had said. 'Call –'

But Avalon had picked up the phone, and before Lily could tell her what information she'd uncovered, Avalon had said, 'I need –'

'What do you need, Ava?'

'I need your help.'

That had been two weeks ago, and Avalon was still ensconced in Lily's tiny Laurel Canyon apartment. She knew she must be frightening people, but she couldn't bother with what other people thought right now. All she could concentrate on was her own mental health. Selfish, perhaps, but Avalon was the queen of self-preservation. She knew exactly what she needed and this was it: Time Out.

Dashiell discovered that he liked the way Sasha looked in his room. She enlivened the place with her bright red hair and uncontainable energy. Besides, she didn't seem to mind at all that there was nothing fancy in the furnishings. If anything, she appeared to appreciate the stark surroundings. Not questioning the fact that he'd spent very little money on the decorations. 'It looks better on camera than a lot of fussy furniture,' she assured him, now moving to kiss his strong chest, working her way in a line down his tight, well-muscled body.

He closed his eyes at the rush of pleasure, but Sasha wasn't having any of that.

'Watch,' she said. 'Watch me. Not the camera. Forget it's there. But watch me.'

Tilting his head to the side, he regarded her with interest.

'How are you going to make me forget?' he asked.

'Don't you worry,' Sasha told him, putting one hand on his chest and pushing him back down on the mattress. 'Trust me. But keep your eyes open. I want you to force yourself to watch every move I make.'

It was a challenge. Dashiell understood that. And as always, he rose to the challenge, this time physically. Watching Sasha, he sucked in his breath as she moved to the bottom of the bed, and then licked her way up the line of his naked legs. She lingered at the indents of the muscles on his thighs, trailing her tongue along the cut ridges. Watching as she headed directly for his already towering erection, he couldn't wait to feel her mouth on him. That moment before she parted her lips and introduced him to the heat of her mouth, that was sublime. Then it got even better as she met the head of his cock and gave it a warm, wet French kiss. Her tongue licked around the knob, then trailed down the length of his rod all the way to his balls. She cradled these in her mouth, bounced them on her tongue, kissed and caressed them.

His gaze flickered over to the camera, but Sasha immediately chastised him. 'No,' she murmured. 'Pay attention to me.'

This was something new. Yes, he'd played with a video camera before. But at the time, he'd been the one cajoling his girlfriend to put out for the camera. Now, he was the star, and he enjoyed every single frame.

19

Deleen would find out. Kelly understood that. She would find out that he was slipping Jessica information for her columns, and she would do something to him. Punish him, or banish him? He wasn't sure. He also wasn't sure exactly why he'd turned into a spy. At first, he'd wanted to prove to Jessica that he missed her. That he wanted her back. But he was no longer sure about those reasons. Jessica accepted the information from him without question, yet she didn't seem interested in resuming their relationship – and did he even want that?

No. He was playing a different game altogether. Showing Deleen that he wasn't afraid of her. Was that it?

DeMarco already knew that he'd broken the rules one time, and he remembered, with a little shudder, what had happened then. The night in her condo, at the top floor, spent outdoors, tied upright, watching as the sky changed colours. Knowing that other normal people were waking up in their beds. Making their coffee, their breakfasts, while his cock grew hard in the cool, morning breeze.

His lover's penthouse overlooked the Malibu beach, and the sea air had stung his eyes, but he hadn't shut them. He'd wondered where she was in the world. Not in her apartment watching him, he knew that. She'd left. Left him to consider what she would do next. He hoped he could survive it.

Was he willing to tempt fate again? To test her wrath? To let her know that he could take it?

* * *

'Interest?' Alex asked. Yes, he understood the word, but used in context with his screenplay, he found he wanted further explanation.

'They like it, Harris,' his agent said. 'They're going to make an offer.'

Alex wanted to say, 'You're kidding.' But he found that he couldn't say anything. His tongue didn't remember how to form words. His movie was going to sell? That's what his agent – a man known for straight talk – seemed to be implying.

'High six figures,' Sam said next, and now Alex found his voice.

'You are kidding. You're fucking kidding.'

'Two studios are interested. One is going to bid first, and they want you to go with them. They want you to say yes now. And, believe me, you will.'

'I will?'

'Dash,' the voice commanded over the speaker phone. 'You'd better sit.'

Dashiell didn't want to sit. Lying down on his favourite leather chair, he was in the prime position for fucking the lovely Spanish woman he'd met earlier that day at the gym. He'd picked up the girl after a brief flirtation by the treadmill, deciding to go for it because of his recent fling with Sasha. He could feel himself starting to like her, really like her, and that meant it was time for him to put some distance there. Time to regain control of his heart. It wasn't in his plans to fall for someone, and the best way to block those feelings was having sex with someone else.

This girl didn't speak English very well, but she did seem to understand the term 'blow job'. Based on what she was doing with her mouth, he thought that the words must be internationally recognised.

'You listening?' the man said when Dashiell didn't bother to respond.

'Don't I always listen to you?' Dashiell asked, adding somewhat snidely, 'I don't have much choice, do I?' He squeezed his eyes shut now as Lucia brought her lips all the way down to the base of his cock and sucked. In his mind, Jessica was the one between his spread legs, working her mouth up and down his tool. Her pink lips parted, her tongue ready to flick against his balls. That was a move that always made him crazy. And when a woman was able to go all the way down, sealing her lips to his skin, that was practically unreal. And then, Jessica was mentally replaced with an image of Sasha. Stunning Sasha, who knew how to please him, how to make him yearn for satisfaction.

'This time it's serious.'

'It's always serious.' Although not as fucking serious as the fact that he was seconds away from shooting. That was the most important thing on his mind right now. Straining, leaning back and coming hard into the mouth of this lovely, dark-eyed plaything. Then flipping her around and returning the favour. He had plans for this evening. Long, detailed plans.

'Send the girl home,' his brother said, making Dashiell open his eyes for the first time since he'd taken the call, 'and focus on the fact that the money is gone.'

The money was gone.

Those four words resounded in Dashiell's head like an echo reverberating within a canyon. Except, instead of receding in volume, growing fainter with time and distance, the words became increasingly louder and clearer. Questions overlapped in his mind, so that he couldn't sort them out. How? Why? When? His older brother had told him to call back when he had processed the information and was ready to listen to what he had to say.

But really, did the 'how' of it even matter? Dashiell had put his faith in his brother's financial skills for years, and things had always worked to his advantage, without any help or hindrance from his own views. He didn't have to think about money. He simply had it. More than he could ever spend. Now, it was gone. How was that even possible?

With a drink at his side and his mobile phone in his hand, Dash steeled himself for calling Ted back. For learning exactly how bad the situation was. For finally focusing on his livelihood. Ted was waiting for him.

'That investment I told you about –' his brother started.

'Which one?'

'You never listen to me,' Ted said. 'You never have. *The* investment. The big one.' Dashiell uselessly searched his brains, trying to replay the conversation from nearly two years before. His brother had been on to some new scheme. Something with hotels. That was it. Theme hotels. But where?

Oh, Christ. Was it on that fucking island? The one with the recent coup. All the carnage on TV news that Dashiell avoided, changing channels to find something more suitable to his interests, like music videos.

'What's left, Ted?'

'What do you have in your bank account?'

Dashiell mentally calculated the figures to the low ten thousands.

'And you own your pad in LA outright, correct? Paid in full?'

'Yes –'

'Then you're doing better than some of the investors.' His brother sounded so matter-of-fact about this. Suddenly, Dashiell had a sinking feeling. A worse feeling than he'd had all evening.

'You didn't put your own money in, did you?'

20

'Here,' DeMarco said, handing a folder to Kelly.

It was in his head to ask, 'What is it?' but from the look in her eyes he found no will to speak. She was giving him something and that was all the information he needed. But fuck, what was it? He waited until he had a break, could go to the trailer to open the folder. And inside were two envelopes. The first held a list of the cast and crew, as well as location sites and a brief plot summary of the movie. His fingers trembled as he held it, but after a moment, he folded the pages and returned them to the white envelope. The second contained a note to him, scribbled in her almost illegible scrawl.

Give it to the girl.

No one in the press had received this much information. A horror film. They knew that. But there was no published cast list, and actors worked on the film at different times, so it was difficult to figure out who was involved, or how many people. The cameos alone contained more star-power than appeared in even huge casts – and here they were all listed.

All for Jessica.

Beneath the first line of the note, Deleen had written her signature DD beneath another scribble. Kelly squinted and then he realised what the word was: love. This was it. His final gift for Jessica before he claimed his status in his brand-new life.

Jessica missed Avalon. She missed Avalon's taste, smell, the way the woman's skin felt beneath the palms of her hands. But mostly she missed the gossip columnist's advice. As she stared at the white roses waiting once again on her doorstep, all Jessica felt was confusion.

Avalon had helped her sort out so many different problems recently, taking the place of Sasha when her roommate had faded into the background. Now, Jessica had nobody to talk to, nobody to discuss what was going on with Kelly – her private gossip source – with Dashiell – who seemed intent on being on-and-off-again in his interest of her – and, most importantly, with Alex. Yes, she now knew that Alex was the one sending the flowers. But what was she supposed to do with the information?

In her room, she sat on the sofa and tried her best to think the way that Avalon would. And then, finally, she went to the computer and sent an email.

For once, Dashiell was using his brains. He was no longer acting on auto-pilot, flitting through life like a spoiled party boy with no consideration for what was going to happen next. Or how he was going to pay for it. The situation demanded his total concentration. He had to think, and he had to work. And for some reason, it felt good. This was the biggest surprise of all. For his entire life, Dashiell had acted on whatever whim appealed to him. If he'd felt like flying to Paris for a weekend, he'd gone. If he'd wanted to buy a new car, he did. Now, he had to focus on minute details that had never interested him in the past, like how he was going to make payroll for his staff.

The small studio apartment had always been suitable for his tastes, but now it seemed not so much like a fake costume set, but like real life.

Sitting at his kitchen table, he spread out the paperwork that represented all of his worldly wealth. Numbers ricocheted through his brain, but rather than numbing them out, he paid attention. He earned some money from the paper – not much, really, but enough to get by. Was getting by good enough for him? It would have to be for the time being.

Alex held the envelope carefully, as if it were a piece of crystal. Or a bomb. From the feel of the hard plastic beneath the paper, he understood he was holding on to one of Avalon's infamous tapes. He felt relief knowing that Avalon was obviously OK. This was the first he'd personally heard from her in months. Yes, they'd known she was alive because she'd left a voicemail request that they tell her readers she was on hiatus. But that was all. What Alex didn't know was whether or not he wanted to hear what was on the cassette.

Finally, tired of being scared, he ripped open the envelope and read the note attached. 'Your sweet girl' was written in Avalon's famous scrawl. That was all, but from that clue he knew that Jessica's voice was captured on the tape. But what was she doing, and what was Avalon doing with it? Those were the questions.

The thing that he did know was that Avalon had given it to him as a dare. Did he dare put the tape in the machine and cue it up? Or was he destined to fuck away his life on regrets? Coming to a quick decision, he snagged his tape recorder and headset, lit up a cigar, and prepared to listen to whatever Avalon had so badly wanted him to hear.

Like Jessica when she'd first heard the tape of Avalon and Kelly fucking, he wasn't altogether sure what he was listening to.

Then, slowly, he started to understand.

Avalon, and her handsome soap-stud roommate, had experienced a threesome with Jessica. A kinky threesome, from the sound of things. And, oh, sweet Jesus, Ian had spanked her. Alex closed his eyes tighter. He instantly understood the emotions he was having. Not jealousy, because he and Jessica had never even shared more than that simple New Year's kiss. And he wasn't upset in the slightest that Jessica played darker than he'd have guessed. No, he was feeling excitement. Because what he learned now was that he and Jessica were perfect together. Fucking perfect.

Now all he had to do was explain that fact to her.

Avalon was coming home.

But first she was coming.

Lily, with her knowledgeable fingers, had spread Avalon's lips apart and was tap, tap, tapping a melody up and over her clit. Pulsing circles were followed by four-pronged diamonds. Intricate designs that felt like Lily was ice-skating her fingertips in Avalon's generous juices.

God, it was sensational. The way those delicate fingers danced and played, probing without the slightest bit of caution deeper inside the columnist's pussy. A quick thrust and then a slow withdrawal, making Avalon clench her eyes shut and groan.

Yes, Lily was an expert.

But Avalon was an expert, too. An expert at knowing the right time to act. She'd received Jessica's email – despondent, desperate – and had realised that it was time to go back home. The paper was in a tangle of chaos without her. Maybe what had been missing from her life wasn't a permanent partner, as she'd thought when watching Ian's belongings leave her apartment. Maybe what truly was lacking from her world was that feeling of being needed.

And here were the facts: her readers needed her, Jessica needed her, and even Alex needed her, since he still hadn't taken charge and made his move. Avalon hoped that the tape would stir him to action. Maybe it would. If not, she would help him along.

Like Lily was helping her. With the flat paddle of four stiff fingers, the beautiful bartender spanked her hand against Avalon's throbbing clit. The sound that her fingers made against Avalon's wet pussy turned her on even more. She could actually hear the wetness meeting Lily's fingertips. The liquid connection there.

The pussy-spanking got harder and sweeter, because right before climax, Avalon was always able to take a firmer touch. Lily knew it, just as she knew the second that Avalon started to come. And now the lovely brunette bent her head and kissed Avalon's clit. Licked it and kissed it, taking Avalon so high up she felt she'd never come down.

Book Four:
Bound for Summer

Ain't love the sweetest thing?

– U2

21

Fourth of July was always a big deal at the paper. Each year, *Zebra* rented a yacht in Marina del Rey, stuck everyone out on the water, and drank until the fireworks went off, physically and emotionally. But this time was different. The relationships between the staff members had been irrevocably altered, and most of the crew decided to fend for themselves. Those left over made do with a box at Los Angeles' famous outdoor amphitheatre, the Hollywood Bowl.

Five people. Alex. Dashiell. Josh. Jessica. And, surprise, surprise, Avalon, who had returned from her self-imposed hiatus, showing up suddenly at work in a flurry of activity, as if she'd never been gone. The uneven number of partiers was made even more uneven because of the twisted situations tying the group together. The five sat outside, under the deep purple sky, drinking good wine and talking when the music stopped as if everything was normal. But after several glasses, the atmosphere changed.

'What do you want?' Avalon murmured, her voice slurred.

Four people turned to look at her. 'Who?' Dashiell finally asked.

'You. Any of you. What do you want?'

'From what?' Josh asked, his voice serious.

'Life,' Avalon said, and then she started to laugh.

'You can't play us like that, Granger. We know when you're taping,' Dashiell told her forcefully. 'We're not your sappy little interview subjects.'

At his words, Jessica flushed, and Alex immediately looked over at her. Before he could speak, Avalon stood unsteadily and reached into her pocket for her recorder. While the others watched, she took out the tape and slit the fine cellophane with one of her spade-shaped crimson nails. Slowly, she pulled out the glistening strands, wrapping them around and around one wrist until they took on the appearance of punk-rock jewellery. The music started up again, but there was notable silence in their private box, as the stunned partiers stared at their drunken mate.

'We're all grown-ups. We all have wants. Needs. Can't you name them?'

When they continued to stare at her, she said, 'Fine, I'll start.' Moving back to sit against the pillowed chair, she sprawled out so that her feet were in Josh's lap and he absent-mindedly began to stroke them. It was obvious to Jessica then that they were lovers, something she'd never realised in the past. That was a weakness in her observation skills, she thought. A better journalist would have caught on to the fact that their public declarations of distaste were simply a well-crafted disguise to hide what was going on in their bedroom after hours.

'I want to get off the merry-go-round,' Avalon said. 'That's why I went away. I am tired of riding the ride.' She closed her eyes and rested her head on Jessica's shoulder, and Jessica thought this was Avalon's way of saying, 'Tag, sweetheart, you're it.' But Jessica had no idea what to say. She'd seen movies like this, where characters came clean about their inner secrets, revealing things that nobody in real life ever did. In the darkened safety of a movie house, she'd always found herself jealous of that type of freedom. Now that it was available to her, she couldn't compete.

It turned out that she didn't have to. Josh, his hands making slow and steady circles along the balls of Avalon's feet, took charge. 'You can get off the ride any time, Ava. You know that. You've always known that.'

The gossip columnist opened her eyes and stared at him, and the defiant angle of her chin jutting in his direction challenged him to keep talking. Other people nearby were staring at them, wanting to tell them to be quiet, Jessica thought, but not daring to interrupt. There was fire in Avalon's green eyes and in the heat of her expression.

'This isn't really the place,' Dashiell said calmly, a look of bemused wonderment on his face. Had he also not realised that Josh and Avalon were lovers? She tilted her head to look over at Alex, and there she saw flat-out recognition. He was the only one who'd understood the connection between the two staff members, and he was simply waiting to see how it would play out.

'There never is a good place,' Josh told Dashiell, although he kept his eyes on Avalon. 'Never a good place to drop the mask.'

'Who wears a mask?' Dashiell asked, obviously trying to keep the party at a light-hearted level, when they all knew that each one of them wore masks. Dashiell was more guilty of this, perhaps, than anyone else.

Josh didn't answer him. 'You ready, Ava?'

There was so much emotion between the two that Jessica felt as if she could see it, like the kaleidoscope of multicoloured lights that suddenly began to explode over the open concert hall. Now there was literally no way to speak. Rockets lit the sky and the reverberations of the firecrackers made talking an impossibility. But Josh didn't need to talk. Instead, he slipped one hand into his jacket pocket and took out a thin blue box. Jessica felt her heart race, and when she looked to Avalon, she saw tears in the gossip columnist's eyes.

Luminous red and gold showers of light streaked across the sky. The orchestra reached the fevered crescendo. And Avalon Granger put her hand out to touch the side of Josh's face as she started to cry.

When the finale was over, the fireworks done both outside the booth and within, Josh cleared his throat. 'You wouldn't let me talk,' he said. 'Now it's about time.' At these words, he pulled out a beautifully crafted ladies' watch and fastened the band around Avalon's wrist. The columnist smiled through her tears as she looked down and saw the second hand ticking away.

'It's about time,' he repeated, his voice the most serious that she'd ever heard it. 'Time for you to get over that tough-girl attitude you like to show off. Time to take me seriously, Ava.' He paused, and then softly asked, 'Are you ready?'

After that, five became three. Josh and Avalon left together, off to sort out the rest of their life, Jessica thought, or at least the rest of the evening. She, Alex and Dashiell remained in the box as the audience filtered out. There was no hurry. Especially once Dashiell had revealed an unopened bottle of eighteen-year-old Scotch. There weren't any glasses left, but that didn't bother the three remaining *Zebra* staff members. They passed the bottle around, lips drinking directly from the glass.

Alex stared from Jessica to Dashiell and back to Jessica again. Dashiell had a faraway look in his eyes, unreadable. Nobody seemed willing to make the first move in the conversation, so Alex sat silent with the others, thinking. Josh had won his game. Had played it correctly hands down. Never pushing his prize. Simply being there for her, to use at her will, and then finally letting her see who he truly was. The one who loved her.

It was a strange sight when masks came off, wasn't it?

Was it time for him to take his own off with Jessica?

If only he could be sure.

* * *

'You thought what?' Josh asked, staring down at Avalon, surprise gleaming in his eyes.

'Tiffany,' she said.

'You're crazy,' he told her, kissing the line of her neck to soften the words. 'That's why you stopped talking to me?'

'Who else?' she asked. 'When I heard you'd gone shopping, I assumed you were buying a ring.'

'I don't do things based on ultimatums,' Josh said. 'You should know me that well.'

Avalon sighed, then looked down at her watch, which was the only thing she was still wearing. 'When you get used to digging for secrets, sometimes it's difficult to put things in perspective.'

'But now?'

She kissed him back as an answer, and then she pulled him towards her, so that they were joined again. Sitting up in the bed, Avalon's thighs were over Josh's, and the two locked eyes as they grew as close together as they possibly could. Staying perfectly still, their bodies responded silently to each other. Avalon's pussy squeezed and released on Josh's cock, drawing him even deeper inside of her. Making him one with her.

As the power flowed between them, creating a full circle of pleasure, Avalon realised that Tantric sex was something that you could really only do with someone you loved. And this was no game.

22

'A million,' Sam said.

Alex blinked hard, staring at the man standing on his doorstep.

'A million even.'

'Don't fucking fuck with me.'

'For a screenwriter, you sure resort to the same lines over and over, don't you? Come on, man. We need you to spice up that dialogue. 'Fucking fuck?' What kind of shit is that?'

Alex backed up until he hit the wall behind him, letting his agent into the apartment. Then he sat down hard on the floor, not even looking around for a chair. His mind was spinning so fast that he felt as if it had taken the room with it. Nothing seemed clear in his line of vision; everything blurred.

'Ten per cent for me. Fifty per cent to the government. You'll clear maybe four hundred. Next time, you can expect to see a little more. Once you're in, they have to pay. They'll want to see the others. All the stupid screenplays you've been sitting on all these years. You'll probably make more deals in the next few weeks than you ever will again in your life. That's how it always goes. One script hits, and boom.'

Well, he'd be able to pay the rent increase. That was for sure. And at that thought, Alex started to laugh. And once he started he couldn't stop.

Sasha felt that she was being dealt more than her fair share of bad days. Mentally, she was so distant on stage that the management actually noticed and fired her from the strip bar. The news stunned her, and even though she was certain she could get another job quickly, she couldn't shake off the dizzying feeling of being knocked down too many times.

She responded to the news as she always did when she was depressed, by taking herself out for a drink. To wallow, she'd chosen a tiny bar on Ocean Boulevard habited by surfers and skate rats. The casual atmosphere, complete with a splattering of sawdust on the concrete floor, made this the last place she'd expected to meet the owner of *Zebra*.

Dashiell ignored her 'unapproachable' scowl, coming towards her table with two bottles of imported beer and handing one over. He didn't try to speak over the music, and he seemed not to notice the fact that she hadn't bothered with make-up, with doing anything to her turbulent curls. She was wearing clothes she'd simply picked up from the floor of her closet, an old pair of jeans and a black long-sleeved T-shirt with the words 'Tony's Pizza. Had a Piece Lately?' on the front.

Together they listened to the heavy beat of one of Santa Monica's many garage-style trios. But when the band took a break, he said, 'Alone?'

'Jess isn't here.'

'Not what I asked,' he said, 'or why I asked it.'

Sasha suddenly felt as if her heart was beating in her throat. What was this man doing here? Yes, they'd had several good times together, a crazy fling when he'd seemed to be dallying with her while waiting for her roommate to fall in love with him. Yet they'd made a pact that nothing would come of it. She would never hurt Jessica. Not intentionally. She wouldn't have let things go this far if she'd been thinking clearly.

Dashiell said, 'I hate it when a pretty girl looks sad for no reason.'

Sasha didn't have a response to that. She felt sad. That was why she'd come to the bar. To feel better. Even if it was only as long as the alcohol was buzzing through her system. But running into one of Jessica's admirers wasn't part of the plan. Not until he said, 'I'd like to make you look happy.'

'How are you going to do that?'

'Just give me a try.'

She remembered how Jessica spoke about Dashiell. That he was always out for a conquest, constantly keeping a track record in his mind. But maybe what she needed tonight was to be conquered. To have her misery physically knocked out of her and replaced by pleasure. Even if it was the most fleeting kind.

Dashiell looked at her again and put his hand on top of hers. She felt the passion between them, remembered what it had been like to be in bed with him. He knew how to touch a woman, how to talk, how not to talk. Like right now, the looks he was giving her told her everything that she needed to know.

Sasha said nothing as Dashiell took her hand and led her from the bar and into a moonless night, to his vintage truck, waiting right outside. They didn't speak as he drove towards his place in Hollywood, didn't say a word as he sped along Wilshire to Doheny. Didn't even speak in the elevator on the way to the top floor. He unlocked the door, kicked it open, and carried her to his living room, where the only thing she had to think about was his body on hers as they moved together.

It was good, as it had always been good. Every time they'd connected. But this time was different, yet again. Unlike the occasions they'd spent outdoors, when they'd seemed to share power, or the time when she'd directed him for her X-rated movie, Dashiell took charge, holding Sasha in his arms, pressing her up against the wall in his living room.

He lifted her legs and helped her position them around his naked waist, and he entered her forcefully, driving in deep. Each thrust made her forget her misery. Each time his steel-hard cock slipped inside her, brought her closer to bliss.

Sasha leaned her head back and closed her eyes. As if in response, Dashiell licked in a line down her neck, pressing at her pulse point before nipping her there. Biting her. She felt alive in his arms, and she sighed as she grew closer to climax, letting Dashiell know the moment when he should set her down on the sofa, push her thighs wider apart, slip one finger up and down her clit. Stroking her. Teasing her.

Taking her there.

But he wasn't satisfied with simply making her come on his couch. As she trembled with the power of the climax, he was lifting her again, this time spreading her out on his bed, taking both of her hands in one of his, holding them over her head. She looked up at him while he tied her down, and the spark of anticipation made her thoughts come slower. All she could focus on was the fact that Dashiell had a hook in his wall, hidden behind a pillow, and that he was now sliding a pair of handcuffs on her wrists and capturing her to that silvery hook.

'Bound for pleasure,' he said, explaining himself, and then making the statement come true in the slowest, most decadent way possible.

So many of the girls Dashiell had dated – not just fucked, but dated – knew his history, his finances, and couldn't keep thoughts of money or power out of their minds. Sasha hadn't seemed to care about any of that from the beginning. Could her attitude be for real?

He looked at her, sleeping peacefully on his mattress, her hands free of the cuffs and now tucked under her chin, and he had an instant flash of their lovemaking. The sweet smell of her arousal, all around him, filling his senses. The way, when he'd reached down to touch her clit, to stroke it with the ball of his thumb, she had sighed and bitten into her bottom lip, hard enough to leave marks afterwards, deep indents in the soft flesh that he'd kissed to take away the pain.

The rush of the experience echoed through his body and he shuddered at the thought of pleasure he'd experienced less than an hour before. She was a fucking dream in bed, that was for sure. Yet there was something again that was different about her. No personal agenda. She hadn't seemed like she was trying for anything, striving forward, lost in a future pleasure. No, she'd been right there with him, every step of the way. Enjoying it as it unfolded.

That's what made her the most special. Carefully, so as not to disturb her, he slipped away from the bed. He felt ready now to really take care of business, and he knew exactly what that meant. He was going to talk to his advisors and sell the paper.

For Dashiell, at age 40, it was finally time to grow up.

23

Avalon's last column. That's what it was. While ensconced in the safety of Lily's private bungalow, she'd decided that sniffing for information was getting old. What she wanted to do was write, as she always had, but write about real things. Not trash. Not secrets. Now that she was back, and with Josh, she felt more secure in that decision. Look where misusing secrets had gotten her?

Still, because she was Avalon Granger, she went out with a bang.

She typed 'Digging the Dirt' for one final time. It felt good. It felt like saying goodbye. Then, focused hard, she typed straight through for an hour. The piece would be way too long to print, but that was OK. It wasn't intended for the average *Zebra* reader. It was intended only for Alex.

The column was waiting for the managing editor on his desk, tucked away in a manilla envelope with the word 'Private' scrawled over the flap and a glossy crimson lipsticked kiss to seal it. Alex smiled as he saw that silly precaution, Avalon's attempt to make sure that nobody else would sneak into her gossipy world ahead of time. It was good to have her back at the paper. Part of the magic of the way *Zebra* worked was Avalon. He'd realised that during her absence.

At his leisure, Alex slid the disk into his computer and waited for the file to open. But once he started reading, he felt as if Avalon was in the room with him, watching and laughing at his response. She would, too. It was why she was such a good gossip columnist. She spared no one.

After reading the entire file once, he stood, paced the office, then returned to his desk for a second go-through, trying to keep his head. The column both confirmed several things that he already knew and shed light on other events that he'd never even considered. The piece stated that Avalon had been with Kelly. And that Kelly had been with Deleen DeMarco. And that Dashiell was out of money. And that Todd was fucking Marina. But none of that mattered. None of it. Because of what was at the end:

Dashiell hadn't been with Jessica, he'd been with Jessica's roommate Sasha.

At the very bottom, there was a bit about him. Congratulations at selling the screenplay. Avalon was the first to have heard about it. He was keeping mum until the cheque cleared. 'All right, dude,' the last line read. 'You've taken your time. Played the round of poker with that dead-pan expression. Now I'm calling your hand. Time to show what you've got.'

Alex understood perfectly. Avalon was behaving the way he did with some of his more difficult writers. She was being heavy-handed, demanding and taking charge, and she was right, wasn't she? But Alex had to do it in his own way.

'I've got a job for you,' Alex said when Jessica picked up the line.

'Spill it, Harris,' she said tersely. She'd picked up quite a few habits from Avalon, hadn't she? He tried to figure out how to pose the assignment. Even the most established writer would have a difficult time in such a confusing situation. Her ex-boyfriend was with the most famous director in the world. DeMarco was going to make Kelly a superstar. But more than that, she was going to make him her own. Wrap him up in her silky web and capture him for life. Jessica knew all of that, but Alex still wasn't sure whether she'd be up for what he was asking.

'A real review,' he said after a moment. 'With a by-line, of course. I'm sending you to review the DeMarco movie *Objects*.' I want your honest opinion.'

How could he say the rest?

'Look,' he added, 'I've got something else to ask you. If you say no, that's fine. And if you say yes, well, that's fucking great. But I don't want you to say anything yet. I want you to think about it. Promise?'

'Yes, Alex,' she said softly. 'I promise.'

Jessica attended the screening alone, wandering down the red carpet in a daze, showing her press pass to the prissy-looking man standing guard outside the doors. Begrudgingly he let her in, and she took her time to enjoy the walk through the lobby. The theatre was one of Jessica's favourites. An old-fashioned relic from the fifties, with a fancy, neon-lit marquee.

She was dateless this evening, and although she wished for a moment that she was with one of her friends, with Avalon specifically, as soon as she entered the theatre those thoughts were forgotten. Down in the very front, she could see Deleen DeMarco. In honour of the opening festivities, the director had changed not one thing about her appearance. Wearing a black silk turtle-neck and black pants, her dark hair pulled back in its normal severe style, the woman looked as chilling as always. The only real difference was her companion. At her side, Kelly leaned in to whisper something, and whatever he said to her made the woman's face melt into a smile.

So she was human, Jessica thought, watching as

DeMarco used one finger to stroke along Kelly's forehead, pushing his wheat-blond hair out of his handsome face. A strong yearning tugged inside Jessica's chest. She remembered the feel of Kelly's skin beneath her own fingertips, the smell of his hair, the way he held her. But had something always rung false in their relationship? Perhaps, because he seemed so completely at ease to star in the new role of his life.

Kelly had accepted his place.

That brought another question to the front of her mind. What was her place? And who should be cast at her side? Then Jessica stopped thinking about connections as the theatre darkened and the movie began to play.

24

It made perfect sense to Alex. He loved the paper. He didn't love screenwriting. Thought he would. From the start, he had dreamed of living the life shown in movies from the forties. Writer hard at work at his typewriter. Pounding out pages daily accompanied by that satisfying whiz-clatter sound of fingers on a keyboard. But, actually, what he really liked was the day-to-day juggling life of running a paper. And Dashiell didn't.

So he'd make the man an offer.

Put it out for him.

Dash needed the money, didn't he?

And what did Alex need? While he waited for Jessica to respond to his question, he needed a life.

Halloween. Sasha wouldn't go out drinking this time. Yes, Dashiell had made her feel better, driving her bad mood away and taking her thoughts off her problems. But the rapture had been fleeting and now, holding the formal acceptance letter to the festival she'd most desperately wanted to attend, she felt her dreams dying. They'd taken her movie based on the trailer, but there was no way to finish the film. Flat out. Plain and simple.

She held the crisp white letter from The Gates in one hand, and a bottle of vodka in the other, still icy cold from the freezer where it had been hiding beneath several packages of frozen peas. An extra-extra emergency, she thought, remembering Jessica finding her coffee when she needed it.

Slipping beneath the blood-red down comforter

draped over her bed, she brought the bottle to her lips and swallowed hard.

The two men stared seriously at each other over the empty, polished surface of Dashiell's desk. His work area differed greatly from Alex's in every imaginable way. Unlike the nightmare of paperwork, files and movie stubs that littered Alex's desk, there was no clutter here. No papers covering the floor. Nothing tacked to the bulletin board except a postcard of Los Angeles in its heyday, when the sign up in the hills still read 'Hollywoodland'. Pristine and almost unused, the environment looked less like the desk of an editor-in-chief and more like some unused set decoration. There was no evidence that anyone actually worked here.

'You did it, Alex,' Dashiell said grinning. 'Way to go, man.'

'The movie business just isn't for me,' Alex said, trying to explain. 'The whole –' He gestured uselessly, then reached in his pocket for a cigar, as if he needed to do something with his hands. But he didn't light the thing, playing with it instead, rolling the fragrant staff of tobacco leaves back and forth in his fingers. 'This is what I love.'

'Your cigar?' Dashiell said. 'What would Freud say?'

Alex laughed. 'This,' he said, gesturing broadly to the room, encompassing the whole of the office with his outstretched arms. 'This whole stupid business.'

'I think I tried to tell you that once.'

'You did,' Alex agreed. 'You said that I was an old-fashioned newspaper man, and that I should fucking get used to it.'

'And you said that I put the job of running a paper on like an actor putting on a costume.'

'Sorry,' Alex said. 'It came out meaner than I meant it.'

'But you were right,' Dashiell agreed, briskly signing his name on the document and handing it over. 'I put on costumes. Try things on for size. Never getting too close or too serious. I'm going to change that now.' He nodded to himself, as if he needed that extra affirmation. 'It's all yours, Alex. *Zebra* is now your fucking headache.' He looked down at the agreement, at the dollar figure that put him back in business, and he smiled.

There was someone he needed to call right away.

And that somebody was Jessica.

Marina was going to end it. This wasn't the way she'd planned her life, wasn't why she'd come to Los Angeles in the first place. LA was the original city where dreams could come true. Well, her dream wasn't to be attached to an up-and-coming musician. Yes, it looked good for Todd, but she'd witnessed close at hand from watching Alex what Hollywood could do to a person's dreams. And she didn't want to see Todd get crushed by the wheel of fame.

Still, why couldn't she get the words out? Whenever she called him, she wound up saying something else. Something entirely different from the script she'd practised in her head. Not 'I can't see you any more.' but 'I have to see you now.'

So when Todd arrived at her apartment early, let himself in and found his way to the side of her bed, she prepared herself to finally say what she had to say. Which turned out to be, once again, entirely different from the words she'd planned.

'The phone's for you,' Jessica said, holding the black receiver out to Sasha. Her flaming-haired roommate shook her head miserably, her curls bouncing in a jubilant way that entirely belied her current emotional state. It looked to Jessica as if even this minor action hurt.

'I'm not in.'

'You're in for this call.'

'No, Jessie,' Sasha moaned as she clung to the side of her mattress, the room still spinning like the roundabout ride at the Santa Monica pier. 'I can't talk to anyone right now. Take a message.'

Jessica leaned over and hit the button on the base of the phone, activating the speaker. 'Dash,' she said, 'You're on.'

'Can you hear me, Sasha?'

At the sound of his voice, Sasha's cheeks reddened, and she nodded, but didn't answer. Her eyes were focused on Jessica's face, but as soon as Jessica looked in her direction, Sasha stared down at the wood floor. This was not the way she'd wanted the affair to come out. Never would have been the appropriate time in Sasha's point of view.

'Jessica knows, baby doll,' Dashiell said. 'She knows everything, and it's OK.' He and the intern had spent an hour discussing the tangled situation. He'd wanted Jessica's help, and her honest opinion of how her roommate felt about him. She'd given him both.

Now, Sasha looked back at her best friend, and there were instant tears shining in her eyes. 'I'm sorry, Jess –' she started but Jessica put up a hand. Dashiell hadn't finished speaking.

'We can discuss the rest of it later,' he said. 'All the history about who was doing what to whom, and when they were doing it. But there are more important things to talk about today.'

'Like?' Sasha managed to murmur.

'Like your movie.'

The tears started to streak down Sasha's freckled face now. In her pocket, she still had the folded letter from The Gates Film Festival.

'Is the executive producer position still open?' Dashiell asked.

Sasha's voice left her completely, and she found herself unable to speak for a moment. Finally, Jessica nudged her, and Sasha whispered, 'You're not serious.'

'He's dead serious,' Jessica said, smiling. 'Dash never jokes about money. Not any more.'

'Better shake off that hangover and get moving,' Dashiell said, and Sasha's cheeks went ever redder. How had he known? 'Slide into those beat-up jeans of yours, kick on your boots, and then open the front door and let me in.' Both girls rushed to the window, where they looked out to see Dashiell sitting casually on the front step, talking on his cellphone. 'The bank closes in less than an hour.'

'Coming with us?' Sasha asked, dressing quickly and grabbing her coat. She was recovering from this hangover fast.

'Not today,' Jessica said. 'I've got a meeting with my editor before the party.'

Once Sasha had left, Jessica entered her closet, looking at the costume she'd chosen for the paper's annual ball. It was perfect, made total sense. No longer an innocent Little Red Riding Hood, trying to learn all she could, she was now so much more knowledgeable. The costume, that of a fortune teller complete with a crystal ball, showed the transformation to the extreme detail. For the rest of her outfit, she'd bought a lace scarf to cover her dark hair, and a matching lace mini-dress that cinched in tight at the waist. The fabric, air-light, was barely there at all, only partially covering her lithe body. Nobody else would have chosen anything quite so daring, she was sure of it, and that made her feel even more pleased with herself.

As Jessica finished getting ready for *Zebra*'s annual Halloween party, she thought about all she'd learned in a single year. Yes, she could turn in a piece written perfectly in pyramid format, could finagle a meeting out of the most reluctant celebrity, could meet a deadline when a story was due 'yesterday'. But as she put the finishing touches on her make-up, she met her gaze in the mirror and thought of how she'd really used her journalistic skills, discovering the *when*, *why*, and *how* her heart had fallen for one particular *who*.

Todd stared at Marina, waiting for her response. His heart beat with the resounding pulse of one of his band's rowdier songs. In any other situation, he would have been writing down music, hearing a new melody in his head. Instead, he was frozen in place, watching silently.

Marina lifted the simple platinum ring from the tiny black box and slid it on her finger. She stared down at the engagement ring, and the look on her face was one of total peace. That was all Todd needed to come back to life, reanimating instantly, thrilled by her action.

'OK, let's go,' he said, hustling her into her bedroom.

'Right now?' she asked. She gazed at him with a look that bordered on worship.

'You've got such a dirty mind. It's one of my very favourite things about you, but I'm not talking about what you think.'

She sighed. 'The party. We don't have to go.'

'Yes, we do,' he told her, as Marina's eyes focused on the ring on her finger.

Alex sat alone in the office, contemplating his new world status. A knock interrupted his thoughts, and he hurried to open the office door, but he didn't hurry fast enough. Jessica opened it herself, and then stood in the doorway, smiling at him. He remembered the first time he'd seen her, that innocent little freshman standing in the office. He also remembered what Pete had said – 'You'll ruin her' – and his own response, 'If Dash doesn't ruin her first.'

None of that had come true. Instead, she'd been the one to turn his life upside-down, easily, as if she knew all the rules while he was a first-time player. And she was still making him feel topsy-turvy inside, because he couldn't tell from her stance what her answer was. Shouldn't he have a handle on her body language by now? Maybe, but he didn't. He couldn't tell anything even as she walked towards him, handing over a blue plastic computer disk and saying confidently, 'Met my deadline, right?'

He looked first at the clock on the wall and then at the disk in his hand. Finally, he forced himself to stare back at Jessica. Her dark hair was up in its standard high ponytail, revealing a pair of shoulder-dusting silver hoop earrings. He noticed her smoky-rimmed eyes, red-glossed lips that were slightly parted, as if she were on the verge of telling him a secret. How he wished she would take a step closer, go up on her tiptoes, press her lips to his ear and whisper the dirtiest, filthiest secret she knew.

'Always,' he said honestly. 'You're the one person on staff who does.'

'Read it and let me know what you think,' she said. 'It's in pyramid format. You can cut from the bottom.'

He stared at her, at the way her glorious body was so perfectly outfitted in that tiny little black lace dress. She had on a pair of over-the-knee boots that laced in the back, and sheer black stockings that were dusted with a silver sparkle. Feeling stunned, he slowly slipped the disk into the drive on his computer and clicked it open. There was only one file waiting for him, and he double-clicked the tiny square icon, and then leaned forward anxiously, reading the words on the screen. The same word over and over:

Yes. Yes. Yes. Yes. Yes. Yes. Yes. Yes. Yes. Yes. Yes.

The question had been simple on the surface – would she go to the party with him? But both knew that it was much more of a serious invitation than that. All the flowers and all the fantasies had come together in that single query.

It had been a year since Alex had thought of spanking Jessica at the Halloween party. He remembered standing there in his velvet suit, a vision of paddling Jessica over his red-flocked lap. Santa punishing a naughty Red Riding Hood. This evening, as he was about to escort Jessica into the party, he bent his head and asked her, 'What do you see in your crystal ball tonight, birthday girl?'

Jessica stopped at the threshold and looked up at him. Then she slid her hand into his and pulled him back to the foyer. 'You knew it was my birthday?' she asked.

He nodded. 'You're not the only one who can read people's minds.'

'Then what am I thinking now?'

His hazel eyes shined as he smiled and led her away from the throng of people, back into the elevator and down to the street. No need to share tonight with anyone else. He took her to the closest place he could think of, the empty *Zebra* office. There he sat down on one of the leather sofas and reached for Jessica's wrist. Her skin was warm to the touch, and he revelled in every second of the interaction, in every single moment they had together. Because this was a fantasy come to life.

Jessica willingly draped herself over his lap, and she drew in her breath as he lifted the thin lace dress, revealing her black panties beneath. There was a moment while both partners processed the situation. She was going to get a spanking, such a birthday spanking, and he was going to get rock-hard while giving it to her.

In that sliver of time, Alex remembered all of the different X-rated visions of Jessica he'd enjoyed over the last year, viewing them in speeded-up motion in his mind: Jessica tied to his bed; Jessica sucking his cock underneath his desk, her deliciously warm mouth on him; Jessica undressed and open, her legs spread, ready for him to dine on for hours. And then he stopped daydreaming and started acting. He slipped his fingers beneath the waistband of her panties, then pulled them down past her knees, leaving them dangling there, reminding her that she wasn't naked, only stripped. Then he set one hand against her pale skin, letting her feel the weight of it.

It was the most amazing moment. That beat of time they shared before he began to spank her. Then he started. His hand came down hard on her naked rear, and Jessica sighed deeply at the instant pleasure that accompanied the pain. He knew exactly the pressure she needed, wasn't playing any games with her. Alex spanked her hard and fast. Taking the job of tanning her bare bottom seriously.

This was real. This was right. They both knew it.

What a perfect birthday present – 21 spanks on her beautiful ass.

Epilogue

Alex stared down at Jessica, admiring the way she looked in the sheer white nightgown he had bought for her. The style suited her perfectly. Sweet in its design, because that's what she truly was. But the charm of the nightie didn't stop there. The gown was naughty in its transparency, and this was perfect because she was a bad girl too. He sucked in his breath as he thought that. He had so many different ways that he wanted to play with her. Years and years of games in store for them.

He watched her breathe slowly, gently.

They had spent the early part of the night fucking, and then he'd left to go back to the paper, overseeing the printing as he always did on Thursday nights. It was early in the morning now. Too early to force her out of bed. But he simply couldn't wait.

For a moment, he thought of all the different ways that he might wake her. He could lift the nightgown, bend down and lick in long, slow lines up the insides of her slender legs. She would stir when his tongue finally made contact with her clit. Or he could kiss the back of her neck, lift her heavy black hair and press his lips to that most treasured spot at the nape. Breathe in, smelling the scent that was truly her. But finally he chose a way that was more perfect than any other.

Crinkling the newly printed paper in his hand, he fanned her face, creating a soft breeze that waved over her until she rolled over and stared up at him. While she watched with her big, dark blue eyes, he opened the newspaper to show the newly revised masthead. Then he carefully underlined the words that he wanted her to read.

Jessica's eyes followed where Alex pointed.

Alexander Harris – Editor-in-Chief
Avalon Granger – Managing Editor
Josh Charles – Advertising Executive

Then there it was. The reward for all of her hard work in simple black letters on a white background.

Jessica Taylor – Writer at Large

Jessica looked up at Alex, a smile dancing in her mesmerising blue eyes, her dangerous lips parted to speak. But instead, she opened her arms wide and drew him in close, so close that she could feel his heart beating against hers.

Alex bent his head against her, and she felt his long hair tickling her skin, felt his breath on the back of her neck. His touch sent a shiver through her, and he held her even tighter in his embrace. And suddenly, Jessica smiled. She knew exactly how to tell him what the masthead meant to her.

She could tell him everything she needed to with her body alone, and he would know precisely how to read between the lines.

Visit the Black Lace website at
www.blacklace-books.co.uk

LOOK OUT FOR THE ALL-NEW BLACK LACE BOOKS – AVAILABLE NOW!

All books priced £6.99 in the UK. Please note publication dates apply to the UK only. For other territories, please contact your retailer.

DEMON'S DARE
Melissa MacNeal
ISBN: 0 352 33683 8

It's 1895. Traded as payment for her aunt's gambling debts, southern belle Vanita is whisked off to a decaying plantation mansion where Franklin Harte and his curious family are quite happy to receive her. She is to marry Franklin's son, Damon, whose bizarre hobbies and even more bizarre sister are enough to send Vanita's head spinning. Their games of weird and freaky eroticism intrigue her and certainly prove distracting. To reclaim her lost property, however, she has to figure a way to escape Franklin's obsessive humiliations, making good on a vow Pearce Truman dared her to accept. Despite the Hartes' peculiarities and perversions, the elusive Pearce seems the darkest demon of all. Historical, darkly weird and freaky! From the best-selling author of *Devil's Fire*.

ELENA'S CONQUEST
Lisette Allen
ISBN: 0 352 32950 5

On a summer's day in the year 1070, young Elena is gathering herbs in the garden of the convent where she leads a peaceful but uneventful life. Lately she's been yearning for something sinful: the intimate touch of the well-built Saxon who haunts her dreams. When Norman soldiers besiege the convent and take Elena captive, she is chosen by the dark and masterful Lord Aimery le Sabrenn to satisfy her savage desires.

Captivated by his powerful masculinity, Elena is then horrified to discover she is not the only woman in his castle; the sinister Lady Isobel – le Sabrenn's wife – is a cruel but beautiful rival and is out to destroy her. This classic Black Lace reprint is packed with brawny Saxons and cruel Normans. Travel back in time and witness sexual jealousy in the time of William the Conqueror.

Coming in April 2002

KING'S PAWN
Ruth Fox
ISBN 0 352 33684 6

Cassie is consumed by a need to explore the intriguing world of SM – a world of bondage, domination and her submission. She agrees to give herself to the inscrutable Mr King for a day, to sample the pleasures of his complete control over her. Cassie finds herself hooked on the curious games they play. Her lesbian lover, Becky, is shocked, but agrees to Cassie visiting Mr King once more. It is then that she is initiated into the debauched Chessmen Club, where she is expected to go much further than she thought. A refreshingly honest story of a woman's introduction to SM. Written by a genuine scene-player.

TIGER LILY
Kimberley Dean
ISBN 0 352 33685 4

When Federal Agent Shanna McKay – aka Tiger Lily – is assigned to a new case on a tough precinct, her shady past returns to haunt her. She has to bust drug lord, Mañuel Santos, who caused her sister's disappearance years previously. The McKay sisters had been wild: Shanna became hooked on sex; her sister hooked on Santos and his drugs. Desperate to even the score, Shanna infiltrates the organisation by using her most powerful weapon – her sexuality. Hard-hitting erotica mixes with low-life gangsters in a tough American police precinct. Sizzling, sleazy action that will have you on the edge of your seat!

COOKING UP A STORM
Emma Holly
ISBN 0 352 33686 2

The Coates Inn Restaurant in Cape Cod is about to go belly up when its attractive owner, Abby, jumps at a stranger's offer to help her – both in her kitchen and her bed. The handsome chef claims to have an aphrodisiac menu that her patrons won't be able to resist. Can this playboy chef really save the day when Abby's body means more to him than her feelings? He has charmed the pants off her and she's now behaving like a wild woman. Can Abby tear herself away from her new lover for long enough to realise that he might be trying to steal the restaurant from under her nose? Beautifully written and evocative story of love, lust and haute cuisine.

Coming in May 2002

SLAVE TO SUCCESS
Kimberley Raines
ISBN 0 352 33687 0

Eugene, born poor but grown-up handsome, answers an ad to be a sex slave for a year. He assumes his role will be that of a gigolo, and thinks he will easily make the million dollars he needs to break into Hollywood. On arrival at a secret destination he discovers his tasks are somewhat more demanding. He will be a pleasure slave to the mistress Olanthé – a demanding woman with high expectations who will put Eugene through some exacting physical punishments and pleasures. He is in for the shock of his life. An exotic tale of female domination over a beautiful but arrogant young man.

FULL EXPOSURE
Robyn Russell
ISBN 0 352 33688 9

Attractive but stern Boston academic, Donatella di'Bianchi, is in Arezzo,
Italy, to investigate the affairs of the *Collegio Toscana*, a school of visual
arts. Donatella's probe is hampered by one man, the director, Stewart
Temple-Clarke. She is also sexually attracted by an English artist on the
faculty, the alluring but mysterious Ian Ramsey. In the course of her
inquiry Donatella is attacked, but receives help from two new friends –
Kiki Lee and Francesca Antinori. As the trio investigates the menacing
mysteries surrounding the college, these two young women open
Donatella's eyes to a world of sexual adventure with artists, students,
and even the local *carabinieri*. A stylishly sensual erotic thriller set in the
languid heat of an Italian summer.

STRIPPED TO THE BONE
Jasmine Stone
ISBN 0 352 33463 0

Annie has always been a rebel. While her sister settled down in Middle
America, Annie blazed a trail of fast living on the West Coast, constantly
seeking thrills. She is motivated by a hungry sexuality and a mission to
keep changing her life. Her capacity for experimental sex games means
she's never short of partners, and she keeps her lovers in a spin of erotic
confusion. Every man she encounters is determined to discover what
makes her tick, yet no one can get a hold of Annie long enough to find
out. Maybe the Russian Ilmar can unlock the secret. However, by
succumbing to his charms, is Annie stepping into territory too dangerous
even for her? By popular demand, this is a special reprint of a free-
wheeling story of lust and trouble in a fast world.

Black Lace Booklist

Information is correct at time of printing. To avoid disappointment check availability before ordering. Go to www.blacklace-books.co.uk. All books are priced £6.99 unless another price is given.

BLACK LACE BOOKS WITH A CONTEMPORARY SETTING

☐ THE TOP OF HER GAME Emma Holly	ISBN 0 352 33337 5	£5.99
☐ IN THE FLESH Emma Holly	ISBN 0 352 34498 3	£5.99
☐ A PRIVATE VIEW Crystalle Valentino	ISBN 0 352 33308 1	£5.99
☐ SHAMELESS Stella Black	ISBN 0 352 33485 1	£5.99
☐ INTENSE BLUE Lyn Wood	ISBN 0 352 33496 7	£5.99
☐ THE NAKED TRUTH Natasha Rostova	ISBN 0 352 33497 5	£5.99
☐ ANIMAL PASSIONS Martine Marquand	ISBN 0 352 34499 1	£5.99
☐ A SPORTING CHANCE Susie Raymond	ISBN 0 352 33501 7	£5.99
☐ TAKING LIBERTIES Susie Raymond	ISBN 0 352 33357 X	£5.99
☐ A SCANDALOUS AFFAIR Holly Graham	ISBN 0 352 33523 8	£5.99
☐ THE NAKED FLAME Crystalle Valentino	ISBN 0 352 33528 9	£5.99
☐ CRASH COURSE Juliet Hastings	ISBN 0 352 33018 X	£5.99
☐ ON THE EDGE Laura Hamilton	ISBN 0 352 33534 3	£5.99
☐ LURED BY LUST Tania Picarda	ISBN 0 352 33533 5	£5.99
☐ THE HOTTEST PLACE Tabitha Flyte	ISBN 0 352 33536 X	£5.99
☐ THE NINETY DAYS OF GENEVIEVE Lucinda Carrington	ISBN 0 352 33070 8	£5.99
☐ EARTHY DELIGHTS Tesni Morgan	ISBN 0 352 33548 3	£5.99
☐ MAN HUNT Cathleen Ross	ISBN 0 352 33583 1	
☐ MÉNAGE Emma Holly	ISBN 0 352 33231 X	
☐ DREAMING SPIRES Juliet Hastings	ISBN 0 352 33584 X	
☐ THE TRANSFORMATION Natasha Rostova	ISBN 0 352 33311 1	
☐ STELLA DOES HOLLYWOOD Stella Black	ISBN 0 352 33588 2	
☐ SIN.NET Helena Ravenscroft	ISBN 0 352 33598 X	
☐ HOTBED Portia Da Costa	ISBN 0 352 33614 5	
☐ TWO WEEKS IN TANGIER Annabel Lee	ISBN 0 352 33599 8	
☐ HIGHLAND FLING Jane Justine	ISBN 0 352 33616 1	

☐ PLAYING HARD Tina Troy	ISBN 0 352 33617 X
☐ SYMPHONY X Jasmine Stone	ISBN 0 352 33629 3
☐ STRICTLY CONFIDENTIAL Alison Tyler	ISBN 0 352 33624 2
☐ SUMMER FEVER Anna Ricci	ISBN 0 352 33625 0
☐ CONTINUUM Portia Da Costa	ISBN 0 352 33120 8
☐ OPENING ACTS Suki Cunningham	ISBN 0 352 33630 7
☐ FULL STEAM AHEAD Tabitha Flyte	ISBN 0 352 33637 4
☐ A SECRET PLACE Ella Broussard	ISBN 0 352 33307 3
☐ GAME FOR ANYTHING Lyn Wood	ISBN 0 352 33639 0
☐ FORBIDDEN FRUIT Susie Raymond	ISBN 0 352 33306 5
☐ CHEAP TRICK Astrid Fox	ISBN 0 352 33640 4
☐ THE ORDER Dee Kelly	ISBN 0 352 33652 8
☐ ALL THE TRIMMINGS Tesni Morgan	ISBN 0 352 33641 3
☐ PLAYING WITH STARS Jan Hunter	ISBN 0 352 33653 6
☐ THE GIFT OF SHAME Sara Hope-Walker	ISBN 0 352 32935 1
☐ COMING UP ROSES Crystalle Valentino	ISBN 0 352 33658 7
☐ GOING TOO FAR Laura Hamilton	ISBN 0 352 33657 9
☐ THE STALLION Georgina Brown	ISBN 0 352 33005 8
☐ DOWN UNDER Juliet Hastings	ISBN 0 352 33663 3
☐ THE BITCH AND THE BASTARD Wendy Harris	ISBN 0 352 33664 1
☐ ODALISQUE Fleur Reynolds	ISBN 0 352 32887 8
☐ RELEASE ME Suki Cunningham	ISBN 0 352 33671 4
☐ GONE WILD Maria Eppie	ISBN 0 352 33670 6

BLACK LACE BOOKS WITH AN HISTORICAL SETTING

☐ PRIMAL SKIN Leona Benkt Rhys	ISBN 0 352 33500 9	£5.99
☐ DEVIL'S FIRE Melissa MacNeal	ISBN 0 352 33527 0	£5.99
☐ WILD KINGDOM Deanna Ashford	ISBN 0 352 33549 1	£5.99
☐ DARKER THAN LOVE Kristina Lloyd	ISBN 0 352 33279 4	£5.99
☐ STAND AND DELIVER Helena Ravenscroft	ISBN 0 352 33340 5	£5.99
☐ THE CAPTIVATION Natasha Rostova	ISBN 0 352 33234 4	
☐ CIRCO EROTICA Mercedes Kelley	ISBN 0 352 33257 3	
☐ MINX Megan Blythe	ISBN 0 352 33638 2	
☐ PLEASURE'S DAUGHTER Sedalia Johnson	ISBN 0 352 33237 9	
☐ JULIET RISING Cleo Cordell	ISBN 0 352 32938 6	
☐ DEMON'S DARE Melissa MacNeal	ISBN 0 352 33683 8	

ELENA'S CONQUEST Lisette Allen .... ISBN O 352 32950 5

BLACK LACE ANTHOLOGIES

CRUEL ENCHANTMENT Erotic Fairy Stories .... ISBN O 352 33483 5 £5.99
  Janine Ashbless

MORE WICKED WORDS Various .... ISBN O 352 33487 8 £5.99

WICKED WORDS 4 Various .... ISBN O 352 33603 X

WICKED WORDS 5 Various .... ISBN O 352 33642 0

BLACK LACE NON-FICTION

THE BLACK LACE BOOK OF WOMEN'S SEXUAL .... ISBN O 352 33346 4 £5.99
  FANTASIES Ed. Kerri Sharp

To find out the latest information about Black Lace titles, check out the
website: www.blacklace-books.co.uk or send for a booklist with
complete synopses by writing to:

> Black Lace Booklist, Virgin Books Ltd
> Thames Wharf Studios
> Rainville Road
> London W6 9HA

Please include an SAE of decent size. Please note only British stamps
are valid.

Our privacy policy
We will not disclose information you supply us to any other parties.
We will not disclose any information which identifies you personally to
any person without your express consent.

From time to time we may send out information about Black Lace
books and special offers. Please tick here if you do not wish to
receive Black Lace information. ❏

Please send me the books I have ticked above.

Name ....

Address ....

....

....

....

Post Code ....

Send to: Cash Sales, Black Lace Books, Thames Wharf Studios, Rainville Road, London W6 9HA.

US customers: for prices and details of how to order books for delivery by mail, call 1-800-343-4499.

Please enclose a cheque or postal order, made payable to Virgin Books Ltd, to the value of the books you have ordered plus postage and packing costs as follows:

UK and BFPO – £1.00 for the first book, 50p for each subsequent book.

Overseas (including Republic of Ireland) – £2.00 for the first book, £1.00 for each subsequent book.

If you would prefer to pay by VISA, ACCESS/MASTERCARD, DINERS CLUB, AMEX or SWITCH, please write your card number and expiry date here:

....

Signature ....

Please allow up to 28 days for delivery.